What the critics are saying...

"Ms. Agnew has written an outstanding story of the cost of war and that love will not be denied. Blayne and Jemma scorch the pages with some of the hottest sex scenes I have read in a while." ~ *Oleta M. Blaylock Just Erotic Romance Reviews*

"By Honor Bound" is an aptly named and wonderfully written anthology by three fabulous authors...This wonderful anthology gives the reader a look into the lives of a few fictional military men and women who serve their country and still find love in spite of the odds that might be against them. The respect that these authors must have for the men and women in the military shows through in this anthology, and that makes "By Honor Bound" a book for the "to be read again" shelf for me!" ~ *Christine, eCataRomance Reviews*

"Denise Agnew's contribution to this anthology is just the right mixture of suppressed attraction, sensual heat and emotion. You can clearly see how Jemma's family life creates issues that she must deal with before she can decide if she wants Blayne in her life for more than one night." ~ *Enchanted Romance Reviews*

"Ms. Agnew writes a very sensual tale about two people who are trying to find their path along true love's course...This is one very sexually charged tale...Highly emotional, deeply romantic..." ~ *Love Romances*

"Kate Hill, Denise Agnew and Arianna Hart do a superb job weaving the three stories together seamlessly... an anthology of military romance that will linger in your mind long past bedtime." ~ *Romance Junkies*

"The three authors compliment each other's writing styles perfectly to bring you an anthology of military romance that will linger in your mind long past bedtime." ~ *Kim, Romance Junkies*

"Arianna Hart knows how to heat up the pages until they combust! This is a tale full of action, bullets flying, run and hide, fears faced and lots of hot sex." ~ *Valerie, Love Romances.*

"As a great fan of men in uniform, this is one of the best books written so far. Each author has written a descriptive story on a member of the Forbes family so well, it was as if I was experiencing every second of a Marine's life. I enjoyed reading each member's struggle for love." ~ *Suz, Coffee Time Romance*

Praise for Silver Fire

"Arianna Hart's SILVER FIRE was an absolutely stunning and gorgeous read. Her sure fire brand of hunky and hard hero is once again present and the plot is captivating and thrilling as is her usual best." ~ *Lady Novelistic, Romance Junkies*

Kate Hill
Denise A. Agnew
Arianna Hart

BY HONOR Bound

BY HONOR BOUND
An Ellora's Cave Publication, May 2005

Ellora's Cave Publishing, Inc.
1337 Commerce Drive, Suite #13
Stow, Ohio 44224

ISBN #1419951920

Other available formats: ISBN MS Reader (LIT), Adobe (PDF), Rocketbook (RB), Mobipocket (PRC) & HTML

Edited by: *Briana St. James and Martha Punches*
Cover art by: *Syneca*

Warning:

The following material contains graphic sexual content meant for mature readers. *By Honor Bound* has been rated S-*ensuous* by a minimum of three independent reviewers.

Ellora's Cave Publishing offers three levels of Romantica™ reading entertainment: S (S-ensuous), E (E-rotic), and X (X-treme).

S-*ensuous* love scenes are explicit and leave nothing to the imagination.

E-*rotic* love scenes are explicit, leave nothing to the imagination, and are high in volume per the overall word count. In addition, some E-rated titles might contain fantasy material that some readers find objectionable, such as bondage, submission, same sex encounters, forced seductions, etc. E-rated titles are the most graphic titles we carry; it is common, for instance, for an author to use words such as "fucking", "cock", "pussy", etc., within their work of literature.

X-*treme* titles differ from E-rated titles only in plot premise and storyline execution. Unlike E-rated titles, stories designated with the letter X tend to contain controversial subject matter not for the faint of heart.

Contents

His Sister's Kiss

Kate Hill

Chapter One

December 23, 1967
North Carolina

Oh goodness.

Angela Christine Franco stared at the six-foot-three-inch hunk of Marine. Deep set blue eyes gazed at her from beneath an almost primitive brow. Broad shoulders, set straight and proud, filled her doorway. Beneath the uniform, his powerful chest tapered to a lean waist and the longest legs she'd ever seen on a man. Her heart fluttered and desire coursed through her as her mouth suddenly went dry.

"Miss Franco? I'm Abraham Marley Forbes." His deep voice made her toes curl and her body tingle in all the right places.

Guilt washed over her. Lust should be the last thought inspired by this man.

Two months ago, Angela had learned her brother, Jim, a gunnery sergeant in the corps who had been missing in action in Vietnam, had died in a prison camp. Abraham, Jim's good friend, had been with him at the time.

In spite of his handsome looks, captivity shone in the thinness of his big-boned frame and the scar above his right eye.

She grasped the hand he extended and shook it. Warmth spread up her arm and her temperature rose from his touch. "Please come in."

With a slight nod, he stepped into the hallway and followed her to the parlor.

"It's good of you to come by," she said.

"I'd hoped you wouldn't object. Jim spoke so much about you and Polly that I almost feel I know you."

Angela smiled. "I understand. He mentioned you several times in letters."

"I wanted to see for myself that you're both all right and let you know you can depend on me for anything you might need."

Angela drew a deep breath, thinking she needed to know if his lips felt as soft as they looked. *Damn you, Angela! Get a hold of yourself. It's certainly not the first time you've seen a man in uniform!* But she'd never seen one quite like this. Virility oozed from his every pore. He emanated such power and authority. Those cool sapphire eyes fixed on her and she resisted the urge to squirm in her seat. Her belly tightened in an unaccustomed feeling of sexual desire.

"That's generous of you, but we're fine. It was rough going at first, trying to make Polly understand that Jim's gone." Angela paused, shaking her head and swallowing hard. "God, usually I handle it better than this."

"It's all right." His voice softened a bit. "Jim was a damn good man. He saved my ass—I mean my life—more times than I can count."

"He said the same about you."

"There are some things Jim wanted me to tell you. I promised that if I ever got out of there, I'd make sure you'd know. Polly, too. Is that her?" He glanced at the picture on the coffee table.

"Yes. She looks like Jim, doesn't she?"

"Sure does." Abraham touched the brass frame.

"As you probably know, her mother died shortly after she was born."

He nodded, his penetrating gaze fixing on her again. This time she noticed emotions burning beneath the calm surface of his eyes.

"How are you?" she asked.

"I'm fine, ma'am."

"I can't begin to imagine what you must have gone through."

"That's good. I'm glad you can't and hope you never have reason to find out."

"Are you on leave?"

"Yes, ma'am. For the next three weeks. I just got out of the hospital a couple of days ago."

"It's nice you'll be able to spend the holidays with your family."

"No family, ma'am."

"None?" She felt a twinge of sadness. How awful that this man who had been captured, tortured, and finally rescued had no family to welcome him home.

"No, ma'am. The holidays never meant much to me anyway. I'm not one for celebrations."

"This year Polly and I are keeping it quiet. Making a big fuss so soon after Jim's death just wouldn't feel right."

"I—"

"Hi!" called a small voice. A girl of about five ran into the room. She stopped in front of Abraham, her blue eyes wide.

"Polly, this is Master Sergeant Forbes," Angela explained.

"He looks like Daddy." She crawled onto the couch beside him, sitting close.

Abraham swallowed visibly, his eyes gleaming with emotion that broke free for all of two seconds.

"Polly, why don't you come sit with me and give him some room?"

"It's all right." Abraham placed an arm around the girl who gazed up at him. "Polly, I came here to talk about your dad. He and I knew each other for a long time and he told me a lot about you and your aunt."

"I miss him."

"I know. So do I."

Abraham spoke to Polly for about an hour. As Angela listened to him relay her brother's messages, part of her wished it was Jim sitting with them while another part of her was grateful Abraham had survived.

She knew a good man when she saw one, and she had no doubt that Abraham was one of the best.

*****

"Polly, go get washed up for dinner," Angela said.

"Is Abe staying?"

Angela's gaze met the Master Sergeant's. Her mouth went dry. Standing, she moistened her lips. "If he wants to."

"No. I have to go." He stood and straightened his jacket.

"Oh." Angela wondered if she appeared as disappointed as she felt. Not that it mattered. Polly looked disappointed enough for both of them. "It would be no problem for you to stay."

"I wouldn't want to be any trouble, ma'am."

"You won't be. There's plenty of food, but if you stay I must ask you one favor." He lifted an eyebrow and she grinned. "Stop calling me ma'am. Polly, wash up and set the table. Abe, you can help me peel potatoes."

"KP I can handle." He smiled, following her into the kitchen as Polly hurried upstairs.

Moments later, Angela and Abe stood side by side. He washed and peeled potatoes in the sink while she chopped them. In between cutting, she glanced at him from the corner of her eye. He'd removed his jacket and rolled up his sleeves, revealing powerful wrists and sinewy forearms dusted with dark hair. His huge, long-fingered hands were far more graceful than she'd expect from a man like him.

"Would you like to spend the holidays with us, Abe?"

He paused and turned to her, holding her captive with his deep blue gaze. He drew a long breath and released it slowly. "I don't think it would be appropriate."

"Jim's dead. Neither of us are in the mood to celebrate, so why don't we be miserable together?"

A slight smile touched his finely drawn lips. "When you put it that way, it's hard to say no."

"We're eating at four o'clock tomorrow night, but come early if you want. The weather is supposed to be bad."

He nodded. "Thank you for the invitation."

"You're welcome."

Angela resumed chopping. Her belly fluttered at the thought of spending Christmas with him. Polly obviously adored him, so Angela told herself it was for her niece's sake that she'd invited him. She didn't want to admit how much he stirred her libido.

*****

Abe inhaled deeply, cold air filling his lungs. The weather was surprisingly harsh for these parts, even for wintertime.

For months he'd dreaded the thought of visiting Jim's family. Few people had meant anything to him in his life, but Jim had been one of them. They'd gone through much together—boot camp and two tours of Vietnam. It was that last time they'd been captured—the only survivors of an ambush. How many times had they wished they'd died with the rest of their squad?

Abe considered himself a strong man and a good soldier. He thought he'd seen just about everything, but nothing had prepared him for the hell of the prison camp. Shitting himself while chest-deep in swamp muck became a way of life along with beatings and other abuses he didn't want to remember.

About a month after their capture, Jim died of an infection. Abe had actually envied him, except for one thing. He had a family, a daughter in the care of his sister, a young woman who earned her living as a tutor. Jim talked about them often, sharing with Abe a family life he'd only dreamed of. In spite of his decent looks and a body most men would kill for, Abe couldn't seem to hold onto a woman. He just couldn't relate to most people. Orphaned as a boy, Abe had spent his life shuffled among distant relatives until finally ending up in a home where he lived until joining the Marines at eighteen. Always a focused young man, he'd taken well to military life. He'd never regretted joining, even while suffering in that Vietnamese shit hole. The Corps was his life, the only place where he'd ever really belonged, so he couldn't help admiring Jim's family life. Before Jim died, Abe had promised that if he ever made it home, he'd see that Jim's sister and daughter never wanted for anything.

Almost a year after his capture, Abe was rescued. Nearly dead from starvation and disease, he'd spent the past couple of months hospitalized and in counseling to help him "deal with" what he'd gone through. He'd rebelled at first, wanting to work through his ordeal in his own way. The Corps didn't agree, however. Unless he wanted to continue as a prisoner in his own country, he'd take the counseling provided.

Abe had needed it more than he realized. Anger, fear, and pain were bottled inside him. Those emotions still hadn't dissipated and he doubted they ever would. Then there were the nightmares. At night instead of resting, he was back in 'Nam, fighting for his next breath. The leave hadn't been his idea. The last thing he wanted was three weeks of nothing to do but think about where he'd been and what he'd seen.

That was why Angela's invitation was so welcome. Normally Abe would never have agreed to spend Christmas with anybody. Hell, he didn't even celebrate holidays. Ever. The minute he'd looked into her beautiful hazel eyes, the second he'd stepped into that warm, cheery little house, he'd felt strangely comfortable. Perhaps it was because Jim had spoken of her so much, but he felt as if he and Angela weren't strangers at all.

It's her terrific body, he told himself. Those gorgeous breasts that filled out her black and white checkered dress belted at her waist and draping hips so shapely that his mouth watered. Damn, his health must be returning after all. It had been quite a while since he'd thought about taking a woman to bed.

What the hell is wrong with you, Forbes? This isn't some two-dollar whore from the docks. She's your deceased friend's sister, so don't treat her like anything but a lady.

Then there was Polly. Looking at the kid breached the icy barrier years of loneliness had erected around his heart. She had eyes like Jim and Angela. Talking to a child at an age when she was so honest and wondering refreshed him in a way he never imagined possible.

Jim should be here instead, enjoying his family. Why was Abe, a man with no strings attached to anyone, alive and Jim, a man with so much to live for, dead?

Just one of those questions to which there would never be an answer.

Chapter Two

Angela's stomach churned so much she wondered how she was going to eat the Christmas Eve dinner she'd spent the day preparing. Whenever she thought of Abe, heat rose in her face and her heart raced like a love-struck teenager's. Something in the man's steady blue eyes and sexy Texas drawl did things to her emotions she never imagined possible.

Most women her age were married with families of their own. She'd had offers from several decent young men her parents loved, but they hadn't stirred her.

"You're throwing your life away searching for a dream," her mother often told her. "Romance is an illusion. Marriage is about hard work and sacrifice. It's about not growing old alone, like what's happening to you."

Angela refused to make sacrifices for someone she didn't love. Jim and his wife had love. They'd been happy together, but where had it gotten them? At least now they were rejoined in death.

Shaking her head, Angela finished sprinkling cheese over the pan of baked macaroni and placed it in the oven to keep warm. This season without Jim was depressing enough. Why make herself even more miserable and ruin the night for Polly and Abe?

Abe with his broad shoulders and long, hard-muscled legs. Abe who weakened her with a single look.

"How's that, Aunt Angela?" Polly gestured toward the table she'd just finished setting.

"It looks lovely. Why don't you get Abe's present and put it on the coffee table?"

Polly hurried to retrieve the gift they'd shopped for that morning. Unsure of what to buy on such short notice for a man she scarcely knew, Angela had decided gloves were a safe enough choice. Besides, his large, long-fingered hands would look rather sensual in the black leather gloves.

No sooner had Angela placed the basket of sliced bread and butter on the table than the doorbell rang.

"I'll get it!" Polly shouted, racing ahead of her aunt and pausing in front of the door. "Who's there?"

"It's Abe."

Polly tugged open the door.

Angela grinned at the sight of the towering Master Sergeant carrying two boxes wrapped in red and green paper.

"Abe, you shouldn't have," Angela said, taking the gifts he handed Polly.

Shrugging, he met her gaze. A shiver ran down her spine. She told herself it was from the cold, but would the cold make her tingle and buzz in places that made her blush?

"Come in and sit. Dinner's ready." Angela glanced at him over her shoulder. "I hope you like macaroni."

"When it comes to food, I like just about everything, but I must say, Angela, your cooking smells especially good."

"I hope it doesn't disappoint you."

"It would be hard for anything about you to be disappointing..." He held her gaze and looked almost sheepish before adding, "ma'am."

Angela's pulse skipped. This man liked her. She was sure of it. Not just any like. This was the deep-down, giddy, I'm-thinking-of-the-wedding-night kind of like she'd always dreamed about.

Drawing a deep breath, she took the food from the oven and told herself to get a grip on her emotions. Her brother was dead. This was his best friend who had come to offer some comfort. Maybe her mother was right. She was a dreamer getting desperate with longing for the impossible relationship she'd imagined.

Polly sat at the table, nabbing Abe's attention with a flurry of questions and stories about school and tomorrow's visit to her grandparents.

Though Angela didn't get along well with her parents, she felt Polly deserved a relationship with them. Jim had felt the same, which was why he'd made Angela his daughter's legal guardian.

"I hope we don't get a storm tomorrow," Polly said. She glanced at Abe. "Aunt Polly won't drive to Grandma and Grandpa's in bad weather."

"Don't worry. We'll get there." Angela tugged the girl's ponytail. All day long the news had been filled with stories of the ice storm moving toward North Carolina.

"I'd be glad to drive you," Abe said.

"We wouldn't want to impose."

"It would be no imposition."

"I'll call Grandma and tell her Abe's coming." Polly darted for the phone.

"Would that be a problem?" he asked. "Because if you think they wouldn't want to see me, I don't mind giving you the ride. I don't want to upset them any more than they must already be."

"If you're driving us, then you're coming to eat. Besides, I think they'd like to meet you." Angela dished out the macaroni, giving Abe an extra helping. "You look like you can use this."

The corners of his lips tugged up in what might have been a smile. He always looked so serious and stern it was hard to tell. "I haven't had a home-cooked meal since I was about nine years old. Mess hall food's not bad, though. I kinda like it, especially after the shi—" He glanced at Polly. "I mean garbage I was eating this past year."

Angela shuddered to think about what he and Jim had gone through. She had the strangest urge to offer him comfort in every way imaginable. This man was getting under her skin and no matter how she tried keeping her thoughts decent and pure, it just wasn't happening.

After dinner, the three sat in the living room and exchanged gifts.

"It's a dog!" Polly beamed, tugging the shaggy brown stuffed animal from the box.

Angela smiled. "She loves dogs."

"I know. Jim said so lots of times." Abe glanced at the present on Angela's lap.

She tore off the paper and opened the box.

"Oh!" She lifted out the snow globe with a deer family standing in front of a log cabin with a pine tree nearby. "It's beautiful. Thank you, Abe."

Again that faint smile flickered across his mouth as his gaze held hers with such intensity that her belly tightened. Thank goodness for the heavy sweater disguising her pebble-hard nipples. The beauty and depth of the man's eyes turned her to liquid.

"Are you going to open yours?" she prodded, anxious for his gaze to fix on something other than her.

He unwrapped the gloves and tried them on. "These are great, ladies. Just what I needed."

"Polly, it's time for you to get ready for bed."

"Can I sleep with my dog?"

"Sure can," Angela said. "Don't forget to brush your teeth."

"Goodnight, Aunt Angela. See you tomorrow, Abe."

"Goodnight, darlin'."

Angela smiled. Though that particular darlin' was meant for her niece, the sound of his deep, sexy drawl caressing the words made her tingle with desire.

Sitting on her end of the couch, Angela folded her arms beneath her breasts and smiled.

"What?" he asked.

"You're not what I was expecting, that's all."

He tilted his head to one side and narrowed his eyes. "That a good thing?"

"Feels that way."

"Me too," he murmured and stood. "I should go, ma'am."

"Why?" Angela's brow furrowed and she approached. Maybe he didn't like her after all? Why was that thought so alarming? She couldn't have any real feelings for him. For heaven's sake, they'd only just met!

"Because." He drew a deep breath and released it slowly. Emotions gleamed behind the cool sapphire surface of his eyes. "I want to kiss you, Angela, and that would be a despicable thing right now."

Angela's heart fluttered and her mouth went dry. Kiss her. That was exactly what she wanted and felt just as guilty about it as he looked.

"I'm sorry," he said, reaching for his cap and jacket hanging on the brass coat rack by the fireplace. "I don't know why I said that."

"Maybe because it's true."

"You must think I'm some kind of snake in the grass, coming here with Jim dead and—"

"Jim was my brother, not my husband." Angela placed a hand on his forearm. Beneath his sleeve, his arm felt so hard, so powerful. What was wrong with her? She'd met this man once and already she couldn't imagine life without him. Was this fate or desperation for both of them? He'd just gotten home after a year in hell. He had no family, no one besides military shrinks to share his problems with. In a strange role reversal, Angela found herself concerned that *she* was taking advantage of *him*.

"Please don't go," she said, vowing not to do anything either of them would regret. "It's Christmas Eve."

"You heard what I just said."

"Yes."

"And you don't care?"

"I care. I just don't..." She sighed, shaking her head. "I don't want you to go."

For a long moment they stood, their gazes locked. Simultaneously they walked to the couch and sat, though not at opposite ends this time. One of his long, hard thighs pressed against her leg, distracting them though they talked of the coming storm and other trivial matters.

Suddenly his hand cupped her face, his thumb gently stroking her smooth cheek as he stared deeply into her eyes. His warmth seemed to reach out and enfold her in powerful yet invisible arms that refused to let her go.

Angela's heart thumped against her ribs and she moistened her lips with the tip of her tongue. As Abe leaned a bit closer, his firm lips parted slightly.

God, she thought. *He really is going to kiss me.*

He gently drew her face closer to his. Angela's eyes slid shut when his mouth touched hers. The sensation was unlike anything she'd ever experienced. Abe's firm yet soft lips moved tenderly against hers. She'd never imagined sensing a man's emotions through a kiss. Lust, yes, but nothing else. Not like what she felt from Abe. How could a man she just met pour so much affection into a kiss?

Warmth from his body spread through her. She edged closer, slipping her arms around his neck. God, she'd never been in the arms of a man this big and strong. The back and shoulders beneath her palms felt like steel. Her breasts flattened against a chest of warm granite. Her nipples swelled, aching for his touch. He smelled so good, too, so clean and male.

Abe kissed both corners of her mouth then buried his face in the hollow of her shoulder. As he licked her neck, a shudder rippled down her spine. Heat emanated from her belly, spreading lower and settling deep in her pussy.

In the midst of her rising passion, she felt something hard and oh-so-arousing pressing against her stomach. In all her life, she'd never felt a man's erect cock. The sudden urge to unzip him and touch all she'd been missing was almost overwhelming.

He stood suddenly and ran a hand through his ultra-short hair. "I'm sorry about that."

"Are you?" Her pulse racing, she approached and touched his arm.

"No. Actually I'm not." He reached for his jacket and cap. "Thank you for a lovely Christmas Eve, Angela."

"Thank you for coming, Abe."

Angela's belly fluttered. He'd only held her once, but she missed the sensation of his embrace and his soft, moist lips against hers. Somehow she knew the rest of the night would seem empty without him.

God, she was falling in love just like a schoolgirl.

"I'm glad you can join us tomorrow," she continued, walking him to the door. "I have to warn you about my parents, though. They can be a little difficult."

"I can take it."

"I don't know. Jim used to say boot camp was nothing after Ma and Daddy."

A smile turned up the corners of his mouth. "I believe I recall him saying something like that, but you're lucky to have a family."

"Oh, I appreciate them, as long as they're not complaining about how I'm not married yet."

"To be honest, I've wondered about that myself." His gaze held hers and Angela's pulse raced. "Just tell me to mind my own business, ma'am."

"Actually it's because I haven't found a man I could imagine spending the rest of my life with."

Until now. The image of her and Abe married with a bunch of kids appealed to her almost too much. Another image of him disappearing overseas and never coming back shoved her out of her reverie. He was a Marine. There was always the chance that, like Jim, he might lose his life while serving his country.

"Goodnight, Angela." His warm, callused hand curved around her nape as he kissed her again.

If Polly wasn't upstairs, she might just consider asking him to stay a bit longer. If her mother only knew the thoughts running through Angela's mind at the moment, she'd probably faint.

"Goodnight," she said, watching him slip on his new gloves. "Drive safely."

Nodding, he held her gaze as he opened the door and stepped outside. Halfway across the driveway, he glanced over his shoulder at her.

Angela waved again, cursing the tingling warmth that enveloped her body each time he so much as looked at her.

Chapter Three

"I hope my coming here isn't any trouble, ma'am." Abe broke the heavy silence. He, Angela, and her parents sat in the living room. Polly settled on the floor next to the stuffed dog Abe had given her and played with a deck of cards.

"Of course not." Mrs. Franco forced a smile. "Any friend of Jim's is welcome here, even if he did choose to leave our grandchild with a young, single girl instead of a proper two-parent family."

"Ma!" Angela snapped.

"It's true. I can't say any more, though." Mrs. Franco nodded in Polly's direction. "Big ears on little people. I wouldn't want to confuse the child."

"Damn it, Patricia," Mr. Franco growled from where he sat on an easy chair, staring at television with the sound turned down. "Can't we get through a single holiday without an argument? And who knows, maybe Abe here will marry Angela and we won't have to worry."

"Dad!' Angela glared, then turned her gaze to Abe. "I'm sorry about this."

He shrugged, amusement gleaming in his eyes.

"Are you married, Abe?" Patricia asked.

"No, ma'am."

"Have you ever been married?"

"That's enough, Mother!" Angela stood. "Isn't it about time to eat? I'll help you get the table ready."

Patricia touched Abe's arm as she stood. "She's basically a good girl, but can be a bit pushy."

"And too damn stubborn for her own good," Mr. Franco grumbled.

"Grandpa, will you play cards with me?" Polly approached.

"Sure."

"Abe, you want to play, too?" Polly gazed up at him.

If Angela hadn't been so embarrassed by her parents, she would have laughed at Abe's expression of relief. At least if they were playing cards the stupid conversation would end.

Dinner wasn't much better. Though Mr. Franco was too busy eating to be much of a conversationalist, his wife talked enough for both of them. Angela had to admit Abe's patience impressed her. By the time dessert was served, Angela had taken about all she could of her mother's innuendos and her father's sarcasm.

"Looks pretty icy out there." Angela glanced out the window over the kitchen sink as she washed the last of the dishes.

"Thank goodness Polly is staying with us for the next few days," Patricia said. "I hate to think of her in a car with all that ice out there. Maybe you should stay, too, Angela."

"No!" Angela exchanged glances with Abe. This time he couldn't help smiling. "I'd much rather go home. I have planning to do for some students."

"Honey, you could do that here."

"No, Ma. I'm better off at home."

"You mean with him?" Mr. Franco jerked his head in Abe's direction.

Angela's teeth ground. She was about to snap when Abe said, "You don't have to worry, Sir. I have the utmost respect for your daughter."

"Uh-huh. I know what young Marines are like."

"I appreciate your concern, but I'm no longer a young Marine, Sir."

"I think we should go now." Angela dried her hands and walked to the closet, grabbing her coat and Abe's. "Before the rain starts and everything freezes even worse."

"But we haven't had dessert yet!" Patricia said.

"We'll get it later."

Abe's brow furrowed as Angela threw his coat over his shoulders and dragged him toward the front door.

"Polly, you have fun and be good for Grandma and Grandpa," Angela called.

"Bye, Aunt Angela." Polly rushed to the door and hugged her Aunt. She tilted her face up to Abe. "Bye, Abe."

"Bye, darlin'." He ruffled her hair then turned to Mr. and Mrs. Franco. "Thank you for dinner. It was delicious, ma'am."

"You make sure Angela brings you by more often. You need to get fattened up a bit."

"Yes, ma'am." Again his eyes gleamed with repressed laughter.

When they reached the car, he chuckled, the deep, amused sound warming Angela to her toes and soothing her frustration after visiting with her parents.

"I told you!" she said. "Now do you understand why Jim didn't want them to raise Polly? I'm surprised the two of us grew up without losing our minds completely."

"I think they mean well."

"They drive me crazy!"

"Your Ma's a good cook."

"Food. Is that all men care about?"

"Not *all*." He glanced at her. The look in his eye made her shiver with desire. It was exactly how he looked last night before he kissed her. She had the feeling that if he hadn't been concentrating on maneuvering the car down the icy road, he would have done so again.

It was dark with they reached her house. The freezing rain had stopped and moonlight bathed the front yard.

"Thank you for inviting me for Christmas," he said as he parked the car and turned to her.

"Thank you for the ride."

"You're welcome."

His eyes burned into hers. In spite of the frigid weather outside, she'd never felt warmer.

"Would you like to come in, Abe?"

"Would you like me to come in?"

She swallowed, her gaze sweeping his handsome face as she recalled the softness of his lips and the hardness of his body. "Yes, very much."

Brushing a fingertip across her lips, he drew a deep breath. With a slight nod, he stepped out of the car. As Angela searched through her purse for the house key, he opened her door and held out his hand. She looked up, feeling almost like Cinderella stepping out of a pumpkin coach into the arms of her prince.

She took his hand. Her high-heeled boots slipped on the ice, but he steadied her, one arm wrapped around her waist and holding her close to his tall, steely body.

"I…I'm fine. Just clumsy." She tilted her face up, feeling the warmth of his breath against her lips.

His mouth covered hers, his lips soft and moist, his tongue gently caressing hers. Angela's arms wrapped around his neck and she giggled as he literally swept her off her feet.

"What are you doing? Put me down."

"I don't want to let you go."

She swallowed hard, her heart racing. God, she didn't want him to let her go! Never in her life had she experienced such a reaction to a man. It was as if their souls were intertwined. Though she couldn't explain how, she felt she knew Abe, that somehow they belonged together.

You're being a fool, Angela. He's trying to get you to bed. That's all. In truth, she wanted to get him in bed as well. All through her teens and her adult life, she'd never slept with a man. She'd always told herself when the right man came along, she'd know it and there would be no hesitation. Now here he was and she knew without doubt it was right.

When they reached the door, he placed her on her feet so she could open it.

"It's cold in here," Angela said as she stepped inside. "Would you like coffee or tea?"

"Whatever you're having is fine."

Angela rubbed her hands together to warm them. "I think I'll build a fire."

"I'll do it." He headed for the living room. "Might as well make myself useful."

Oh, he was going to be useful all right, Angela smiled.

Her head spun as she stepped into the kitchen to prepare tea. Just when she thought her life would settle down, something completely unexpected had to happen. Her attraction to Abe was so powerful that she couldn't help feeling the elation of new love, yet part of her feared the future. What if she did fall madly in love with him and, like Jim, he left her far too soon? Yet, that was the risk everyone took. Life had no guarantees. She knew that well enough.

She jumped as arms encircled her from behind and Abe's stubbled face and warm lips nuzzled her neck. He moved so quietly for such a large man.

"Don't think this is a common thing for me," she said, trying to keep coherent thoughts as he kissed her neck and hugged her close to his powerful frame. Her eyes half-closed, she reached up and stroked his face. "I don't usually act like this with men I just met."

"I know."

"How do you know?"

"Just a feeling. Sometimes that's all you have to go with."

She turned, gazing up at him. His sapphire eyes stared intently into hers. Her hands slid up his arms and across his impossibly broad shoulders. What did he feel like under all those clothes? Was his chest smooth or hairy? Did he have scars? He must. What did his cock look like? Was it big and veined like the ones in dirty magazines her girlfriends had gotten hold of in high school? Was it ruddy or pale? What would it feel like? She couldn't imagine.

"I won't lie, Angela," he said in a hushed voice. "I want to take you to bed."

"I know."

"I should go."

Clasping the back of his neck, she tugged his face closer as she stood on tiptoe and whispered against his lips, "No you shouldn't."

"The fire's going."

Taking his hand, she walked to the living room and knelt on the rug in front of the fire. Abe unfastened the top buttons of his shirt and stretched out on his side. He tugged her alongside him and stroked wisps of hair from her face. He kissed her forehead and each eyelid.

"Abe?" She slid her hands up his torso and began undoing the rest of the buttons on his shirt.

"Yes, darlin'."

There it was. That endearment spoken in his deep, sultry drawl just for her.

"What's going to happen tomorrow?"

His brow furrowed.

"I mean, what's going to happen to us tomorrow?"

"You're not getting rid of me fast, if that's what you think."

She smiled. "No, that's not what I thought."

"Yes, you did." His eyes glistened with amusement. "Like your Daddy said, you think I'm some wild Marine with bad intentions."

"What if I'm the one with bad intentions?"

He smiled slightly and kissed her, pushing her gently onto her back and stroking the column of her throat. Covering her mouth with his, he parted her lips with his tongue. Hers met it, so warm and tender, as they caressed one another with long, slow strokes. His deft fingers unbuttoned the front of her dress. The tops of her plump breasts were exposed above the neckline of the cream-colored slip she wore beneath. He kissed the soft, pink-tinged flesh while stroking the slight swell of her belly and the curve of her hip.

Angela kicked off her shoes and slid her foot up his calf.

"You're a beautiful woman, Angela," he said.

"Thank you." She caressed his smooth nape. "You're not so bad yourself."

He sat up, shrugged off his shirt, and tugged his T-shirt over his head.

Angela's mouth went dry at the sight of his long torso. Without a pound of spare flesh, every bone and muscle shone like a granite statue chiseled by the most talented artist. Scars marked his torso, some faded white, others still pinkish. Closing her eyes, she swallowed passed tightness in her throat. The idea of him suffering combined with the knowledge that Jim had died enduring the same tortures was almost too much to tolerate. She drew a deep breath and shook her head. If Abe had lived through it, then she wouldn't turn chicken on him now.

Instead, she concentrated on the light dusting of hair that covered his chest, tapered down his flat abdomen, and disappeared beneath the waistband of his trousers. She sat up and splayed her hands across his back, her fingertips tracing several jagged scars.

"Are you going to be cold down here on the floor?" he asked.

"Somehow I doubt that."

While he finished undressing, Angela did the same, rolling off her stockings and sliding out of the dress. She was about to remove her slip, but her gaze riveted to Abe. For a moment, she was unable to move, only stare. She'd never seen a naked man in the flesh, but Abe was far better than anything she'd looked at in those stupid magazines.

His legs were incredibly long, dusted with hair, and curved with rock-hard muscle. With narrow hips and buttocks big and tight enough to make a woman's heartbeat skip, he personified male beauty.

Again, he stretched out beside her. Angela inched closer as he drew her into his arms. Closing her eyes, she rubbed her cheek against his chest and inhaled his sexy scent of clean, male flesh. His body was so warm and hard. Nothing compared with being wrapped in the arms of a man like this!

"I want you so bad, Angela," he said in a husky voice, one of his hands pressed against her back, the other buried in her hair, stroking tenderly.

"Then take me, Abe." She tilted her face upward and gazed into his eyes, her pulse racing. "Take me."

Abe's hand swept down her shoulder and arm. It slid across her lower back then cupped one of her smooth bottom cheeks. He kissed her temple and cheek before claiming her lips in a kiss that made her forget everything else.

"Oh, Abe," she murmured, refusing to take her hands off him even as he sat up.

Angela's breathing quickened. He looked so gorgeous, kneeling there, his lips slightly parted and his eyes burning with lust. Reaching up, she caressed his chest and brushed a fingertip across one of his flat, pink nipples peeking through the crisp hair. It felt soft, the nub scarcely visible. Her hand trailed lower, feeling his ribs and the hard, defined abdominal muscles.

Her gaze fixed on his cock. It stood, thick and pinkish, above a nest of dark hair. The balls dangling below were large and looked so full, so alluring, that she couldn't resist taking them in her hand. They spilled over her palm as she gently squeezed, loving their softness and warmth. He drew a deep breath as her fingers ran up and down his cock. Now *that* felt hard. Stiff and hot, like steel covered in warm velvet. The little eye in the smooth, bulbous head fascinated her. She ran her thumb over it and around the underside.

"Do I pass the test?" he grinned.

"Looks good to me," she replied, gazing at him through her lashes and tossing him a coquettish look. "Not that I have anything to compare it to."

"You know, Angela," he slid the straps of her slip down her shoulders and inched toward her feet where he tugged off the entire flimsy piece of satin and lace, "I kinda hope to keep it that way. Are you going to take off those undergarments, or do you want me to do it?"

Her heart leapt and she licked her lips as a sudden case of nerves struck her. In moments, she would be completely naked with a man who stirred her like no one ever had. Was she nervous? Of course. Did she still want him? More than anything she'd ever wanted in her life.

Sitting up, she unhooked her bra. The heat of his gaze was almost tangible as she bared her breasts and tossed the bra aside. They were full, rounded globes tipped with rose-colored nipples now elongated with desire. Her entire body was covered in smooth, creamy flesh tinted delectable pink. She was pleasantly rounded with flaring hips and long, curvaceous legs. Abe could scarcely wait to be buried deep inside her. But he would have to. He knew without question this responsible and pretty tutor was innocent in the ways of love. Though he sensed no fear in her, curiosity such as she exhibited, as well as the naïveté of her touch told him she had little experience with men.

Damn, he felt lucky. It was as if after a year of the worst kind of hell, he was being rewarded by finding the woman of his dreams. Reaching out, he brushed his hand down her arm. Her skin was so soft and warm. Not only did she arouse him physically, but she reached inside him and touched upon buried emotions. All his life he'd longed for the true affection only offered by a family. As a child he'd been denied the love of his parents. Into adulthood, no woman had ever breached his cool, warrior's heart. Maybe it was fear, like one of the shrinks had suggested. Fear that if he did love somebody, they'd be snatched away. He protected himself with his loneliness. What he didn't have, he couldn't miss.

Now he realized exactly what he had been missing. This woman did things to him he'd never felt before. She twisted his insides and wrapped his soul in hers, breaching his mental defenses when even the VC couldn't.

A slight blush on her cheeks and a sexy little smile on her lips, Angela lowered her eyes as she hooked her thumbs in the waistband of her white satin panties and slid them off. The triangular patch of dark hair between her legs made his breath catch. It seemed everything about her was beautiful.

He cupped one of her calves in his hands and stroked upward, over her soft, smooth thighs and ran his fingers through the arousing thatch of curly hair. With one of her hips in his hand, he used his other to continue stroking her soft mound. His thumb found the ruddy peak of her clit and he stroked over it. She drew a sharp breath at his touch.

Tenderly, he parted her thighs and circled her clit with this fingertip, pushing it in slightly. She felt so hot and wet that his erection leapt. It seemed he turned her on as much as she aroused him.

Removing a wet fingertip, he circled her clit.

Angela shivered and fell back on the rug, closing her eyes as he stroked and caressed where she was so warm and aching. Her clit throbbed as he stroked faster.

"Oh, Abe!" she gasped. His free hand moved up her ribs and found her breast. His thumbs rolled over her nipple and clit simultaneously. Angela was going to shatter, but she didn't care.

He was giving her something she so desperately needed. So desperate—

"Ahh! Oh, God! Oh, Abe!" she panted, her entire body convulsing in hot waves of throbbing pleasure. As they crashed over her, she couldn't see. Her heartbeat echoed in her ears. Every muscle in her body convulsed in the most exquisite manner imaginable.

She lay still for several moments, her eyes closed as her breathing returned to normal. Angela had orgasms before. She enjoyed masturbating every now and then, just to rid herself of natural sexual urges. Never in her life had she dreamed an orgasm so intense. It must have been because she'd been under Abe's control. The thought of him touching her was as exciting as the actual sensations. The combination created almost unbearable pleasure.

"That had to be the most beautiful thing I've ever seen," Abe said, lying beside her and stroking her throat.

Opening her eyes, she smiled. "That had to be the most beautiful thing I've ever felt."

"It will get even better, darlin'. I promise."

"I know." She cupped the back of his neck and drew his face closer for a kiss. "I want to feel you inside me, Abe. I want to know what it's like."

Reaching for his trousers, he tugged something out of his pocket. She watched as he opened the condom and rolled it on.

With a raised eyebrow she asked, "You always come prepared or were you planning this after all?"

"I won't lie. I was hoping for it."

"Well, you are honest." She lay on her back and stared at the ceiling.

"But I wasn't hoping just for tonight, Angela." He turned her face toward him. "I can't explain how I feel. I'm a man of action. Always have been. I can't rightly put these emotions I have into words."

"Try."

"The other day when you opened the door, I felt like somebody had kicked me in the gut. You grabbed hold of my heart and you're not letting go. That's never happened to me before."

"Me either, but I always hoped it would." She smiled. "Either I'm the biggest fool in the world or I'm right about you being..."

"Being what?"

"If I say, I'll probably scare you off."

Lying beside her, he pressed her body close to his as he stared deeply into her eyes. "You're never scaring me off, understand? I'll go if you ask me to, but other than that you're not getting rid of me any time soon. How do you feel about a broken-down Marine set on making you his woman?"

His woman!

"Abe, we're moving too fast, aren't we?"

"Way too fast." He smiled, nuzzling her neck.

"You know, I don't care. This is the first time in my life I've ever been this happy."

His gaze held hers. "I'm glad, Angela."

"So am I." She clutched his head as he kissed her.

Looming above her, his hands braced on both sides of her head, he gazed deeply into her eyes as the tip of his cock pressed against her pussy lips.

Abe resisted the urge to groan with pleasure as he inched his way inside. She was so warm and soaked with passion that he longed to plunge in hard and fast, but he couldn't. Angela was not some two-dollar dock-hanging whore. Beneath him, she stiffened a bit and drew a sharp breath as her tight, virginal pussy rebelled a bit against his thickness and length.

"Try and relax, sweet thing," he murmured against her lips.

Her arms slid around him and she gripped his back tightly as he moved with agonizing slowness. Finally he remained still, buried hilt-deep. After a moment, she relaxed and wiggled her hips. A smile curved her delicate lips and her hands stroked his back. It felt so damn good buried inside her that it was all he could do keep his thrusts slow and easy.

Angela's eyes slid shut as Abe thrust. Wrapping her legs around him, she pressed her heels against his calves as her hips joined his rhythm.

"Oh, Abe!" she gasped, clinging to him tightly.

His thrusts quickened. Other than the rasp of his breath, he remained a quiet lover, his lust and desire simmering inside, waiting to burst forth.

"Ahh!" she cried, convulsing in waves of pleasure.

A couple more thrusts and he came, his silence broken with a throaty groan of pure ecstasy. "Damn it, woman! Angela, oh, God!"

Orgasm shot through him, wrapping him in pleasure from head to toe. He collapsed atop her and listened to the slowing of their breathing.

Lifting his head from her shoulder, he gazed at her.

"You all right?" he asked, stroking wisps of hair from her forehead.

She smiled. "Better than all right."

Angela snuggled close. Wrapped in each other's arms, they gazed at the flames crackling in the fireplace.

Chapter Four

Angela awoke to the aroma of coffee and the sound of rhythmic chopping. Flinging off the covers, she smiled as cool air fanned her naked body. What a marvelous night it had been. The memory of Abe's gorgeous, powerful body claiming hers with such tenderness and affection was better than any fantasy. Running a hand over his side of the bed, she longed to see him again as soon as possible.

Reaching for her robe, she slipped into it as she walked to the window to find out the cause of the annoying chopping sound. Tugging up the shade, she blinked against the sunlight. Again she smiled. Abe shoveled ice from her front walk. As if sensing her stare, he turned, his lips curving up in the slightest half-smile as he waved.

Feeling giddy as a schoolgirl, Angela waved back and disappeared into the bathroom where she washed and fixed her hair and makeup.

Naked, she walked into the bedroom just as he stepped inside. Gasping, she covered her breasts, then realized how silly that must appear after last night.

"Sorry," he said, his gaze sweeping her. "Should have knocked."

"I guess it's a little late to be shy." She tried sounding nonchalant in spite of the blush heating her face.

"God, you look beautiful."

She placed a hand on her hip. "So are you going to keep looking or let me get some clothes on?"

"I apologize, ma'am." He looked amused as he left her to pull on her underclothes and a sleek black-and-white polka dot dress with a red belt that matched her lipstick. Slipping her feet into black pumps, she glanced at herself in the full-length mirror behind her door. It must have been the happiness she felt being with Abe, but she hadn't looked this good in weeks.

In the kitchen, he stood, barefoot and shirtless, making more coffee. Angela licked her lips, her pulse racing. The sight of his big bones and hard muscles had her more than ready to head right back to the bedroom.

He glanced at her over his shoulder as she approached and ran her hand from his forearm to his shoulder.

"Took off my shirt and shoes. Picking ice can be as messy as shoveling snow. I drove back to my place early this morning. I needed a change of clothes and you needed salt for your walk."

"Thanks for doing that. Would you like eggs with your toast?"

"Scrambled."

"Fine."

As Angela cracked eggs into a bowl, her heart fluttered as she asked, "How many days' worth of clothes did you get at your place?"

He chuckled. "Is that 'cause you're afraid I'll overstay my welcome?"

"Actually I was hoping you'd stay for a few days. Polly will be with my parents for the rest of the week."

His arm slid around her from behind and his hand folded over hers as she used a wire whisk to beat the eggs. Taking her earlobe in his teeth he licked it gently then kissed her cheek.

"If I stay here for a week, it'll be awful hard to leave."

"Maybe not." She turned, gazing up at him. "We might find we can't stand living with each other."

"So maybe we should make like a couple of those long-haired hippies and try out living together."

"Excuse me, Master Sergeant, but just because I slept with you doesn't mean I'm a—"

"Hold on, darlin'." His brow furrowed and he grasped her shoulders, turning her to face him. "That blood on those sheets this morning surely wasn't from some two-dollar whore practicing free love and all that. I guarantee if I stay here I won't want to go."

"You'll have to. With Polly—"

"I'd never do anything to hurt your reputation or expose that girl to a damaging situation."

"Then what are you saying, Abe?"

He dropped his hold on her and walked across the room, running a hand over his peach-fuzzed head. What the hell was he saying? That the short time he'd spent with her had given him a taste of what he'd been missing all his life? That he was tired of having no one to come home to after spending months in strange places having his ass damn near blown off by enemy fire? Was it really Angela he wanted or the illusion of what she offered? No. He'd never been a man ruled by dreams and fantasies. He was thirty-three years old and had never gotten this close to any woman. Sure, he'd had sex, but he'd never hung around afterward to chop ice off her front walk and look at her whip up scrambled eggs. Just seeing her in that prim, high-necked dress with a strand of pearls around her neck and her hair combed just so as she cooked breakfast made his gut twist with tender feelings he'd never experienced. Earlier, when he'd walked in on her, the sight of her blushing face and gorgeous naked curves had not only given him an erection that would have shamed a breeder bull but stirred his emotions.

"Abe, I really want you to stay," she said, "but I'm afraid."

"Of me?"

"Of doing something I've been told all my life is wrong."

"Then I'll go." He cupped her face in his hand. "Just tell me we can see each other again?"

Angela sighed and took his hand. She kissed his palm. "And I'm afraid because—"

"What?"

She was falling in love with him. Falling fast and hard. Unless she stopped herself, he'd probably end up breaking her heart. Not intentionally, but as a side effect of his duty. Losing Jim had been terrible, but she couldn't imagine losing a husband to war. Something told her that if she and Abe continued as they were, they would undoubtedly marry. She didn't buy for one moment her insinuation that after living together they'd find they weren't compatible. Like any other powerful emotion, love was often immediate. The brain registered hate, pain, hunger, thirst, and jealousy right away, so why not love?

The phone rang. Glad for the interruption, Angela reached for it. "Hello?"

"Sweetheart, it's Mother."

"Hi, Ma. How's Polly?"

"Just wonderful. She's playing with her Christmas gifts. I wanted to make sure you got home all right."

"Is the Marine there?" Her father shouted in the background.

"That's none of our business if he's there!" Patricia snapped. "Just as long as you don't do anything you'll regret later, sweetheart. Remember, if a man can get his butter for free, why pay the dairyman?"

Angela gritted her teeth. "I got home fine, Ma. I was just about to eat breakfast. Can we talk later?"

"Uh-huh." Patricia sounded all-knowing. "He's there, isn't he?"

Yes, Mother, he's here and after breakfast he's going to take me upstairs and fuck me even better than he did last night.

Abe glanced at her with a raised eyebrow as he placed aside his coffee mug and squatted beside her, sliding a hand up her skirt and stroking her clit through her satin underwear.

Stop it, she mouthed the words silently, resisting the urge to giggle.

"Sweetheart?"

"Mother, I have to go before my eggs get c-cold." Angela's pulse raced and she tried to keep her voice steady as Abe tugged down her panties and stroked her clit with his index finger while his thumb slipped partway into her damp pussy.

"Angela, are you all right? You sound strange."

That was probably because Abe was now under her dress, his tongue and lips toying with her clit. Shock combined with sensation almost knocked Angela off her feet.

"I'm fine, Ma. Just st-starving. I need to eat. Bye."

Angela slammed down the receiver and leaned against the kitchen cabinet, panting, her pulse racing.

"Abe, stop it!"

His tongue thrust into her pussy then ran down her clit and circled it with sinful skill.

When he pulled back, she thought she'd die from need. This man's touch was becoming an obsession. Her body ached for him as much as her spirit cried out for him.

"You really want me to quit it, Angela?"

"No. God, no." She closed her eyes as his hands cupped her buttocks and he resumed licking and sucking her swollen, aching clit.

"Crazy, I must be crazy!" she gasped. "Oh, Abe! Oh!"

Her words turned to a high-pitched cry of fulfillment as he rested the flat of his tongue to her clit and pressed with quick pulsations until she came. If not for his hands clasping her bottom, she probably would have fallen on the floor. Smiling, she rested limply against the cabinet, warmed from the inside out. The man roused giddy yet sensual feelings from deep inside her. He nourished them with loving caresses, masculine, throaty whispers, and tenderness reflected in eyes that had seen the worst life had to offer. Knowing that he could treat her with such care, that he hadn't grown completely hard in spite of all he'd endured, touched her profoundly.

Abe ducked from under her skirt and slid up her body, holding her close. The thickness of his erection pressed against her and she couldn't resist reaching down to trace it through his pants.

"Never in my life have I imagined anything like that, Abe." She touched a hand to her cheek. "I must be blushing like crazy."

"Yeah." He grinned. "Your pretty cheeks are about as red as the devil's hiney."

She grasped a dishtowel and playfully slapped him with it. "That was a wicked thing you did! I was on the phone with my mother!"

"And you looked mad enough to say something you might have regretted later. I was just trying to save you from yourself, darlin'."

Angela laughed. "You, Master Sergeant Forbes, are incorrigible."

"And damn hungry. So how about those eggs?"

While Angela finished preparing breakfast, Abe switched on the small television at the end of the table and turned to the news.

"Maybe they'll say something about when this ice will melt," he said.

"Good idea. I hope it's not too—" Angela's voice faded as she approached the table, spatula in hand, and stared at the television screen. Rage boiled inside her at the sight of police attempting to restrain a group of screaming war protestors. Shouts of baby killers and murderers accompanied hand drawn signs depicting anti-war symbolism.

"Stupid bastards!" Teeth clenched, she turned off the set.

"I suppose that's why we fight, so stupid bastards like that can have the freedom to protest if they want to."

She turned to him, her stomach twisting. "I really don't give a damn about them. All I know is my brother is dead while these protesting weasels sneak across the border or sit in some college lecture hall to avoid their duty."

"Not everyone has the guts to do what Jim did."

"Or what you do." Some of her anger faded as she slipped her arms around his neck and he tugged her onto his lap. "Don't get me wrong, I have no problem with anyone who's against fighting, but they have no right to treat you badly. I shudder to think what would happen to this country without soldiers protecting us."

"I knew a boy from the Army against fighting in 'Nam. Nice kid. He protested by not carrying arms." A far-off expression clouded Abe's eyes and Angela nearly shivered. "I watched him die. Legs blown off. He had guts, though, in his own way. I have to respect him for holding onto his beliefs but not shirking his duty."

"I can't stand to think about what you went through over there, Abe. When I see those *people* shouting, waving signs, and spitting at soldiers, I feel mad enough to wring their necks!"

Lifting his head he smiled and took her chin in his hand. "I'll be damned if you don't have quite a temper, Miss Franco."

"When it comes to people I care about not being treated right, I can get riled very easily."

"So it's safe to say you care about me, even though we haven't known each other long?"

"I care about you, Abe." She held his gaze. "If I didn't want to sound like a fool, I'd say I'm already in love with you."

"You could never sound like a fool, Angela." His lips hovered over hers. "Not to me."

His lips grazed hers when she jerked away, startled by the scent of burning food.

"The eggs!" She jumped off his lap and raced to the stove where smoke rose from the charred eggs in the bottom of the frying pan.

While she turned off the stove and flung the pan in the sink, he opened the kitchen window to clear the air.

Raising an eyebrow, he said, "So much for scrambled eggs."

"I'm not usually such a bad cook. I guess I'm distracted by a handsome hunk of Marine sitting in my kitchen."

A hint of a blush colored his ears, yet he teasingly said, "The ladies find us boys irresistible."

"And modest." She winked. "Jim was just a shy wallflower, too."

He couldn't resist another hug and kiss. Keeping his hands off her was next to impossible. Why hadn't he accepted Jim's offer years ago to visit his family? He and Angela would have gotten together long before now and been able to spend time with Jim, too. Abe mentally chastised himself. What good would have come out of them meeting sooner? Then she would have had two POWs to worry about.

Damn it, Forbes? How dumb are you? He swallowed hard. If this relationship continued, it certainly wouldn't ease her concerns. He was a United States Marine. It was all he knew how to be. Would she want to spend the rest of her life with him, traveling from base to base, waiting months, sometimes years, for him to come home, hopefully alive and in one piece?

"Keep kissing me and we'll miss breakfast completely." She gazed at him with those big, beautiful eyes and his heart, frozen by battle, melted. "How about some hotcakes?"

With a nod, he released her and watched as she opened the cupboard and got out supplies for making hotcakes. He imagined what it would be like if they were married. What would she look like plump with his baby inside her? How would it feel knowing that no matter where he was or what happened, she was waiting for him?

Selfish son-of-a-bitch. But he couldn't help it. Master Sergeant Abraham Marley Forbes had fallen in love.

Chapter Five

Knees bent, crouching as low as seventy-five pounds of equipment strapped to their backs would allow, Abe and his unit moved silently through the jungle. Their senses so heightened by survival instinct they could almost hear their heartbeats, they knew death was out there, waiting. They smelled it, felt it. How many times had they already escaped it and when would their luck run out?

Abe motioned with his head for them to start moving in the direction of a clearing. The village was ahead. They were friendlies. The unit had lived with them for a while, providing some much-needed medical care and getting to know some of the families. If they were lucky they could stop there now.

It took only moments to reach the village. Strange. No one was around, even though it was the middle of the day. Abe tensed, sweat trickling down the back of his neck, his gear suddenly too heavy. He took a step closer to one of the huts and the gear pushed him ankle deep into the muddy ground. Glancing around, he noticed several of the others were already waist-deep in the muck. Another step and Abe was in it to his knees. His hand tightened on his rifle and his pulse raced. He tried licking his parched lips, but his tongue was just as dry.

A little more and he'd be at the nearest door.

He reached out to push on it and shouted, shielding his eyes as the door blew off. His skin burned, but to his surprise he was still in one piece, though waist-deep in mud. Pushing through what was left of the door he stared for a moment at the carnage. Severed heads, the eyes wide in horror, scattered around him. Scraps of wood, dark with blood, lay amidst piles of bloody feet, arms, legs, and hands.

*****

"Abe!" Angela shook his shoulder, her pulse racing.

He turned so fast she didn't have a chance to react and pinned her beneath him, his eyes glaring into hers. Sweat misted his face and his breath came in short pants. His anger faded suddenly and he sat up, glancing around the room.

"I'm sorry." He rubbed his eyes with his thumb and forefinger. "Must have forgotten where I was."

Still shaken, Angela also sat up, pulling the sheet around her. Moments ago, she'd awakened to his groaning and thrashing. Moonlight bathing the room told her it was late and Abe was having one hell of a nightmare.

"Are you all right?" She cupped his cheek in her hand. "Want to talk about it?"

"No." He jerked away from her touch.

She rested her hands on his chest. "But—"

"I said no!" He grasped her wrists and placed them firmly at her sides before lying down with his back to her. "Go back to sleep."

Angela gritted her teeth. A smart woman would have been afraid of an angry six-foot-three Marine, but a smart woman wouldn't have slept with him so fast in the first place.

"Give the orders to someone else, Master Sergeant," she snapped. "I'm not one of your damn soldiers!"

Not bothering to see if he'd reply, she left the bed, taking the covers with her, and trudged to the living room.

She'd just settled onto a corner of the couch and closed her eyes when she felt the cushion beside her sink. Abe wrapped his arms around her and held her to his chest. Still angry, she contemplated shoving him away as he had done to her.

"I'm sorry," he said, kissing the top of her head. "I shouldn't have turned you away like that."

"I was just worried about you, that's all. When I woke up I wasn't sure what was wrong at first."

"It was only a dream. I get 'em sometimes."

"Was it about what happened to you?"

"It was about 'Nam, if that's what you mean."

Slipping her arms around his waist, she tilted her face up to his. "Isn't there someone who can help you with...with that kind of thing?"

"What, you mean a shrink? I've been talking to them. They can't just fix it, though. The mind isn't like some broken part of an engine or something. At least that's the kind of shit they tell me."

"I'm sorry."

"I don't need pity. I'm proud of the job I do."

"I don't pity you. I guess I'm sorry we need people like you to experience those horrors so the rest of us don't have to."

He cupped her face in his hand and stroked her cheek with his thumb. She was so soft, so gentle, yet there was underlying strength to Angela. Not only was she getting over the loss of her brother, but she was raising his child on her own while dealing with those crazy parents of hers. She shared her thoughts and feelings with Abe, and she encouraged him to do the same. How many other women would take some battle-scarred Marine into their bed and want to know about the nightmares haunting his sleep?

"It's late. We should go back to bed," he said. "Unless you're afraid to sleep with me now."

"Terrified." She smiled, grasping his wrist as she stood and tugging him to his feet. "Let's go. Maybe I can think of something to get us both tired enough to collapse into a deep, dreamless sleep."

Raising an eyebrow, he followed her to the bedroom and remade the bed.

She slipped beneath the covers and settled between Abe's spread legs.

"Umm," she moaned with lust as she slipped an arm beneath his rock-hard thighs and pressed her lips to his balls. His cock twitched awake from where it lolled in its nest of hair. She laved it and traced the head with her tongue.

His fingers wove through her hair and he bent his knees. Sliding her hands from his legs, she cupped his balls in one fist, squeezing gently, and clasped the base of his rapidly stiffening cock in her other, pumping the shaft as she continued licking and sucking the head.

"Damn it, woman, you're a fast learner!"

She smiled around his cock, loving the warmth of his soft skin textured with veins, the muscle beneath rock-hard. Taking the head between her lips, she sucked quickly over and over until his breath rasped. One thing about Abe, he wasn't a man who moaned and groaned as passion grew. Only at the final moment would he let loose a cry that made her shiver from head to foot just from hearing it. Knowing that her kisses and caresses provided enough pleasure to shatter the control of this modern day warrior thrilled her. She waited for that cry of surrender, that audible proof of his need for her touch.

Taking his cock so deep into her mouth that the head brushed the back of her throat, she withdrew it slowly. It popped free and she kissed the tip before sliding lower, wrapping her arms around one of his thighs and rubbing her breasts against it. The sensation of his curling hair and hard muscle hardened her nipples and made her wet with need.

"You have the longest, sexiest legs of any man I've ever seen," she breathed, kissing him from thigh to knee. "I feel like I'm making love with a granite carving of Odin or Zeus or something."

"I guess I'm a classical beauty, huh, darlin'?" Amusement laced his voice.

"From what I can see." She kissed his hips and lapped his hard, muscle-ridged belly. God, she could kiss him day and night and never grow tired of it! "And taste."

"And feel?" He grasped her arms and hauled her up his body until her breast dangled over his mouth. He took her nipple between his lips and sucked it gently. As his tongue swirled over the sensitive nub, she gasped. Clasping his sides with her knees, she took his cock and slid it inside her.

"Umm," she groaned, reluctantly pulling away from his teasing mouth so she could ride his big, sleek body as fast and hard as she liked.

As she bucked and writhed atop him, her hot, drenched pussy filled by his thick, hard cock, he fondled her breasts. Pleasing him inspired such passion within her that she couldn't leave him even if it meant her life. She needed him so badly! His thumbs rolled over her nipples and he watched her through half-closed eyes.

God, she was beautiful, with her head thrown back, lush breasts thrust toward his hands, and curvaceous hips working against him. The soft, smooth expanse of her bottom continually brushed his thighs. So many sensations had him panting, his cock straining as he tried holding off his climax just a little longer, just a little—

With a throaty cry of fulfillment she came, her face and breasts flushed, her moist lips parted, and her eyes tightly closed. Abe's eyes squeezed shut and he groaned deep in his chest as his hips lifted and he pumped into her. Intense pleasure shot through his entire body.

Angela melted onto his chest. His arms wrapped around her, and he murmured, "I love you, Angela Franco."

"I love you, too, Abraham Marley Forbes," she whispered in a drowsy voice before they both drifted into a deep, contented sleep.

Chapter Six

"Angela! Where are you, darlin'?"

"Abe?" she shouted from the basement. He opened the door, watching as she trudged up the steps, her rubber boots squeaking. "It's flooded down here! One of the pipes broke."

He opened the door, his brow furrowing as he glanced from her to the water on the floor below. She could only imagine the sight she made, dressed in her old dungarees and plaid shirt with her hair tied up in a red kerchief.

"You look cute."

"Sure I do," she muttered. "I look like a mess!"

"Fine to me." He kissed her.

"I talked to the plumber. He's had so many calls that he won't get here for a while. I hate to think what the basement will look like by then."

"I'll take a look." Abe walked down the steps. "See if I can stop the leaking until he gets here."

Angela smiled, relieved. "Thank you. I'll get cleaned up and fix lunch."

Nodding, Abe stepped into the water with a splash. It took him a moment to find the problem, but Angela had nothing in her house to patch a broken pipe. He went to the store to pick up some supplies, and when he stepped back in the house, the scent of chicken, vegetables, and biscuits struck him like a shot in the gut. He inhaled deeply and smiled. What the hell was he going to do when he had to return to the barracks where there wasn't a home-cooked meal in smelling distance? Even worse, what was he going to do without Angela warming his bed and waiting at home when he got in?

"Smells good," he said, stepping into the kitchen.

His gaze fixed on Angela who stood by the stove, an apron covering the front of her gray and pink flowered dress with a dainty lace collar. The scarf was gone from her head and her hair was arranged in soft waves about her face. Just looking at the woman warmed him from the inside out and made his cock come alive.

"Will it take long to fix the leak? Lunch will be ready soon."

"Shouldn't be long."

He opened the basement door and switched on the light. The steps creaked a bit as he walked down. His booted feet sank into water that was now to his knees. Moments later, in a dim corner of the basement, he was absorbed in repairing the pipe.

As he moved his boot, water slapped against the wall. A prickle ran up Abe's spine. Someone was there, behind him in all the water and muck.

He spun around, his heart pounding as he stared around the basement. It was empty.

What about under the stairs?

Grasping a wrench in his hand, his senses sharp, he slowly made his way to the stairs. The swamp smell was thick in the air. Winter chill turned to jungle heat. Sweat beaded on Abe's brow and upper lip. It trickled down his neck as he clutched the wrench harder and raised it high as he stepped under the overhang, knowing the scrawny son-of-a-bitch waited, ready to blow his brains out—

Abe turned as someone touched his shoulder. He shoved the plump, red-haired man in white overalls against the wall and cut off his breath by pressing his forearm across his throat.

The man gasped and sputtered, his eyes wide.

"Abe!" Angela splashed through the water. She pulled on his arm, her expression frantic. "What are you doing? This is John, the plumber!"

Abe released him immediately. "I'm sorry. You snuck up on me."

"My mistake," John choked out, rubbing his neck.

"Are you all right?" Angela asked, touching the man's shoulder.

"I think so."

"I'm real sorry," Abe said, placing the wrench aside and climbing the basement steps. He'd nearly reached the front door when Angela grasped his arm.

"Where are you going? Abe, what happened down there?"

"They call it a flashback, Angela." He glanced at her, noting her shoes, stockings, and the hem of her dress were soaked with water from the flooded basement. "I can't stay here with you."

"Why?"

"Last night. Just now. That stuff's going to keep happening. I don't know when—or if—it will ever stop."

"So you're just going to leave?" Her brow furrowed. "I didn't think Marines ran from anything. I know Jim never did, and somehow I doubt you ever have, either."

"I'm not running. I'm doing what I have to for you and Polly, too."

"I love you, Abe! I said it last night and that wasn't just pillow talk, damn it! I meant it! Didn't you?"

"Yeah. I meant it." He took her face in his hands then dropped them before he stepped out the door. "That's why I have to go."

"Abe!" she shouted, but he ignored her as he slid into his car and sped off.

*****

Angela sat in the diner, fidgeting with her spoon and glancing at the door while trying not to appear anxious.

A week after Abe had stormed out of her house, she'd given up on trying to forget him and sent him a letter. Enraged at him for waltzing out of her life after a couple of marvelous days and feeling stupid for believing he was actually going to show up, she'd asked him to meet her at one of the only decent diners in town. The place was tiny and showed wear and tear since its construction back in the twenties, but the owner, Rosemarie Simons, kept the place spotless and served the best food in the state. Rosemarie had been a good friend of Angela and Jim for years.

"Another cup of tea?" Rosemarie approached, her plump frame covered in a flowered dress and white apron.

"Thank you." Angela glanced at her and smiled.

"All right." Rosemarie dropped into the booth and tapped her fingertips on the back of Angela's hand. "Are you going to tell me what celebrity is supposed to walk through that door so I can roll out the red carpet and such?"

Angela looked surprised. "No one. I was just looking in that direction."

"No, baby, you was fixed in that direction like a dog fixin' on a hunk of steak."

"I guess I should try looking less obvious."

"So who is he?"

"Just a friend."

Rosemarie raised a bushy brown eyebrow.

"A friend of Jim's."

"Oh," Rosemarie looked thoughtful. "Another Marine?"

"Yes. He's in the Corps."

"You know you get a gleam in your eye when you talk about him?"

"Do I?"

"Sure do, and I— " Rosemarie jumped up and smiled. "Abe! When did you get back?"

Angela swallowed hard, her pulse racing and hands trembling so much she nearly dropped her fork. *Calm, Angela. Appear calm and disinterested.*

Abe, wearing a blue T-shirt tucked into snug jeans that hugged every long, muscular inch of his legs, strode inside and accepted a hug from Rosemarie.

"Damn, it's good to see you, baby." Rosemarie tugged his face down for a kiss on the cheek. "I was so worried when I heard you was missin'."

"I got out of the hospital a couple of weeks ago." Abe said, though his gaze strayed to Angela. His expression revealed nothing, but his throat moved as he swallowed.

"Couple of weeks? The least you could have done was let ol' Rosemarie know you was all right."

"Sorry. Thought you'd be glad not to have me here every week eating you out of house and home."

"Shit, boy, I know you since you was a skinny eighteen-year-old private, and you thought I wouldn't care what happened to you?"

Abe smiled at her, though his gaze again wandered to Angela. This time Rosemarie noticed. She watched as Abe approached and slipped into the seat across from Angela.

"He's a good man." Rosemarie rested a hand on Abe's broad shoulder.

A powerful shoulder that led to a long, gorgeous arm of rock-hard muscle. Angela's mouth went dry. *Don't let him know he's got you, Angela. Look nonchalant.*

"And she's a good girl." Rosemarie shook the shoulder she clutched. "You treat her right, hear me, Abraham Forbes?"

He glanced at her. "Yes, ma'am, I do and I couldn't agree more. She is a good girl."

"If you two are finished talking about me like I'm a pet dog, Abe and I have to discuss some things."

Rosemarie raised an eyebrow. "I'll make myself scarce and fix you some lunch. Want the usual, Abe?"

"That'd be fine, Rosemarie. Thanks."

"How about some of my House Special Stew and a nice chunk of sourdough bread for you, Angela?"

"That sounds good. Thank you."

Rosemarie left them staring at one another.

Abe's pulse raced like he was about to hit the beach into a storm of enemy fire. Angela was even more beautiful than he remembered, with her large, innocent eyes and luscious curves beneath her blue and white striped dress. She did things to his insides no one had ever done before. That was why he had to meet her today. Her letter had gotten under his skin and pissed him off, though his anger was mostly directed at himself.

"How's Polly?" Abe asked.

"She's fine. She talks about you a lot."

"She's a good girl."

"Like me. A good girl?"

"Not like you, and you know it, Angela."

"I assumed you thought of me as a child, since you treated me like one."

"What's that supposed to mean?"

"It means you don't think I can decide for myself the sort of man I want to see."

"I told you it's for your own good. I'm a Marine."

"Don't you tell me about Marines! My brother was one. I'm raising his child. I know what you do and the risks you take."

"And you want to tie yourself up with that all over again? Jim was your brother. Think real carefully about what it would be like with a husband in the Corps. Imagine yourself with two or three kids along with Polly, raising them for months while I'm away. What do you think of that picture?"

"I'm not some delicate flower who'll shrivel at the first sign of frost, Abe!"

"What about what happened in the basement with the plumber?" He lowered his voice and drew a deep breath. "What if that was you I'd grabbed instead?"

"I'm not afraid of you."

"Maybe you should be." She held his gaze and he shook his head. "You're a damn fool, woman. And what the hell did you mean in that letter when you said I used you?"

She shrugged, flinging him a haughty look. "I figured all that line about you leaving for my own good was just an excuse for you to take off after you got me in bed."

"There's not a bit of truth to that."

"So did you plan on never seeing me again?"

"At the time I thought it was best."

"And now?"

Abe's gaze switched to Rosemarie who approached carrying plates of food. As if sensing the seriousness of their conversation, the woman said nothing as she placed their meals on the table and left.

"Abe, if you don't want to see me, I can handle it, but only if it's because you decided you don't like me after all. If it's because you're protecting me, then you're making a mistake. I've waited my whole life for the right man. I don't care if he's a businessman who'll be around all the time or if he's a Marine whose life is on the line. There are no guarantees for anybody."

"You have one guarantee." He took her hand and raised it to his lips. "That I'll love you until the day I die."

Angela's throat constricted and she blinked back tears. No one had ever said anything so beautiful to her. God, if anything ever happened to him, it would tear her heart out, but it would be worth it. Whether she had him for a single day or the next sixty years didn't matter, as long as they spent what time they had together.

"Want to have dinner with me and Polly tonight?" she asked.

"Yes, I do. Where is she now?"

"Back in school this morning and Daddy picked her up afterward."

"You know I missed you a lot this past week," he said.

"I missed you, too."

"I want to spend as much time as I can getting to know you and Polly."

She smiled. "I'm glad, Abe."

He held her gaze and nodded. "Good. That's good."

"You know what I'm thinking about right now?" She blushed a bit and cast her eyes down to their fingers entwined on the table.

He lifted an eyebrow. "I'm hoping it's what I'm thinking."

"Then let's finish lunch and get back to my place before Daddy drops off Polly."

Abe grinned and reached for his knife and fork. "That's even better inspiration to eat than pure hunger."

Chapter Seven

"How's the leak?" Abe asked as he followed Angela into the house.

"Fixed." She switched on the light, stepped into the living room, and sat on the couch.

A wry smile played around his lips. "How's the plumber?"

"He was fine, Abe. Just a little shaken up." She slipped off her shoes and cast him a sultry look. "Aren't you going to ask how I feel?"

"No." He sat next to her and pulled her into his arms, nuzzling her neck. "I'm going to find out for myself."

"Abe!" She giggled as he tickled her ear with his tongue. Though it had only been a week, it seemed like years since they'd held each other like this. It was such a deep, incredible feeling that no words could fully express it and only his touch could satisfy it.

Settling her onto his lap, he tucked his head in the hollow of her shoulder and gazed at his hands as he began unfastening the front of her dress. "There sure are a lot of little buttons on this thing."

"There sure are."

She ran her hands over his sinewy forearms lightly dusted with hair and he continued with her dress. When she stood almost naked, his gaze lingered over her soft belly and full, plump breasts nearly spilling out of her bra. Abe bent and took one of her nipples between his lips while taking the other between his thumb and forefinger. He sucked and stroked simultaneously while she clutched his head tightly.

"Oh, Abe, I want you so much. I've missed you so much," she breathed, her nipples aching with pleasure from his touch. Her pussy turned to liquid and she squirmed, more than ready for his cock to fill her. From her position on his lap, his hard staff pressed against her bottom in the most teasing, delicious manner. Such overwhelming desire for this one man overshadowed everything she'd ever wanted or needed. Love was the most glorious feeling in the world!

"I want you, too, darlin'." He gently pushed her onto the couch and stood, lifting his shirt over his head and baring his magnificent, steely chest and well-defined abs.

Her breathing quickened as he kicked off his boots and jeans. Oh! He wore no underwear beneath! The sight of those full balls and thick erection tightened her nipples even more. She slipped off her panties and tossed them atop her dress. Angela's pulse skipped as she watched him roll on a condom and sit beside her. Grasping her hips, he tugged her onto his lap. She knelt, one smooth leg on either side of him, and slid onto his cock.

Angela closed her eyes, moaning with pleasure as every hard, marvelous inch slipped into her. While she used her knees and hips to guide their passion, he fondled her breasts, his callused palms rubbing and fingers gently pinching her nipples. It amazed her that he could inspire such wild, hot passion yet remain a tender, caring lover.

"Abe, oh, Abe!" she panted as he sucked first one nipple then the other.

Unable to restrain her movements, Angela flung her arms around his neck. He kissed her, thrusting his tongue into her mouth and exploring as she gyrated upon him.

Orgasm burst within her and Angela cried out into his mouth. His arms tightened around her as he lunged up several times then stiffened, every muscle hard against her as he came.

Angela let her head drop to his shoulder, her lips against his neck as they rested a moment, wrapped in contentment.

The sound of a car pulling into the driveway roused them.

"God! My father and Polly!" Angela leapt off his lap and threw his jeans in his face as she reached for her panties and dress.

Abe smiled as he dressed, his gaze fixed on her.

"Damn all these little buttons!" she said, her fingers trembling so much she couldn't fasten one. Instead she ran for the bathroom, managing to lock herself in just as the front door opened.

"Abe!" Polly shouted as she stepped inside with her grandfather.

"Hey, darlin'." Abe accepted her embrace.

Mr. Franco cleared his throat. "Didn't expect to see you here, Abe."

"Angela asked me over for dinner."

"It's just after lunchtime."

"I'm early."

Mr. Franco made a sound that might have been a growl just as Angela stepped out of the bathroom.

"Hi, Daddy. Polly, did you have a good day at school?"

"Yes. We had to draw a picture from Christmas so I drew this."

She handed Angela a picture in crayon of the family sitting around the table eating dinner.

"See. I drew, Abe, too, and my dog."

"She loves that dog you gave her. Hardly lets the thing out of her sight," Angela said.

"So you asked him to dinner," Mr. Franco said.

"Yes, I asked him to dinner."

"Are you going to marry Aunt Angela?" Polly gazed up at Abe.

"Polly, you know better than to ask a question like that!" Angela said.

"I just thought he was going to because Grandpa said if he didn't, he was a low-down snake in the grass looking for one thing."

Mr. Franco looked properly embarrassed as he edged out the door. "If I'm late, your mother will kill me. See you all later."

"What's the thing Grandpa was talking about?" Polly asked.

"Nothing, honey. Grandpa was just teasing." Angela forced a smile. If her parents ever learned to mind their own business, it would be a miracle. "Go get cleaned up and I'll hang your picture on the refrigerator."

Polly hurried upstairs and Angela turned to Abe. "If you can take me with my parents then I can surely take you and the Marine Corps."

He grinned as he followed her to the kitchen, knowing better than to agree but unable to disagree, either. There were times when it was best to just be the strong, silent type and Abe was smart enough to know it.

*****

A few days later, Angela had just sent her Friday afternoon student home when a note arrived at her door.

She grinned, immediately recognizing the bold lettering on the envelope. Tearing the edge, she slipped out the note.

My Darling Angela,

I would like to escort you to dinner tonight at seven o'clock.

Until then, I'm thinking of you.

Abe

Her smile broadened and she tingled inside. She'd never gotten an actual love letter before.

Seven o'clock! It was four o'clock now. She'd have to hurry. Abe must have remembered Polly was spending the weekend at her parents' house. It was also the last weekend of his leave. Come Monday, she wouldn't get to see him nearly as much. For the past week, he'd eaten dinner at her house every night, taken her to breakfast almost every morning, and picked up Polly after school while Angela had been doing some extra tutoring for a child who was home recovering from surgery.

She'd gotten quite accustomed to having the Master Sergeant around. Though Abe promised to visit her and Polly every moment of his free time, she was going to miss him terribly. Her niece felt the same. Abe had the knack of relating to a child without spoiling her. Polly obeyed Abe like she did Angela and Jim, when he'd been alive. Finding a man who was a good father figure for Polly was just as important to Angela as relating to the man herself. Abe seemed to be the wonderful combination of both. Yet in spite of what she'd told him about not caring if he was in the military, she couldn't help thinking how hard it would be for both her and Polly when he was sent away again.

Enough of such thoughts. He wasn't going away tonight, and she had a date to get ready for.

Angela spent the next few hours bathing, shaving, rubbing on lotion, painting her finger and toenails, and arranging her hair and makeup. Finally, wearing her black dress with a full skirt and a rope of pearls around her neck, she glanced at herself in the bedroom mirror. The results pleased her. She looked pretty good.

The doorbell rang and she hurried down the steps. Abe waited outside, looking handsome in his uniform and carrying a bouquet of red roses.

"They're beautiful, Abe," she said, taking the flowers and closing her eyes as she inhaled their scent.

"I thought they were, until I saw you."

Angela smiled and gazed at him. "I know what you're trying to do. You want to make sure I'll never love another man like I love you."

"Damn right. Are you ready to go to dinner?"

"Just let me put these in some water."

The small town only had a couple of diners and a drugstore lunch counter, so Abe took her to the only decent place around he could think of. Angela had been to the NCO club once before with Jim, but with Abe everything seemed completely different. She didn't really care where she was since all she could see was the blue of his eyes and the warmth of his smile.

After dinner, they drove to the beach and parked nearby, watching the waves lick the shore.

"Angela?" He turned to her, his gaze even more intense than usual.

"Yes, Abe."

"I know we haven't been together very long, but I love you. I said it before but I'm saying it again just to make things real clear."

She nodded, tingling inside. "I love you, too, Abe."

"I care a lot about Polly, too. I think of her like a daughter."

"So do I. She's my niece. She means the world to me."

"How does she feel about me, do you think?"

"She's crazy about you, Abe. You know that."

"Good. You know next week my leave is over."

"Yes."

"I've never spent such a terrific three weeks in my life."

"Neither have I."

"I don't want to rush you, so I think we should give it some time before we set a date—"

A smile touched her lips. "Abraham Marley Forbes, what are you asking me?"

He reached into his jacket pocket and withdrew a ring box. Opening the lid, he held it out to her, revealing a single, pear-shaped diamond. "I'm asking if you'll marry me, Angela."

She laughed, excitement coursing through her.

"Are you poking fun at me, or is that laugh because you like the idea?"

"I don't like it, Abe. I love it!"

"Good." He took the ring out of the box, grasped her hand, and slipped it onto her finger. "I tried getting the prettiest ring I could find, but it's nothing compared to the hand it's resting on."

Angela's heart fluttered as he kissed the back of her hand. Tugging her close, he covered her mouth with his. Angela wrapped her arms around his neck, loving the warmth of his body against hers and the moist, tender stroking of his tongue as it explored her mouth.

"When should we set the date?" he asked.

"Late this year? That should give us more time to get to know one another as well as plan a decent wedding."

"Sounds good to me."

"Now comes the hard part."

His brow knitted in question.

She laughed. "Telling my parents without letting them take over all the plans."

"Let's tell them tomorrow." He nuzzled her neck. "I have some plans to celebrate on our own tonight."

Angela uttered a soft moan of pleasure as he kissed her neck and gently traced the shape of her breasts through the fabric of her dress. "Let's go back to my place."

"You're right." He kissed her upper lip then her lower. "We're a little old to be making it in a car."

She smiled, massaging his inner thigh and stroking his cock with her fingertips. She longed to hold the warm, velvet-skinned rod and run her lips over the smooth head. The thought of feeling it deep inside her again, of being wrapped in his steely arms against his hard, naked body, made her wet with desire. "A bed is much more comfortable."

After one more kiss, he turned on the ignition and headed for her house. She smiled as he took a hand off the wheel to adjust his cock. It was nice knowing he was as hungry for her as she was for him.

During the ride, Abe's hand rested on Angela's knee, stroking gently. If she hadn't been afraid of distracting him, she'd have continued fondling him through his trousers. *Oh well, not touching him just helps build anticipation.*

Not that they needed anything more to spur them on. As soon as they stepped into the house and closed the door behind them, they tore at each other's clothes. They walked up the steps in a tangle of arms and hands, unbuttoning, unzipping, and un-tucking.

Giggling, Angela stumbled on the steps, but Abe caught her and swept her into his arms. As he carried her to the bedroom, he covered her face with kisses.

He placed her on the bed and removed his clothes while she undressed.

When he searched his pocket for a condom, she purred, "Just think. This time next year you won't have to bother with that anymore."

Grinning, he rolled it on. "I can hardly wait."

Naked, except for her stockings, she began slipping off the thigh-high silk, but Abe grasped her hands.

"Let me," he whispered against her lips.

Nodding, Angela leaned back on her elbows, lifting first one leg then the other as he slid off the silk, kissing from her knee to the top of her foot. After tossing the stockings aside, Abe spread her legs and settled himself between them. Closing his eyes, he pressed his lips to her inner thighs before covering each with kisses. Brushing his thumb through the curls partially concealing her clit, he stroked gently while thrusting his tongue into her pussy, tasting and exploring. Her warm flesh, so soft and quivering, squeezed his engorged cock. God, every time he took her, instead of satisfying his need for her, he wanted her more.

She moaned, the sexy, high-pitched sound exciting him. Her buttocks felt so smooth yet firm as he squeezed them, pressing her soft mound close to his face as he swirled his tongue in her pussy then lapped her clit. His lips fastened on the warm, swollen flesh and sucked tenderly.

"Oh, Abe," she panted. "I love it when you do that! You know just how to touch me."

She squirmed, her buttocks tightening and pussy throbbing as she neared her peak. How he loved touching her, pleasuring her! With Angela, he could explore a strange and wondrous side of himself. Emotions, long buried, sprang alive when she looked at him, held him, and panted for his touch. Bringing her joy was his top priority. Her excitement and happiness inspired his own.

Abe knew her body as well as she knew it herself. Just before she came, he entered her with a long, slow thrust. By the time he reached his hilt she throbbed around his cock, her arms and legs clutching him in the most wonderful death grip.

As her orgasm ebbed, he began thrusting in a steady rhythm while he kissed her neck and traced the shape of her ear with his tongue.

Abe resisted the urge to groan. She felt so damn good. Her pussy was hot and wet. Her breath fanned his shoulder, and her fingers kneaded the taut muscles of his back. Every lusty sound that escaped her throat increased his excitement. With a racing pulse, he kept his thrusts slow and steady, ignoring the need to ram into her and satisfy the magnificent, torturous lust building inside him.

"Oh, Abe, sweetheart, I love you so much," she breathed, her hips joining his rhythm and her legs wrapping around him as she approached her climax.

He knew by the rasp of her breath and her frantic squirming that she was about to come. Increasing his pace, he managed a few more fast, hard thrusts before orgasm washed over him at the same moment he felt her erupt in pulsations of pleasure.

Angela cuddled against him, stroking his chest while he ran his fingers through her hair.

"This has been the nicest night of my life," she said.

"Mine too."

Gazing at the ring on her finger, she asked, "How does Angela Forbes sound?"

"Sounds great to me."

"Have you ever asked a woman to marry you before, Abe? Don't answer that. I don't want to know."

"No, Angela. You're the only woman I've ever asked to marry me."

"Really?"

He nodded and kissed the tip of her nose. "You're the only woman I've ever felt this close to. I've never been good at making relationships last, even friendships. Don't get me wrong. In the Corps we'd die for one another, but it's not like what you and I have. This is… I have no words for how I feel about you."

"I know what you mean. When I'm with you, I feel good inside, like you've touched a part of me I didn't even know existed. I had lots of fantasies about what it would be like when Mr. Right came along, but they were all childish compared to what we have."

"I hope I can make you happy, Angela. You and Polly."

"You will. I hope I can do the same for you."

"You already make me happier than I ever thought possible."

She cupped his face in her hand and drew a deep breath. "Just…"

"What?"

"Just be safe wherever you go, whatever you do."

He held her gaze. "I love being a Marine, Angela."

"I know. I'd never ask you to give it up. You'd only end up resenting me."

"I could never resent you."

Smiling, she kissed his lips. "That's sweet, Abe, but you could and you would. I'm smart enough to know it. It's more than a job to you. It's part of who you are. I'm proud of what you do."

"Thanks, darlin'." He squeezed her tighter. "That's good to know."

It was true. She admired Abe and men like him. The Corps meant as much to him as she did, and asking him to give it up or whining because he decided to stay wouldn't be fair. From the moment they'd met she knew what he was. She didn't have to stop him that first night when he was going to leave because he wanted to kiss her, nor did she have to write him that letter when he'd left her after that incident in the basement.

"So tell me, Master Sergeant." She straddled his hips, her hand splayed across his chest as she gazed into his eyes. "Do I get one of those weddings with Marines lined up on either side of me, drawing their swords?"

"If that's what you want." He ran his hands up her sides and cupped her breasts. Amusement gleamed in his eyes as he bucked a bit, his hardening cock rubbing against her. "Speaking of swords, I got one right here that can use a special kind of sheath."

"Maybe I can help," she purred.

"Darlin', I believe you're the only one who can."

Angela's eyes closed with pleasure as she curled her fist around his cock and guided him deep inside her warm, waiting pussy.

Chapter Eight

Two weeks before the wedding

"I think that looks just beautiful." Patricia Franco gazed at Angela who stood in front of a full-length mirror wearing her wedding gown. It was cream-colored satin with a long train decorated with pink seed pearls that matched the pearls sewn along the edge of her veil. "Sweetheart, Abe is such a lucky man."

"I can't wait to marry him, Ma."

"I know. All you and Polly do is talk about him. She's going to make the cutest little flower girl."

"She's all excited about being in the wedding."

"I think it's a wonderful idea that you and Abe are adopting her once you're married."

"He loves her like his own child, Ma."

"I believe he does. You know, when your father and I first met him, we weren't so sure about him, but he's a good man."

"He's the best." Angela smiled. When he'd proposed and she suggested they wait almost a year for the wedding, she thought it would fly by, but waiting so long to become his wife seemed to take forever. Just a little longer and she, Abe, and Polly would be a family by law, though in their hearts they already were.

For the past year, Abe had spent all his free time with Angela and Polly, planning the wedding. They'd decided that after they were married, instead of buying a new home, Abe would move into Angela's. Already he'd made so many of the repairs on it that Angela had been putting off. Her parents were happy about the forthcoming marriage and, as a wedding gift, offered them a generous amount of money to help pay for the expenses.

Angela and Patricia glanced out the window as Abe's car pulled into the driveway.

"He's here early," Patricia said. "Sweetheart, you'd better get out of that dress. You know it's bad luck for the groom to see the bride in it before the wedding."

"Tell him I'll be right out, will you, Ma?"

Patricia closed the door behind her as she left. While Angela undressed and carefully packed away the dress, she heard voices from the kitchen. As usual, her belly fluttered at the thought of seeing Abe. She wondered if she'd ever completely get over that giddy feeling almost every time she saw him.

As she stepped into the kitchen, she knew by his expression he had something to tell her. Even Patricia appeared uncharacteristically quiet.

"I'll go pick up Polly at school," Patricia said, patting Abe on the arm. "I'll see you two later."

"What was that about?" Angela's gaze followed her mother as she left.

Abe approached. "I got orders today. I'm going back to 'Nam at the end of the week."

Angela drew a deep breath, stunned. She shouldn't have been. All along she'd known he could be sent back at a moment's notice.

"I'm sorry, darlin'." He took her in his arms. "I know the wedding's planned and all, but—"

"How long?"

"Eighteen months."

She nodded, forcing a smile. "Are you going to marry me first or wait until later?"

"If you don't mind getting married without the big wedding, I would love to have you as my bride before I go."

"I want that more than anything."

Taking her in his arms, he kissed her forehead and lips. "Then let's tell Polly and your parents."

Angela clung to him tightly, closing her eyes. She wished that moment could freeze in time, so the end of the week would never come, and Abe would never have to leave her.

*****

The day before Abe was to leave for Vietnam, he and Angela were married by a Justice of the Peace with her parents and Polly as guests.

Patricia cooked a delicious meal at Abe and Angela's, but the Francos left early, giving the new family privacy before their separation. That night, Angela listened from the doorway as Abe read Polly a bedtime story.

"Abe, are you scared to go?" the girl asked as he tucked her in.

He sat on the bed and held her gaze. "Everybody gets scared about something at one time or another. When I do, I'll have you and Angela to think about instead. Goodnight, darlin'."

"Goodnight, Abe."

He kissed her cheek and walked to the door. Taking Angela's hand, he switched off the light.

Angela swallowed hard, willing herself not to cry. That would only make it harder for Abe and she certainly didn't want Polly seeing her all teary. What kind of an example would that be? Tomorrow, when Abe was gone and Polly was off playing with her friends, she'd get upset. She could hold back until then.

In their room, Angela climbed into bed while Abe locked their door and pulled the shade. She heard him unzip his jeans and kick off his boots. When he slipped into bed, she snuggled close to his warm, naked body, her cheek resting against his chest. His heart beat steadily against her face. The thought that he might be wounded or killed in action suddenly overwhelmed her. No! She would not let this night be ruined. It belonged to them and she would not poison it for him by succumbing to her fears.

His arms enfolded her. Kissing the top of her head, he slid one of the straps on her nightgown down her shoulder and caressed the smooth flesh.

"Abe," she murmured, straddling his waist and pressing soft kisses to his chest. She licked his nipples and splayed her hands across the hard pectorals, rubbing and squeezing the plates of muscle. Sitting up, she raised her arms, allowing him to lift her nightgown over her head. She wore no underclothes beneath, so her curves were bared to his touch.

"So beautiful, Angela," he whispered, resting his hands on her waist and stroking upward, tracing her ribs with his fingertips. Cupping her breasts, he gently squeezed the full globes. His thumbs rolled over her nipples, circling over and over until they stood out stiff and aching.

While one hand continued stroking her breasts, his other found her clit. He circled it with a callused fingertip, feeling her grow wet against his belly. Rising onto her knees, she lowered her drenched pussy onto his cock, swallowing him inch by delectable inch. She wanted to make him happy tonight, so he could remember the warmth and love they shared whenever he was stuck somewhere terrible, surrounded by danger and yearning for home. Still, keeping her passion under control long enough to tease and please him was difficult when she wanted him so, so badly!

Their hands locked as she rocked upon him, keeping her mewls of desire trapped in her throat, as she didn't want Polly to hear. It was so hard, not verbally expressing her lust as passion grew. Her heart beat frantically and her clit and pussy ached with desire.

Abe strained to see her in the darkness. He made out her silhouette, her gorgeous body gyrating astride him, her breasts so full and thrust forward as she moved sensuously.

Pleasure built deep inside him, centering in his cockhead. She enveloped him like a hot, wet velvet glove sliding over him, loving him on all sides.

Her breath rasped and he knew she was trying like hell to keep silent. Angela was normally a very vocal lover, but with the little girl in the next room, they'd both have to alter their ways a bit.

Abe grinned. It could be fun.

He gently rolled her onto her back without his cock sliding from her. Pinning her hands above her head, he covered her mouth with his and thrust with short fast strokes, pushing her toward a quick orgasm. Just when he sensed she was about to come, he slowed his movements, drawing out their pleasure. All the while he rimmed her lips with his tongue and thrust it into her mouth in time with his hips.

She panted, her body hot as her legs wrapped around him and her hips lifted to meet his.

For the first time, he felt a bit sour about leaving for a tour. Knowing he wouldn't see Angela for eighteen months... Eighteen months! What if they never saw each other again? He wouldn't think that way. He couldn't. When had Master Sergeant Abraham Marley Forbes gotten so soft? Yes, he loved this woman with his heart and soul, but he was also loyal to the Corps. In order to do his best for both his woman and his country, he would give her a happy memory of her wedding night, then go and perform his duty with the single-mindedness that had gotten him through hell many times before.

His thrusts quickened and he immersed himself completely in her soft, feminine body. With her eyes closed and her limbs tight around him, she gasped as she came.

Her hot, wet pussy throbbed around his cock. In a burst of pleasure that stole his breath, Abe stiffened and strained in climax. Tearing his mouth from hers, he gasped against her ear.

"I love you, Angela," he whispered.

"I love you, too, Abe."

"When I come home, you give me a night just like this."

"I will."

"Promise."

"I promise." She hugged him tightly and kissed his cheek.

Chapter Nine

December 1969
Vietnam

Abe sat on the floor of a hut where the army had set up an infirmary. He'd arrived that morning with what was left of his unit. Most had been picked off by snipers a few weeks ago. Many suffered bullet wounds that, while not fatal, left them weak from pain and blood loss. A couple more had fallen prey to traps made of shit-smeared spikes disguised by leaves and branches, rendering them helpless from infection. Abe and those left uninjured took turns carrying the wounded through the hot jungle, infested with vermin, traps, and enemy soldiers.

Shrugging his shoulders, Abe rested his head against the wall. His body had felt sore and sweaty for so long that he scarcely noticed anymore. That's what happened after almost a year in hell. Not that he was complaining. He could be stuck back in the prison camp like last time, getting the shit beat out of him and his arms busted while some bastard fired questions at him. Being stuck in isolation could be just as bad, sitting alone, wondering if you'd ever look at another face like yours again, your head telling you there was no way you were getting out while your heart said your brothers would not abandon you.

Nearby a kid started crying. Medics were too busy to do anything about it. Abe pushed himself to his feet and approached. It was a skinny girl, a little younger than Polly, with bandages on her face and arm. He talked to her, using what Vietnamese he'd picked up, and she quieted a bit.

Funny he could be comforting this one today and busting in on another kid's village tomorrow. No point thinking about it. Unfortunately, there were more times than most people imagined that you could just ponder these thoughts, trying to figure out what was right or wrong. Those concerns faded fast when faced with a deadly situation, though. Survival instinct seemed to win out over almost any other.

The kid fell asleep and Abe glanced around. Civilians gazed at them with wariness in their eyes, even the ones who smiled outwardly. Medics worked. Some of his men sat talking, others in silence.

Lying in a corner, a private, his chest swathed in bandages, glanced in Abe's direction. Abe remembered what it felt like being fresh out of boot camp. He'd been luckier than this kid and not been thrust into combat right away. Training prepared you for the motions, but nothing could prepare you for the emotions of the first real taste of enemy fire.

Abe squatted beside him. "How you doing?"

"Fine, Sir."

"Boring lying there."

"Kind of, Sir. Lots of time to think."

Abe nodded. "Home?"

"Yes, Sir."

"Where's that?"

"Texas."

"That's where I grew up. Near Austin."

"My girl's from Austin. We're getting married when I get home."

"Not too much longer, then."

"That's what I hope, Sir."

"This your first time here, private?"

"Yes, Sir. How many times have you—"

"This is my third." Abe rested a hand on the private's shoulder. "Rest up."

"Yes, Sir."

Looking at the youth's sallow skin and reluctance to move or even talk too loudly due to the pain of the injury, Abe could hardly believe his narrow escapes over the past year. Every time he got through a shower of bullets or discovered a trap before he stepped on it and got his feet punctured or his legs blown off, he was grateful. Being wounded was no picnic, but there were worse things, he well knew.

He stepped out of the hut and leaned a shoulder against the side of it. Reaching into his pocket, he pulled out two letters. They were stained and tattered from being read so much, but just looking at them made him feel better. One was from Angela the other from Polly. They'd given him the letters the morning he left, knowing that it might be next to impossible to reach him during his tour. Polly's was short and sweet, the loving words of a little girl. Angela's was a bit longer and he knew it by heart.

My darling Abe,

You're not even gone yet and I miss you already. I keep thinking about the honeymoon we'll have when you get back.

Sometimes during the day when I miss you, I close my eyes and pretend you're close by. I can just about feel your arms around me and you lips against mine. That's what I'll do while you're away. At night, when I'm in bed, I'll close my eyes and imagine you beside me, stroking my hair, touching my face. I don't know if you'll be able to do the same. I'm sure you'll have too much else on your mind while doing your job, but if you can, think of me and know you're in my heart.

Miles can physically divide us, Abe, but our souls are joined forever.

I love you with all my heart.

Your Angela

He gazed at the letter and ran a fingertip over the words.

I think of you more often than you know, darlin'. I wish more than anything to be with you again, but the only way to do that is to concentrate on my job. That way I'll come home to you.

*****

North Carolina

Angela gazed out the kitchen window from where she sat at the table with one of her students. The boy was busy working on math problems and it was a good time for Angela to daydream.

Always, her thoughts drifted to Abe. What was he doing? Was he safe? She hated to think about how tough life must be for him and the others over there.

The only person she trusted to discuss her fears was Rosemarie. She knew her parents wouldn't be difficult intentionally, but her father would just tell her to bear up because she married a Marine while her mother would go on about the lists of people killed and missing in action.

"Honey, even other veterans are protesting the fighting," she said one afternoon when Angela dropped Polly off to visit. "If not for the damn war, your brother would still be alive."

"Ma, don't talk to me about protestors. You know how I feel about it. No one wants Abe and the others home more than I do, but not supporting the troops and spitting on them—"

"Who's talking about spitting on them? I'm talking about ending this madness!"

Angela stormed out and took a long walk before stopping at Rosemarie's diner. The two women talked about Abe for a long time. Rosemarie even told her stories about him as a skinny young private with a hotshot attitude that made Angela laugh when she thought she'd forgotten how.

When Angela picked up Polly that night, she and her mother seemed to have gotten over their bad feelings, or at least buried them. She'd eaten dinner with her parents then she and Polly drove home.

She and Polly had written to Abe often, knowing that the letters might not get through. Still, it made them feel better talking to him in the only way they could.

Mail from Abe had been scarce. Still, a few letters had gotten to them.

Angela reached into her apron and withdrew the most recent one, several months old. She gazed at his bold writing and felt somewhat comforted.

My Sweet Angela,

You know I'm not a man who finds it easy putting my emotions into words, but I want you to know how much I love you and Polly.

It's not too pleasant over here to say the least, but I won't get into that. I don't want to waste the time when I can be telling you how much I want to be with you again. Remember that honeymoon you mentioned in the letter you gave me when I left? You plan on it, honey. It'll be the best.

I know it's not like the real thing, but let me try giving you a kiss on paper. I'm taking you in my arms now and I can feel yours sliding around me. You're soft and warm. Our lips our touching. Moist, tender. Everything is dark and still. Our hearts beat together. I don't want it to end, Angela, but it does, everything must, but that's a good thing because it means eventually this will end and I'll be home with you again. Then we can have a real kiss and make new memories that I carry with me like the ones I have of you from before I left.

Give my love to Polly and tell those parents of yours I will be back.

I love you with all my heart.

Your husband,

Abe

"Mrs. Forbes? Are you all right?"

Angela blinked back tears, pocketed the letter, and turned to her student with a forced smile. "Sorry, Ronny. Did you ask me something?"

"Can you help me with this problem? I don't get it."

"Sure." She picked up a pencil and leaned over the paper, focusing on her pupil though thoughts of Abe floated in the back of her mind.

God willing, he'd be home in a few months.

Please, God. Please let him come home safely.

*****

July 1970
Vietnam

This is it! Abe thought, running through the clearing toward the chopper hovering in the distance. Pumped with adrenaline, he scarcely felt the weight of his gear and the injured man he supported. He'd feel it soon, that was for sure, when he tried climbing into that chopper. He was keenly aware of his men around him, all heading the same way, and even more conscious of the enemy fire that suddenly erupted around them.

One of the men turned to cover him and fell at his feet, his chest blown open. Abe and several others returned fire and one of the guys picked up the dead Marine. They were almost to the chopper but they sure as hell weren't safe.

This is it. All I have to do is make it to the chopper and I'll be with Angela and Polly again. His family.

The thoughts of them were fleeting, as he concentrated on survival. They sent the injured up first.

Abe's heart pounded as his turn finally came. He was the last man up. The gear weighted him down as he climbed upward, swinging in the wind as the chopper hovered.

He was going to make it! Pain erupted in arm. He was hit but didn't have time to think about it. He finally reached the edge of the chopper and felt helping hands pulling him in.

As he and one of his men tried stanching the flow of blood from his arm, Abe said a silent prayer of thanks. He'd made it. Again he'd escaped with his life. Angela would be waiting for him at home. He laughed in spite of the pain.

"Sir, are you all right?" the soldier helping him asked, concerned at the sight of a wounded man laughing.

"I'm fine, son." Abe drew a deep breath. He was better than fine. He was going on a honeymoon.

*****

July 1970

North Carolina

The phone rang and Angela cursed softly, climbing down from the cabinet she'd been rearranging. It seemed whenever she had her hands in water, went to the bathroom, or climbed into some strange position for housecleaning, the phone rang.

She picked up the receiver. "Hello?"

"Angela, darlin', it's Abe."

Abe! Just the sound of that deep, sexy drawl sent her pulse racing. He was alive!

Angela laughed, giddy with pleasure. "Sweetheart, God, it's so good to hear you! Are you all right? Where are you?"

"I don't have long to talk, baby. I'm fine. I'm coming home. Friday morning."

Thank you, God! Angela felt happy enough to jump up and down like a love-struck teen.

"How's Polly?"

"She's fine, Abe. She'll be so happy to hear you're coming home. You don't know how happy I am. I love you so much."

"I love you, too, darlin'. There's so much I want to tell you, but I can't now. I have to go."

Go! It was too fast. They'd scarcely said anything to one another, yet it was enough. It would have to be. He would be home in a short while and they could talk for as long as they wanted to. Better than talk. They'd be in each other's arms.

"Bye, baby. I love you," he said again.

"Goodbye. I can't wait until Friday."

"Neither can I, Mrs. Forbes."

The receiver clicked as he hung up, but Angela held the phone for a moment. Tears stung her eyes and she told herself to get a hold of herself. Maybe someday she would grow accustomed to their forced separations, or maybe she wouldn't. It didn't matter. Angela had already learned to appreciate what was happening *now* instead of thinking about what might happen *then*.

*****

Angela's heart pounded as she and Polly waited for the returning soldiers to step off the plane. Abe should be there. He'd phoned. She'd actually talked to him. Hearing his voice over the phone had been like the best gift she'd ever received. Until now. This was even better. In a few moments, she'd be in his arms.

Panic set in when other soldiers stepped off with still no sign of Abe. Then she saw him. So tall and handsome, even from a distance, though thinner than she remembered. He turned and her stomach tightened when she saw his arm looked a bit stiff at his side.

"There he is, Aunt Angela!" Polly beamed.

Abe turned to them with a broad smile and waved his good hand.

"Abe!" Polly reached him first. He stooped and hugged her tightly. "Look at you, darlin'. You sprung up like a weed. Pretty soon you'll be as tall as your aunt."

"She did get big," Angela said, unable to contain her tremulous smile. She felt like laughing and crying at the same time. "You're hurt, Abe?"

"It's nothing, Angela." He stood and pulled her into his one-armed embrace, holding her close to his broad chest and kissing the top of her head. "God, I've missed you."

"Oh, Abe." She stood on tiptoe, took his face in her hands, and kissed him with all the love she felt. "I love you so much."

"I love you, too." He kissed her again. His gaze held hers for a long moment. They had so much to talk about, so much affection to share. Glancing at Polly he said, "You, too, girl."

"I missed you, Abe. I have lots of stuff from school to show you."

"I can't wait to see."

Abe drew a deep, contented breath and released it slowly. It was the first time someone was actually waiting for him to come home. It felt even better than he'd dreamed it would.

Chapter Ten

After returning to the house, Abe spent time with Polly while Angela fixed dinner. They shared a meal of chicken, corn, and sweet potatoes cooked with brown sugar with blueberry pie for dessert.

Her parents phoned to welcome Abe back and asked the family to plan an evening at their house for dinner as soon as Abe was settled and rested.

Angela grinned. "Since you left, my father's been bragging to everyone about his Master Sergeant son-in-law who's just about the bravest Marine in the Corps."

"That's a shock." Abe chuckled. "I thought for sure that man had it in for me."

"No, Daddy just likes to talk a big show."

The three talked for a long time, catching Abe up with all that happened during the past eighteen months. Polly had an array of pictures and papers from school and Angela had taken plenty of photos in his absence.

"That's my best friend from school." Polly pointed to a picture of herself with a little red-haired girl. "Her Daddy's a Seabee but she's living here with her grandma while he's away. There's a breakfast at school next week for kids and their daddies. Can she come with us, Abe?"

Abe glanced at Angela, feeling a bit surprised and happy that Polly thought of him as a father figure. He'd better get used to it, since the adoption would hopefully go through soon.

"Sure she can, if it's all right with her grandma," he said.

Angela smiled, her fingertips brushing his as she handed him another photo album.

Finally, he and Angela tucked Polly in and retired to their bedroom.

"How would you like a nice hot bath?" Angela purred. "With a very willing woman ready to soap you down and massage you all over?"

"Oh, God." He grinned, his eyes slipping shut as she unzipped his trousers and slipped her hand beneath his briefs. His cock sprang alive in her hand.

"Hmm," she giggled and whispered against his lips, "that's one heck of a big gun, Sir."

Wrapping his arm around her waist, he pressed her close and wiggled his eyebrows. "How about later tonight I show you how good it fires, darlin'?"

"I can hardly wait."

While Abe undressed, Angela changed into the black lace nightgown she'd bought especially for his first night home. She brushed her hair until it hung, thick and shiny, down her back.

"You look so beautiful," he said, caressing her bare shoulders and kissing her lips. "I almost want to wait on that bath."

"Oh, you won't want to miss it." She grinned, taking his hand and guiding him to the bathroom where she ran the water in the tub and poured in a couple of capfuls of her favorite bubbles.

Abe's lips curved upward slightly as the basin filled and he sank into the hot water. "If anyone ever suggested that Abraham Marley Forbes would be sitting in a tub of bubbles smelling like roses, I'd laugh in his face."

"How does it feel?"

He glanced down, sniffing the water and brushing bubbles from his chest hair. "I think I kinda like it."

Angela was torn between laughter and lust at the sight of the big-boned, hard-muscled Marine with a shaved head and rugged features seated in a tub just a bit too small for him.

"Girl, are you laughing at me?"

Her self-control snapped and she covered her mouth to stifle the giggles. "Sorry Abe."

"Come here."

She shook her head and he stood, extending his hand, bubbles clinging to his water-slicked skin, his hard cock and weighty balls a feast for the eyes.

"You promised me a massage or something. So collect yourself and get on over here," he said, his face arranged in serious lines though his eyes glistened with humor.

"Sit back down." Taking a step closer while repressing more chuckles, she reached for a bar of soap. Her gaze swept his partially healed wound. "How's your arm?"

"Fine."

He dropped into the tub and stared at her, his lips slightly parted. Angela stood behind him and bent, dipping the soap into the water and lathering it over his chest. The sensation of hard muscle, damp hair, and wet skin made her tingle deep inside. God, it felt so good just to touch him!

Dropping the soap, she used her hands to wash and caress his chest. She kissed his neck as she leaned over him, her fingers sliding over his ribs and down his stomach. To better reach his cock, she walked around to the front of the tub, clasped his thick, wet rod, and pumped.

"That feels so good, baby," he said, cupping one of her breasts, his wet hand molding the satin to the flesh. The nipple strained for his touch and he accommodated, rolling his thumb over it and pinching it gently. Wrapping his arm around her, he tugged her even closer and pressed his tongue against her nipple, teasing it through the wet fabric. The nipple was so tight and sensitive that Angela couldn't control a gasp of pleasure. How wonderful it would feel when his lips and tongue played with the bare flesh without the nightgown between them!

As if sensing her thoughts, he pushed down the front of her nightgown, just enough to bare the breast he'd been fondling.

His warm, wet tongue rolled over the nipple and she shuddered. A few more minutes of this, and she might come from the sensation piercing her from nipple to clit. Her stomach clenched and unclenched and her thighs rubbed sensuously together.

Now the nipple was between his teeth and he nibbled tenderly, every once in a while swirling his tongue over the berry-shaped flesh. He shifted position enough to slide his hand under her nightgown. She wore no panties, so his fingers found her drenched pussy and pulsing clit right away. Smoothing her juices over her clit, he rubbed and circled the ultra-sensitive flesh. Gauging her desire, he pulled away before she exploded.

Angela's pulse raced. Her clit ached and pussy throbbed. The sensation of his hands and lips upon her teased her to a fevered height. She felt so hot and wet, so desperate for his cock to fill her and his lips to cover her with kisses that she trembled.

Her breathing quick, she reached between his legs and felt for the bar of soap, unable to resist squeezing his balls and outlining his shaft with her fingers. Finally she found the soap and handed it to him.

"Abe, I think you better finish this bath yourself. And make it fast."

Turning, she hurried to the bedroom where she arranged the pillows and covers on the bed and lay down, waiting for him, her heart pounding with love and desire. Having him home felt unbelievable. She could scarcely wait to cuddle with him in bed, close to his warmth and feel his heart beating against her cheek, but only after he sated the lust raging inside her. Since he'd gone, she'd dreamed of waking with him near her, now it was happening. Her thoughts briefly drifted to men like Jim who never came home and she said a silent prayer for their families. Having Abe back was a gift, just as each moment shared with any loved one was a gift.

Her thoughts faded as Abe stepped into the bedroom wearing nothing but a towel around his waist. Though a bit too slim, he still had the most unbelievable body. All big bones and rock-hard muscles with legs long and steely enough to make a woman lose her breath.

"You are so beautiful," he said, a smile tugging at his lips. "Damn it, woman, do you know how much I've thought about holding you in my arms, of burying myself deep inside you?"

"As much as I thought about the same thing." She stared as he dropped the towel and approached the bed, his cock semi-erect and waiting for her fist to curl around it and her lips to caress its head.

"That bath made me hot as hell."

"Should have used cooler water."

"I'm not talking about the water."

Angela held out her arms to him as he climbed into bed and tugged her close, his mouth covering hers. He took her face in his hands and stroked her smooth skin with his thumbs while his tongue gently parted her lips.

She relished the sensation of his powerful chest beneath her searching hands, the crisp hairs slipping through her fingers. The beating of his heart against her palms seemed linked to her clit. It ached and pulsed with need for him.

"I want to taste every inch of you, Abe," she breathed. Though she still felt ready to burst from need, the thought of tasting and touching him was irresistible.

"I want to eat you up, darlin'. I can't get enough of you." He spoke while pressing kisses to her neck and shoulder.

He slid the nightgown straps down her arms and tugged the satin, still damp from the tub. The delicate black material dropped from her breasts and pooled at her waist. He took a warm, tender globe in each hand and bent, kissing the plump, creamy tops. Angela clasped his head as his lips fastened on the nipple he'd teased in the bathroom. As he sucked the hard, sensitive peak, she wanted to scream with passion. Licking the aroused bud, he guided her to her back.

Lifting his face, he whispered against her lips, "Let me touch you, baby."

Angela nodded, closing her eyes as his lips brushed her forehead and cheeks then fastened on her mouth, his tongue thrusting tenderly inside. He kissed her jaw and throat. His kisses swept across her collarbone and down one arm. Taking her hand, he licked between each finger and kissed her palm before following the same sensual pattern on her opposite arm. His tongue circled one breast, drawing smaller circles as he neared her nipple, which he took between his lips and sucked. Lapping beneath her breast, he moved to her other one and covered it with kisses, savoring the hard, aching nipple with his lips and tongue.

Angela's breathing deepened and her head tossed on the pillow. It was so hard not to moan and pant as the tip of his tongue trailed down her belly and dipped into her navel. His fingertips stroked the curls covering her soft mound before dipping into her hot, wet pussy. The muscles squeezed around his fingers. His cock leapt, yearning to be enveloped by her soft, slick flesh. Soon. Very soon.

With long, slow strokes, his tongue caressed her clit. Angela's lips parted in a silent cry and her fingers tightened on his scalp. Her breath came in quick sips as he licked and stroked. Thighs trembling and hips lifting, she burst in an orgasm that turned the world black.

As she lay catching her breath, her body marvelously satisfied and relaxed, she felt him stretch out beside her. His face rested against the hollow of her shoulder while his fingertips languidly stroked her hip and thigh.

"That," she whispered, "was too wonderful for words. And it deserves payback."

"I'm more than ready to collect, Mrs. Forbes."

Smiling, Angela slid from beneath his arm and knelt beside him. Abe rolled onto his back and gazed at her, one arm bent under his head, his injured one at his side.

"Close your eyes," she whispered, brushing her fingertip across his eyelids for emphasis.

He did as she asked. Angela stared at him for a moment, grateful that he was with her and captivated by his handsome features, those sharp cheekbones, perfectly shaped nose, and lips just made to kiss.

Edging closer, she touched her mouth to his, loving the firmness and slight moisture of his lips. She brushed her cheek against his, feeling the beginnings of stubble on his face. From the bent position, her breasts dangled over his chest, the nipples rubbing against the hair-covered muscle. Her fingers massaged his broad shoulders. She squeezed and caressed the rock-hard muscles of his good arm while gently stroking down the length of his injured one.

Abe's breathing remained soft and steady as her lips and hands traveled to his chest, though when she rested her cheek against its broad expanse, his heart thundered in her ear.

Fingertips danced across his flat belly and hip as they made their way to his cock. She drew a deep, pleasured breath upon grasping the hot, hard staff. She squeezed and stroked, feeling it swell even more against her fingers and palm.

Climbing between his legs, she bent, her hair sweeping his stomach, and took his cockhead between her lips. Her tongue laved and teased, tracing the underside before her lips sucked him fast and her fingertips fluttered up and down the staff. She reached for his balls. The big, warm sac spilled out of her grip.

Abe's entire body tensed. His breathing quickened and his heart pounded. The beautiful girl was going to suck him dry unless he stopped her. Time, he had time. He'd always been able to control the magnificent climb to orgasm.

Angela's tongue trailed over the thick vein on the underside of his cock and swirled around the head as she sucked harder.

"Oh, God, Angela," he panted, grasping her shoulders and pinning her to the bed. Her bath had aroused him, then licking her to orgasm had heightened his desire to the point of shattering. Having her use her hands and lips on him after was nothing short of torture. A man surely couldn't take much more. With a swift thrust he was inside her, stroking longer and faster than he imagined possible.

"Abe, sweetheart," she whispered in his ear before licking it and biting the lobe.

Ignoring the ache in his injured arm, he only felt the intense pleasure in his cock and the love for her warming his heart.

Her smooth legs wrapped around him and her arms clung to his shoulders and back. The hiss of her breath against his ear, the sensation of her soft breasts against his chest, and the sudden burst of her orgasm gripping his cock shattered what was left of his control.

Covering her mouth with his to silence both their cries of passion, he came, surging into her. Rolling onto his back, he cuddled her to his heaving chest and closed his eyes as he caught his breath. Damn, that had felt so good! Plunging into her soft, sexy body and feeling her love wrap around his heart was just what he needed, even more than he'd realized.

"Remember what I said to you the night before I left?" he asked, stroking her shoulder.

"You said a lot of things."

"I mean what I said about when I got back you giving me a night like the one we had then?"

"Yes," she smiled, cuddling closer, "I remember."

"Well, this was even better."

"You mean I outdid myself?" she teased.

"It seems every time I'm with you, every moment we spend together, things just keep getting better and I keep loving you more than I thought possible."

"I remember when you used to say you had trouble putting your feelings into words. You're getting really good at doing just that."

"Am I?"

"Uh-huh."

"I got plenty of practice writing you love letters."

"I kept every one. Polly and I wrote you a lot, too, Abe. I don't suspect you got them all."

"Probably not, but the ones I got, I read so much they're falling apart."

"Yours, too. I've been thinking, Abe, that maybe Polly could use a few brothers and sisters."

He grinned. "That thought has crossed my mind."

"Let's say we make it our duty to see that happens."

"You know I'm always devoted to duty." Abe loomed above her and kissed her lips. Gazing into her eyes, he smoothed wisps of hair from her face and said, "You're the best thing that's ever happened to me, Angela."

"That's exactly how I feel about you, Abe." She looped her arms around his neck. "Are you too tired to do some more honeymooning?"

His hips shifted and his stiffening cock brushed her belly. "What does it feel like?"

Angela's hand slipped between them and curled around his staff. "Feels like you're ready for action, Master Sergeant."

"Ready, willing, and able."

Before she could reply, his lips covered hers and he began showing her again how much he loved her.

Epilogue

Summer 1976
North Carolina

"Son, do you know what it means to cook a burger rare?" Mr. Franco held his half-eaten hamburger under Abe's nose.

"Get that thing out of my face, Sir. Can't you see I'm trying to keep this grill going?" Abe told his father-in-law. He smirked as the man grumbled and took another bite of his food. Abe's brow furrowed beneath the white chef's hat Angela and Polly had bought him as a joke after he'd hosted their first family barbecue several years back. Angela thought he looked almost as cute in it as in his uniform cap. The white apron stained with barbecue sauce wouldn't have looked sexy on many men, but Abe carried it off like a magazine centerfold. Shirtless beneath the apron, every rippling muscle in his shoulders and arms and a good expanse of his powerful, hair-roughened chest was exposed. Snug jeans hugged his long, well-muscled legs.

"I told you to let me take care of the cooking, Abe," Rosemarie teased, trying to take the spatula from Abe's hand and nudge him aside. She didn't stand a chance. Abe had designated himself the official barbecue cook, and no one was going to take his duty out from under him.

Angela grinned from where she sat in a folding chair on the porch. Rosemarie should have known better than to try taking over a task from any Marine, let alone Abe.

"Blayne!" Angela shouted across the yard to her five-year-old son who rolled in the mud with his new puppy. Both were covered in filth but looked so cute she couldn't stay mad at them.

"Get out of that mud and under the water sprinkler, boy!" Abe called. "We can wash the dog later."

"But Daddy, we're just playin'!" Blayne stood, his large, intelligent eyes staring in his father's direction as Abe flipped burgers and toasted buns on the grill. The boy had inherited Abe's determined nature and sense of adventure. He looked so much like his father, too, though according to Abe, he was the spirit and image of Angela.

"Out of the mud!"

"Yes, Sir."

"I'll help him clean up," said Polly, now a lovely fourteen-year-old. The teen had so many boys knocking at the door that Abe teasingly threatened to sit in the front yard with his rifle, just in case.

Polly approached the grill and gazed at Abe with her most innocent expression. "Daddy?"

"Yes, darlin'."

"Dave asked me to the dance at the end of the week."

"The tall, thin boy with the freckles?"

"Yes, Sir."

Abe raised an eyebrow and Angela bit her cheek to keep from laughing. Polly was a good girl, but she wasn't known for sweetness and perfect obedience. She'd inherited Jim's wild streak, all right, and both Abe and Angela knew it.

"I told him I'd have to ask you first."

"I don't see any reason why you can't go to a chaperoned school dance."

"And the beach afterward."

"Not on your life, girl," Abe replied.

"But, Daddy!"

"Don't but Daddy me. He can take you to the dance, he can take you to the movies after school, but he's not taking you to any beach in the middle of the night."

"Mama?" Polly turned her frustrated gaze to Angela.

"I agree the beach at that time of night is no place for you. If Dave wants to come back here after the dance, that's fine."

Polly sighed, making a disgusted face before going to clean up Blayne and the puppy.

With the last burger finally flipped, Abe placed two on a plate, loaded them with mustard and piccalilli, and motioned for Angela to step inside with him. Their guests were busy eating and playing horseshoes, so the couple decided to sneak a private moment.

Angela followed Abe to their bedroom where he closed the door.

"Umm." Angela took a bite of her burger. "Delicious."

"That's what I say." Abe removed the chef's hat and apron and stretched, the hard muscles in his torso tightening in a way that made Angela's mouth go dry. At forty-two years old and after eight years of marriage, he still made her pulse race and her clit tingle.

"Do you think we were too hard on Polly?"

"Nope."

"Is that a father speaking, or a rational, impartial observer?"

"That's a man who remembers being a boy trying to get some girl to go to the beach at night."

Angela grinned. "I suppose I can't argue with that."

"I can think of things I'd much rather do than argue." Abe took the burger from her hand and tossed it alongside his in the dish. He placed the food on the dresser, grasped her waist, and pressed her body close to his.

"You know you are the most gorgeous woman."

"Abe, I am not! I got pudgy after Blayne was born and never quite lost it."

"You're sexy as hell and a whole lot hotter, darlin'." His mouth hovered over hers as he grasped her buttocks in both hands and squeezed.

Angela's heart fluttered as she gazed up at him and looped her arms around his neck.

"Abraham Marley Forbes, are you going to stand in here kissing me while we have a backyard full of guests?"

"Yes, ma'am."

"Well you better go ahead and do it before one of them decides to come looking for us."

"With my luck it'll be your father."

"He can't say anything now. We've been married eight years."

"Somehow I think he'd still find something to say."

Angela's giggle was silenced by Abe's kiss. His moist lips moved tenderly against hers before his tongue parted them. He tasted and explored every inch of her mouth while his hands roamed over her soft curves.

One thing both of them learned from each other, nothing tasted as sweet as true love.

The End

About the author:

A lifelong fan of action and romance, Kate Hill likes heroes with a touch of something wicked and wild. Her short fiction and poetry have appeared in publications both on and off the Internet. When she's not working on her books, Kate enjoys dancing, martial arts, and researching vampires and Viking history.

Website: http://www.kate-hill.com

Email: katehill@sprintmail.com

Kate Hill welcomes mail from readers. You can write to her c/o Ellora's Cave Publishing at 1337 Commerce Drive, #13, Stow, Ohio 44224.

Also by Kate Hill:

The Blood Doctor
Captive Stallion
Darkness Therein
Deep Red
Dream Stallion
Forever Midnight anthology
The Holiday Stalking
In Black
Knights of the Ruby Order 1: Torn
Knights of the Ruby Order 2: Crag
Knights of the Ruby Order 3: Lock
Midnight Desires
Moonlust Privateer
Vampires at Heart

Major Pleasure

Denise A. Agnew

Dedication

To all the soldiers, sailors and marines in harm's way.

Trademarks Acknowledgement

The author acknowledges the trademarked status and trademark owners of the following wordmarks mentioned in this work of fiction:

Ford Focus: Ford Motor Company

Ford Taurus: Ford Motor Company

Chapter One

Fort Carson, Colorado

Major Blayne Forbes felt like hell. He also had an attitude to match.

As he drove his small blue Ford Focus onto Fort Carson, an army post near Colorado Springs, his head throbbed and his eyes burned with the need for sleep. He had arrived back from his deployment after more than four months sweating, fighting, and almost dying with his fellow soldiers in the desert. Instead of chilling at his apartment with a cold beer, he'd felt wired and compelled to visit the one person who could put things into perspective. Jumping into the car and heading to the military post would cure what ailed him.

He hoped.

After countless hours in a military transport aircraft with less than first class jump seats and then another flight in cramped coach quarters, his patience had worn thin. Rigors of deployment didn't bother him. Except for this last time. The battle had been hell, the situation gruesome, and the pain extraordinary.

Most of all, the reason why he'd been sent back to Fort Carson instead of fighting with his men irked him no end.

His hands gripped the steering wheel too tight, and his stomach lurched with sudden nausea. *Get a grip, Forbes. This isn't the way a Forbes reacts to adversity. Punch through it. What would Dad think if he could see you now?*

Dad wouldn't think any less of him. His father had never given him anything but respect and support, even when he'd made some decisions in his life that hadn't rubbed Dad quite the right way. Like joining Special Forces.

An ache rolled through Blayne's healing body. Maybe Dad had been right all along. Perhaps the Special Forces had done more than give him pride and purpose—it had drained his soul and his energy until he had nothing left to offer. Blayne didn't quite believe Dad in that respect. After all, Dad had met and married Mom. And he knew for a fact his warm, caring mother wouldn't have married a man who had nothing to give. He always admired his parents' marriage, even if he didn't think he'd ever find the right woman for him.

Damn, a cold beer, a warm bed, and a hot woman might help what ails me.

Right now none of those things was an option. Beer would probably make the lingering effects of his illness worse, and he needed to vent more than take a woman to bed.

Talking to his buddy Graham Teagan would put his head on straight and his sight on the goal. He could pretend he needed a few things at the exchange and the commissary, and in reality he did. The refrigerator was empty. Plus, he needed shaving cream.

He pulled into the parking area near the building where Graham worked and got out of his car. Winter intruded on the area this October, and although the day sparkled with brilliant sun, a thick line of snow clouds already drifted over Pikes Peak and threatened a significant snowstorm later in the day.

He stepped out of the car and cold frosted his breath. As he headed toward the renovated offices, his head throbbed harder. He'd pick up a bottle of aspirin, too. Just before he reached the entrance the door swung open and out walked Graham's sister, Jemma Teagan. He couldn't repress a grin. Every time he saw her, his gonads did a full stop and double take.

Scratch that.

This time he did more than a double take—his cock stood at full attention. Didn't matter he felt crappy, the heat poured straight into his loins and demanded attention. Seeing her sweet face, sparkling eyes, and heart-stopping smile did crazy things to him that would cure any illness on the spot. He swallowed and reined the animal reaction into submission with difficulty. It wasn't like he could march right up to her and say, *Let me fuck you until I get it out of my system.* In fact, he wouldn't think of saying anything remotely like this to Jemma.

Not if he wanted to live.

Graham would kill him if he knew erotic thoughts about Jemma bounced through Blayne's head every time she came within viewing distance. Blayne had wrestled with his attraction to her more than once, and he could bludgeon his physical interest into acquiescence if he tried.

Pfft. Right, asshole.

Who was he kidding? He wanted her under him, on top of him, any way he could get her as long as he could part her thighs and slide deep inside her wet, tight heat. At the same time, he knew he couldn't screw her without becoming a little too interested in more than her body. She was his best friend's little sister and a damn fine woman.

That was half the problem. The last thing in the world he would do is hurt her. Plus, Graham was extremely protective of his baby sister, almost too protective as far as Blayne could tell. Blayne couldn't afford to become involved with a woman who let her family dictate her social life.

So he shoved aside thoughts of making it with her, regardless of how much his body craved her.

Think of the battlefield. That should do the trick.

When she turned and caught his gaze, her brilliant grin wiped thoughts of death and destruction straight out of his head and launched him into full-on, raw sexual need. Battle often left a residue, a powerful need to connect, that he sometimes satiated with a willing woman. He'd never given into sexual need with Jemma, but right now it sounded damn good. She looked so fuckin' cute.

Sun caught the red highlights in her straight, waist-length light auburn hair. She stood in the doorway dressed for winter with a black beret hat and long black wool coat. He wanted to call out a greeting. Instead he felt a wave of dizziness.

Hell, this isn't good at all.

Jemma saw the big man walking toward her with confident strides. Her heart leapt in surprise and happiness, then thundered with excitement.

She couldn't restrain how her breath quickened and her body hummed whenever she saw him. It didn't matter that months of separation parted them, or that he traveled the world keeping freedom, hope, and democracy intact. No, she responded to him with unadulterated pleasure and lust she couldn't control.

Then reality intruded. What was Blayne doing home? She almost called out to him in greeting, until she saw his slight limp and the tired expression on his face. Pale, with a five o'clock shadow and a haunted look in his eye, he didn't appear like the tough, indomitable soldier she'd known for almost two years. He caught sight of her and his trademark sultry smile started, then came to a dead stop. His mouth opened but instead of greeting her, he put one hand out to prop against the doorframe.

"Damn," he muttered as his eyelids started to flutter.

Worried, she reached up to cup his face in one hand. "Blayne, are you all right?"

The dazed look in his eyes retreated. "Yeah, I'm okay."

With instincts honed by years of growing up with brothers who didn't see the doctor unless their parents hogtied them, she shifted her touch to his forehead. "You're feverish. What's wrong?"

He blinked as if someone had just told him he'd jumped out of a plane without a parachute. "Nothing's wrong. I'm good."

A little surprised by his gruff tone, she withdrew her hand. His stubble-roughened jaw scratched against her palm, and though he looked tired, he could still make the molecules in her body come to a standstill and take notice. No doubt about it, in her personal dictionary under the word hunk, the description said Blayne Forbes. From the first time Graham introduced them, she had a gut-level reaction to the man. Blayne's unique combination of gallantry combined with a dangerous edge intrigued her. So did the soulful, sexually charged nuance in his thickly lashed dark eyes. A short, military cut restrained the curls in his lustrous, thick ash-colored hair. His somewhat crooked nose and strong jaw line added to the craggy image. His incredible, conditioned body spelled sin. In the recipe book of life under scrumptious there should be a picture of Major Blayne William Forbes.

For too long, steamy, sexy dreams of being with him haunted her. It didn't help he looked delicious enough to eat.

Swirling heat filled her loins and mixed with her extreme pleasure at seeing him. *God, the man is gorgeous.*

Today he wore a black leather bomber jacket, thick red turtleneck sweater, and butt-loving jeans showcasing his long, muscular legs. But it didn't matter what he wore because every time she saw him, her libido caught on fire whether she liked it or not.

More often not.

After all, getting involved with a footloose, rough-and-tumble Special Forces officer didn't define her idea of safe and secure. He had a risky job. Chances are one of these days he'd come back from a mission in a flag-draped coffin.

Right now, though, he looked anything but tough and it worried her.

He kept his hand on the doorjamb. "Sorry, Sweets. It's been a long day."

Sweets. Only Blayne could get away with calling her something like that. And she'd been too damn chicken to ask him why he'd pinned her with the nickname not long after they'd met. He never said it in an insulting manner, but always in a warm, teasing tone.

"I didn't know you were coming home," she said. "I figured Graham would have mentioned that your unit was back."

A grim, almost sarcastic smile spread over his face. "Graham may not have heard. I'm back alone."

"Why?"

Clutching at the doorjamb, he shrugged those mile-wide shoulders. "Long story."

Her eyes narrowed as she frowned. "I saw you limping. Is that why you're back?"

His mouth thinned, his gaze sharpening. "Among other things. Is Graham here?"

"I stopped by to see if he wanted to go out to lunch, but he apparently ran out to do some errands."

"I should have called first." He released the doorjamb gingerly, as if unsure he could stand without the support. "It doesn't matter. I needed to come on post anyway."

His gaze centered on Jemma again and this time the way he looked at her brought wild, rushing feelings back to her. Warm and appreciative, his attention caressed her face. Her cheeks flushed under his unbridled interest. As her nipples tingled in response, she wanted to reach up and hug him. Every so often she thought she caught two emotions running across his expression and it always caught her off guard.

Lust and tenderness.

Tingling built in her belly, moistening forbidden areas deep between her legs in a shocking rush.

The man knows how to turn me into mush every time.

"You look good, Jemma." His smile went brilliant, a touch of the old Blayne in his grin. "How are you?"

"I'm great." Before she could thank him, he closed his eyes a second and winced. That did it. She clasped his arm. "I think you should sit down a minute."

"It's no big deal."

"Right. You almost fainted in my arms a moment ago and you look like the semi from hell plowed over you and then backed up and did it again."

He placed his palm over her hand, effectively trapping her fingers against his arm. Big and well-shaped, his hands always inspired some pretty interesting fantasies for her.

He resurrected a wolfish grin. "Big, bad Special Forces officers don't faint."

She rolled her gaze to the sky a moment, then sighed. "Oh, excuse me. You don't faint, you pass out." She tugged on his arm and started to pull him along. "Well, Major Forbes, what am I going to do with you if you fall flat on your face right here? I'll have to call for EMS and that would embarrass you, big bad Special Forces officer or not. Why don't you sit in my car a minute and take it easy."

To her surprise he allowed her to guide him to her Taurus. She opened the door and he slid into the passenger seat. She got into the driver's seat.

When he leaned his head back and closed his eyes, she asked, "So what's wrong? Why did you come back early? Were you injured during the mission?"

The thought of him hurt at any time made her heart drop into her shoes.

He opened his eyes but kept his head back on the seat. "Maybe I should have taken a nap before I drove straight to the post."

"You just got back? No wonder you're out on your feet."

"I changed clothes and came right over. I need to talk with Graham."

"Well, in lieu of my big brother, I can be a pretty good listener."

He shook his head.

She grinned and crossed her arms. "Oh, is this one of those I'd-love-to-tell-you-but- then-I'd-have-to-kill-you things?"

"Yeah, some of it is."

She sensed an undertone in Blayne's voice, something dark and serious beneath the evasiveness.

Go for it, Jemma. "Since my dear brother stood me up for lunch, maybe you could have lunch with me."

He looked at his watch. "You don't have to go back to work?"

"I'm on two weeks' vacation."

He grunted. "You know, I think I'm going to go home and crash." He flicked a warm, almost sensual look her way before opening the door and starting to get out. "Good to see you, Jemma. I'll talk to you later."

Fine. Be that way. She didn't care if she had lunch with him anyway. *He probably has a girlfriend waiting for him at home.* The thought made unwelcome jealousy rise inside her.

Instead of leaving the car, he came to a stop and put his head in his hands. She reached out to touch his broad shoulder. "That's it, Forbes. You're telling me what's wrong. If you're ill, you're going to the doctor."

He removed his hands from his head and managed a crooked grin. "Forbes?"

"Okay, *Major* Forbes." She blushed. "Blame it on my brother. He calls you that."

Although he looked weary, he smiled. "I figured that's where you got it." He shook his head. "I've told you to call me Blayne."

Resistance to the idea remained steady in her psyche. "Tell me what's wrong. You're not healthy. I can see that."

He rubbed his hand over his chin. "I'm getting over the flu."

"I think you should see a doctor," she said. "Then I'll take you home."

His gaze cleared long enough to rake over her with a sudden, blazing energy. Flickering with sensual awareness, his gaze locked with hers, then drifted to her lips.

"Yeah." His voice came soft and sensual. "Maybe I need some nursing."

Jemma's belly fluttered and tingled. *My, oh my*. She couldn't deny the innuendo, and she knew he realized what he'd said. She dared search his eyes, probing for his intentions and enjoying the heated way his gaze moved over her. With any other man, the blatant once-over might have seemed insulting. When Blayne looked at her like this she felt uninhibited and willing to take a dare. Hell, she felt *devoured*.

Did she see desire in his eyes, or had her imagination kicked into overdrive? On a few occasions over two years he'd thrown her this same look. She dared to keep her gaze on him as heat flamed in her face.

"I saw a doctor before I came home from the mission," he said. "All I need is something to eat and some sleep. I'll be great after that."

Somewhat relieved he'd jumped ahead without waiting for her to speak, she grabbed at the chance to keep the subject on less sexual ground. "Okay, it's settled then. Do we need to swing by the grocery store?"

"Yeah, the refrigerator is empty."

"After you get some groceries, I'll drive you back to your apartment. We can eat and then you can crash. How does that sound?"

His mouth opened on a half-formed protest, but then he smiled. "You always were persistent as hell. How could I forget that?"

Deciding she didn't want this conversation to focus on her, she continued in a different vein. "You've been gone almost four months. Maybe the mission cleared away a few brain cells."

One corner of his mouth turned into a crooked smile. "Thanks a lot, Sweets. Always could count on you for an ego boost."

"Don't mention it."

"I shouldn't leave my car here."

She shook her head. "I'm not letting you drive if you're not feeling well."

"Man, you're tough."

"You can get your car tomorrow or something."

Instead of objecting, he smiled. "Let's go to a store off-post, then. They've got better vegetables."

Her temporary pass on her car and the fact she wasn't in the military or a military dependent meant she couldn't enter the commissary on the fort anyway.

She did wonder, as they drove out of the parking lot, if she'd lost her mind. After all, she'd just invited Major Blayne Forbes, sex god in the flesh, to have lunch with her in his apartment. Reality sank in as they rolled into a grocery store parking lot near his apartment complex. She, Jemma Elaine Teagan, never ingratiated herself with men like Blayne, even if her brother couldn't say enough good things about him. Over the two years, she'd seen Blayne in action and had some decent conversations with him at picnics and other social functions and parties. But every time she wanted to talk with him, they never had any privacy.

What would it be like to be alone with him this one time? A wild excitement centered deep in her heart and loins. *Hmm.*

As Jemma and Blayne wheeled the cart around the store, and he quickly picked out what he needed, she offered to make something quick, like omelets.

His paleness and the tired lines around his eyes concerned her. Blayne looked about as relaxed as a man on tranquilizers. She was so used to his urbane wit that his relative silence disturbed her a little. They made it through the crowded store, loaded the groceries, then took off.

They reached Rock Ridge Apartments less than ten minutes later. Situated near a highway leading directly to the fort, the five large blue and gray buildings looked clean and upscale. As a major, Blayne could afford something a little nicer, and these were made more like condos than the typical apartment. After parking the car, she followed him up a stairway to the second floor. As he opened the private entrance and they walked inside, a whirl of confusion centered in her mind. She wanted to know him better, yet caution warned her away. Before she could become caught up in her uncertainty, he closed the door behind them and led the way from the foyer to the kitchen. They dumped the paper grocery bags on the counter.

"I'll get the rest," he said and went outside to grab the remaining two bags.

As she gazed around, she came to a startling realization. Blayne lived with little in the way of knickknacks or furniture, and the place looked immaculate. In the back of her mind she had this idea Special Forces soldiers lived a junky existence. *Nothing like assuming*. Of course, if he didn't spend much time here he wouldn't have an opportunity to mess it up.

Blayne stepped into the high-ceilinged living room with the groceries and kicked the door shut behind him. After putting the bags down on the kitchen counter, he slipped off his leather jacket.

"Take off your coat and relax," he said.

She didn't feel relaxed. In fact, she was suddenly nervous as hell. She did as he suggested, slipping off the wool coat and handing it to him.

He grinned. "You going to wear that hat?"

Blushing, she pulled off the hat and gave it to him. *Real suave, girl. Real suave.*

Still smiling, Blayne placed her hat and coat in the hall closet. When he returned she said, "How about you crash on the couch and nap, and I'll fix lunch."

He slanted a glance at her. "I might not sleep. I've been having difficulty with that lately."

She frowned. "Well, why don't you just chill and I'll fix lunch anyway?"

"I'll help. There's no way I'm lounging around while you slave away."

She grinned. "You're worried I'll destroy your kitchen."

A warm grin touched his mouth again. "Not much in there to annihilate. Besides, I'm not dead yet. I can help with lunch."

As they moved around in the kitchen, she caught his masculine, spicy-warm scent and it made tendrils of heat flare inside her. *Wonderful. The man smells so delectable and is distracting as hell. If he gets any closer I just might melt into a puddle.*

As they diced tomatoes, ham, cheese, and mushrooms for omelets, she said, "I'm sorry about earlier. I was being a mother hen, wasn't I?"

He cracked a grin. "Yeah. Graham told me you're overprotective."

She shrugged. "I see cute little animals and I want to take care of them."

One of his eyebrows lifted, and he gazed at her with an intensity that burned straight into her soul. His regard targeted her like a laser, the question in his eyes making her face heat. She saw undeniable physical interest barely held in check and it excited her as much as it scared her. She swallowed hard and poured eggs into the hot pan. She couldn't remember being around any man as rugged, tough, or as damned sexy as Blayne. Dealing with how she felt around him seemed to be taking up all her oxygen and concentration.

Maybe I'm in over my head here.

"So I'm a cute little animal," he said.

"Well, maybe an animal."

"Damn straight." He laughed. "I was starting to worry. If you thought I was cute, then I'm in trouble."

How did she take *that* statement? "No chance of you being cute and adorable, Major."

The glance he threw her, as a matter of fact, sparked with his trademark sensuality. Power exuded from his posture and gaze, the sure sign of a primal male always ready for action.

No, the man didn't have a cuddly bone in his body.

The Major defined rugged masculinity. Authority radiated

from him though she knew he didn't feel his best. He grinned, the heart-stopping smile sending a tingle straight down her body where it pooled warm and liquid in her stomach.

No denying the feeling. Pure sexual attraction tugged at her, demanding acquiescence. But she couldn't do anything about it. Not with Blayne, a powerhouse with secrets she could never know. Besides, he probably knew plenty of women to take care of his sexual needs.

Jemma tried to sound casual as she worked at the stove. "I can't make omelets worth a damn."

"I can't either," he said. "In fact, I'm one of the worst cooks in the world."

"I was thinking of taking a cooking class."

"Sounds great."

"I'll have to squeeze it into my schedule. I'm busy as it is."

"A full life can be good. As long as you enjoy things you want to do and not just things you have to do."

"Isn't that the truth?"

How many things did he want to do, and how many chores in his job did he find tedious and maybe distasteful? She could only imagine. They made decaf coffee and soon the kitchen filled with tantalizing aromas.

When the eggs were finished they took their plates to the small chrome and glass dinette set off the side of the kitchen.

Silence entered the room as they enjoyed lunch, and the unfathomable look in his eyes made her wonder what changed him in the last few months. Beyond the occasional hooded, mysteriously seductive look he threw her way, something dark and worrisome resided in his eyes that she didn't remember seeing before.

Jemma remembered the first time she met him, and her heart sped up. She'd stopped by her brother's office and the Major arrived a few moments later in dress blues. Ready for a military ball, he'd cut a devastatingly handsome figure.

Remembering his handshake made her fingers tingle with heat to this day. His presence had captured her, defining the man as more than a guy who could handle weapons and kill with his bare hands. He'd given her a dazzling devastating smile. How any man packed that much warmth into one grin, she'd never understand.

She'd responded to his touch with a full body arousal, as amazing and searing as anything she could imagine. Her response to him had stunned her. When he'd left she'd seen a beautiful blonde woman in the car with him.

For days after their meeting, she wondered what made him so different from other soldiers she'd met.

"Earth to Jemma." Blayne's deep voice cut her reverie.

"Oh...um, sorry." She swallowed and licked her dry lips. "What were you saying?"

"I said thanks for the compliment earlier. You took me by surprise."

"Women don't compliment you?"

"Not very often."

"I don't know too many men who would enjoy being called cute."

"Well, cute is a bit..." He shrugged as if he couldn't think of the right word.

She took a bite of egg so she wouldn't have to reply right away. After she chewed and swallowed she said, "Not macho enough?"

He winked. "You said it."

Silence came again except for the clanking of their utensils.

Blayne took a long swing of coffee and then leaned on the table. "Why did you insist on helping me today?"

Her thoughts poured free and she almost said, *Because I want to get you alone. I want you naked so I can touch every inch of your no doubt gorgeous body and explore to my heart's content.* Or, if she felt really frisky, *Let me lick you from head to toe. How does that sound?*

In an effort to hide her flustered state, she pushed her plate back and stirred cream into her coffee. "I wasn't going to let you maybe have an accident on the way home."

His gaze kept her pinned, as if he feared she'd get away. "Thanks."

All teasing left his gaze and heat eased his eyes into melting dark chocolate. Almost black, his eyes trapped and wouldn't release her. As she inhaled deeply she caught his musk and sandalwood scent again and it teased her in a forbidden, exciting way.

"You're welcome." She had to get her thoughts back on track instead of mooning over him like a teenager. "How are you feeling now?"

"Great, thanks to you." He leaned back, sliding down until his head was propped on the chair back. He sighed and closed his eyes. "I didn't realize how hungry I was."

She stood and took their plates to the kitchen. After rinsing them and putting them in the dishwasher, she came back to the table. "I'd better go. You need some rest."

His eyes popped open, and though he looked tired, his voice came strong and sure. "Please, don't go. Stay awhile and talk."

Surprised, she stared at him for some time without answering.

He grinned. "Come on. I promise I don't bite."

She couldn't help it; a soft snort of laughter parted her lips. "Right. Sure you don't."

He gave her a mocking frown. "I'm harmless. If old ladies and little puppies can trust me, so can you."

"Okay, but wouldn't you be more comfortable on the couch? You could stretch out."

"Damned if that doesn't sound good."

She settled into a cozy dark blue chenille recliner almost

across from the matching sofa. An oblong glass-topped coffee table sat between the chair and couch. Once he'd taken off his boots and stretched out on the couch, the man looked mouthwatering sprawled in careless abandon.

His tall body, muscled to perfection, tantalized her imagination. When he stretched one arm over his head, his sweater inched up. A strip of naked flesh came into view. Muscled and flat, his stomach was covered by a sprinkle of dark hair. Her gaze coasted down to the generous bulge in his jeans.

God, if his cock is that big without an erection –

Her entire body tightened in sensual appreciation and wicked thoughts kicked in with a vengeance. Somehow she knew, with soul-deep certainty, that this man would be a ravenous, highly sensual, fantastic lover. She shivered and not from the cold. He would caress, soft and sure, bringing her to heights of ecstasy she'd never experienced. Would the first time he made love to her be fast and hard, or soul-stirringly slow? Jemma didn't have to guess that no matter how fast or slowly he took her, Blayne would drive her to levels of arousal that would make it easy to accept his generous cock deep inside. She visualized how she would feel if he wedged his steel-hard erection into her.

She gulped.

Her gaze snapped up to his and a lazy, sensual smile touched his mouth. "So what do you think?"

Oh, man. Had he realized she'd been ogling his package? She cleared her throat. "About what?"

"About anything. You're sitting there looking nervous and earlier you seemed at ease. What's wrong?"

She should have known he'd be sharp as hell. She'd heard from Graham that Blayne spoke Arabic and German fluently, and he'd somehow managed to obtain his Master's Degree in International Relations between missions. Not any easy thing to do considering his occupation.

"Nothing is wrong." She shifted and tried to relax. She

allowed her left hand to finger the chair arm. The soft texture beneath her fingers soothed her nerves. "So why are you back from the Middle East?"

His expression altered, eyes glittering with slow-boiling anger. "Bureaucracy is one reason. I hurt my knee, but not enough to send me back to the United States." He took a deep breath and some of his ire seemed to ease. "Then I got the flu."

Jemma frowned, sensing immediately something wasn't right. "You're right. That doesn't seem to be enough reason to separate you from your unit and send you stateside."

He scrubbed his hand over his jaw, then sat up and leaned against the arm of the couch. He kept his legs up on the couch. "How has life been treating you?"

She figured his blatant subject change meant he didn't want to explain the whys and wherefores of his return to the United States. Curious, but willing to go along, she allowed him to shift gears. "Frankly," she said, "things have been a little boring lately. I need to get a life."

Blayne cocked one eyebrow. "Why? I thought your legal assistant job and your volunteer work at the art museum was enough."

Surprise made Jemma pause. "You remembered about the museum?"

"Of course, why wouldn't I?"

Why indeed? She shrugged. "Not many men remember that much about me, I don't think."

"They must be idiots. How could they forget *anything* about you?" His voice turned husky. "From the first time I met you, Jemma, you made an impression on me."

Stunned, she allowed his clear admiration to absorb. Despite her resolution she couldn't become involved with him, his blatant appreciation pulled her heart closer and closer to him. "Was that a good or bad impression?"

"Very good." Again he stretched and looked ready to fall asleep. "When I first met you I was curious. Graham told me what a great sister you were. Then when I saw you...well...I wanted to know everything about you."

A little surprised, she asked, "Graham said I was a great sister?"

He grinned. "He thinks the world of you."

Deep inside the gratification felt good, although she wished Graham could say the words to her face. Then again, Graham had trouble expressing what he felt when it came to family. Instead he tried to show his affection through deeds.

"You'd rather he tell you face-to-face," Blayne said.

Startled by his dead-on assessment, she narrowed her eyes. "That's exactly what I was thinking. How did you know?"

Another heart-melting grin touched his mouth. "My mother and sisters trained me. I remember to say I love you on a regular basis."

I love you.

Her heart did a flop, a stutter and triple-timed. Not even the guys who'd tried to coax her into bed had claimed to love her. The very idea of Blayne saying those words to her made her heart pound. On the other hand, the concept of him declaring his feelings to another woman, a woman he wanted in his life forever, made her stomach clench with unwanted jealousy. Floundering for a suitable answer, her mind seemed to turn to jelly.

Humor, girl. Try humor.

"That's good to know," she said. "That you can be trained, I mean."

The words came out sounding more taunting, more challenging than she wanted. He sat up and swung his feet off the couch.

With a sleepy-eyed expression that looked too damned sexy, he said, "No one can train me unless I want to be trained. I control my destiny."

She crossed her legs and pondered how they'd jumped into

the cavern-deep side of the ocean so fast. "That sounds like a heavy subject."

"Don't you believe people have ultimate responsibility for themselves?"

Jemma frowned. "Why do I feel like we've catapulted straight into something far more serious than training?"

She worried how he'd take her statement. He'd either find it too obtuse or believe she mocked him.

"That's the bottom line, Sweets. We're in control. For example, you've decided your life is boring right now. But you're the only one who can change it from boring to the best life you've ever had."

She nodded. "Got the book, wore the T-shirt. You're preaching to the choir here, Blayne. When I said I needed to get a life, I meant I would have to do the work."

His own nod held solid affirmation. "Good." He leaned forward and his forearms rested on his thighs. "What about you? Can you be trained?"

The heat in his tone assured Jemma he meant the double entendre. Excitement entered her veins as she absorbed the electricity jumping between them. She could almost feel the anticipation pumping. A sensual ache started deep inside, moistening her with arousal. Her nipples tightened into sensitive points.

Okay, she'd play along. She flipped her hair over her shoulders. "To do what?"

"Reveal your secrets."

"I don't have any secrets."

"Yeah, right. Everyone has secrets."

She felt like she'd plunged right into a *Truth or Dare* game. "Okay, I'll bite. But watch out. When I bite it can be very painful."

His eyes widened and his lips parted. "I think I like the sound of that." His chest rose and fell, the deep inhalation and exhalation catching her attention. "What is your deepest secret, Jemma?"

She wondered if she'd made a mistake. If she let him in on her biggest secret he'd probably run in the other direction. A smile touched her lips. On the other hand, she doubted he'd ever run from anything in his life.

No, she couldn't tell him the biggest secret...that she wanted his body so much she could barely keep her hands off him. But she could tell him a little one. "My life is a pretty open book. Nothing too exciting has happened to me."

"I don't believe that."

"Believe it. When I was about five I was a kleptomaniac."

A startled laugh burst from him. "What?"

She blushed. "I was a little thief. For about two weeks I stole erasers out of a couple of kids' desks."

He grinned. "Why?"

"Beats me. I still can't believe I did it and got away with it. I stopped doing it partially because I was ashamed and because I figured I'd get caught."

"So you punished yourself rather than let anyone else do it. Sounds like good impulse control."

"You could say that. I never did it again." She frowned. "I've never told anyone about it until now."

His smile remained, albeit smaller. Instead his intent, caressing look said he not only liked what he saw, but liked what he'd heard. "Thanks for sharing with me."

For some reason telling him a little secret, an itty-bitty confession she'd never revealed before, made her feel closer to him. "Whatever you do, don't tell my brothers."

Blayne had met her other brother, Davis, last Christmas before Davis had taken a U.S. Marshall assignment in Denver.

A mischievous glimmer entered his eyes. "Why didn't you tell them yourself?"

"Are you kidding? They'd tease me unmercifully."

"Isn't that what brothers are for?"

Wondering about his first cousin and adopted sister Polly and his other sister Anne made her ask, "Have you tortured your sisters with their past indiscretions?"

"Indiscretions. Now that's an intriguing way to put it. You make it sound old-fashioned."

She sighed and then smiled. "Sue me. I've been told I'm a little old-fashioned."

This time his grin held pure disbelief. "I don't believe that."

"Really. I had this guy at a bar tell me I looked like a schoolteacher."

Once again his gaze danced over her, as if he liked surveying her at every opportunity. "What do schoolteachers look like anyway?"

"That's what I asked him. He said I appeared staid and pure." She shook her head and her thick hair fell like a blanket across her shoulders.

Doubt entered his expression. "The guy must be nuts. Your hair reminds me more of fire. Brilliant, hot fire." His voice dropped, warming her insides with the heat-laced tone. "More like Lady Godiva."

Her mouth popped open in surprise. "Blayne."

She tried to remember if a man's attention had ever made her feel this special, this flustered. No. Only Blayne could send her out of control, his notice a precious gift.

"The idiot needed to have his head rearranged," he said. "Was he a soldier?"

"How did you know?"

He clasped his hands together. "A lucky guess. This town boasts about three times as many men as women. There's a good chance single women in a bar are going to run into a soldier." His gaze hardened. "Wait a minute. How long ago did you meet this guy and are you going out with him?"

With any other man Jemma might have resented his

inquisition. Instead she heard an edge in his voice that rocked her foundations.

Jealousy and protectiveness. And damn it all, she liked it.

Boldness reared inside her, something that seemed to happen the longer she stayed near Blayne. "Why do you want to know?"

His face tightened a little, then she saw his Adam's apple bob as he swallowed hard. "I'm sorry. It's none of my business."

His bashfulness, so unlike the self-assured man she knew, made her heart melt. "You're right, it's none of your business. What I want to know is why you asked it in the first place. Men always think they know me better than I know myself."

He nodded. "So they can impress you enough to get you into bed."

"Maybe."

It happened so fast she didn't have time to think. He rose from the couch and walked toward her, his movements smooth.

Putting his hands on the arms of the chair, he leaned in close and spoke in that toe-curling deep voice. "I wanted to know if I needed to kick the guy's ass for being stupid enough to think you were anything less than beautiful."

His warm scent and masculinity enveloped her. His dark eyes sparked, determined and unwilling to give an inch. She saw raw desire there, and perhaps an emotion she couldn't define. Her lips parted and Blayne's gaze dropped to her mouth. For one overwhelming moment, she thought he would kiss her. Her heart leapt in wild anticipation tempered with panic. Everything inside her stilled and waited.

Instead he straightened, retrieved her empty cup, and headed toward the kitchen without another word.

Jemma stared at the wall above the couch and couldn't move, her brain befuddled and every fiber hot with longing. She couldn't suck in a breath for a few seconds, her heart pounding. Disappointment mixed with relief. Staggering arousal surged and flowed inside her, demanding an immediate outlet.

How could she be disappointed and relieved that he hadn't kissed her all at the same time? Had she lost her mind?

Sure, I could just grab him and kiss him first. Maybe the tension would be gone then, and I wouldn't have to put up with this crazy, knee-weakening attraction that keeps slamming me in the gut. Her thighs tightened and she tried to deny the throbbing between her legs. Her clit felt sensitive to the slightest movement, the ache inside growing by the second.

"Want more coffee?" he asked.

She cleared her throat. "Um. No."

Good response, Jemma. The guy's going to think he's rattled your cage. And damn it, he has. She could scarcely form a coherent thought.

When he wandered back into the living room his expression betrayed nothing. Self-consciousness intruded and she wondered if he'd decided not to kiss her because he didn't find her attractive.

Dolt, he just called you beautiful.

Then again, even if he thought she could launch a thousand ships it didn't mean he would kiss her.

He settled on the couch again. This time he stayed on the edge, and she wondered if she'd overstayed her welcome. She found she didn't want to leave.

Anxious to fill the silence, she asked, "What do you do to impress women?"

"I don't much care what other people think of me. If a woman likes me, great. If she doesn't like me, no sweat."

Once again her mouth spoke before she could think. "I don't imagine you have to worry. Women probably swoon at your feet."

A crooked grin parted his lips. "Is that a compliment, Sweets?"

What if he does know you like him? Let it hang loose for a change. "Oh, come on. You've got to know that women find you attractive."

She thought he'd smile at her teasing tone. Instead frown lines formed between his eyebrows. "Life's been a little too damned busy lately to notice."

Deciding danger lurked down the path of flirting, she switched gears. "How are you feeling now?"

"Good. A little tired, maybe, but nothing sleep won't cure."

Cue number one. She needed to flee so he could have some rest. She also must get away from him before he realized her interest had exploded into a full-blown crush.

That's what it had to be. Why else would she feel like drooling like a teenager over him?

She stood and headed for the window. While she'd vaguely noticed the snow coming down earlier she hadn't paid much attention to the amount. Wind whistled around the eaves and snow sliced across the window as a heavy gale battered the apartment complex.

"Man, would you look at that?" Blayne came up behind her. "I thought this snow was supposed to hold off until tonight."

"Me, too." A sinking sensation entered her stomach. "I'd better get out of here before I'm snowed in."

She turned and almost bumped into him, but he didn't budge. His hands came down on her shoulders. "You're not going out in this weather. It looks icy as hell out there."

"But—"

"No argument." His fingers caressed her arms, warm and tantalizing. "It could be dangerous."

A tiny panic welled up, one born of fear of the unknown. And right now being this close to this gorgeous man was starting to ramp up her libido and send her thought process into total disarray.

"It's not that bad," she said in defense.

He frowned. "Look, I'd be worried as hell if you went out

there now. Wait until it blows over."

"That could be morning." Her voice came out sounding breathy.

He gave her a gentle smile overlaid with teasing. "Yeah."

Chapter Two

Jemma's heart seemed to stop in her chest. Part of her wanted to run as fast as she could, the other wished to explore what would happen if she became snowbound with this intriguing man.

She dared look into Blayne's eyes. Dark and mesmerizing, his gaze made her want things, made her visualize tangled sheets, naked skin, and the incredible prospect of his hard cock wedged deep inside her. She craved connection, to experience what she knew within her primal instincts would be a mind-blowing escapade. If she understood nothing else about him, she realized he owned a sensual intelligence and masculine aura that radiated intoxicating sexuality.

Oh, God. It has been ages since I've slept with a man. Two years, to be exact.

Two years.

She hadn't had a date, much less sex, since Blayne walked into her life. Afraid of what that meant, she shoved the insight to the back of her mind.

His hands felt big and strong on her shoulders, but he held her gently. Maybe if she kissed him, allowed him to pull her into his embrace and give her one of those heart attack producing lip-locks she dreamed about, she'd realize he was only human. He wouldn't be the hero of her dreams, or perhaps fling material for a one-night stand.

As if I would have a fling. Thoughts jumbled in her head. Perhaps she should consider a quick affair for as long as Blayne stayed in town. She could remove this itch she needed to scratch, plus she would know what it would feel like to make love with him.

Correction. Fuck him. That's all it would be, without commitment or promises. An incredible experience, but a fuck all the same. Going to bed with him wouldn't have the taste of lifelong lovemaking, but the explosive need of two people no longer denying an awesome attraction.

What surprised—no, shocked—her was that she didn't care. She'd always thought of herself as a woman who must have love and commitment before she had sex. With Blayne she simply had to have him.

She sighed. No matter how much she might *want* him to be ordinary, the man in front of her far surpassed her wildest dreams. There was nothing the least boring about this soldier and she knew it.

Unfortunately, she knew if she kissed him it would lead to more. She knew it by intuition, the way a woman always detects when a man desires her. She saw passion in his eyes and craved to know his taste, to touch him, and give everything she could.

Feeling vulnerable and eager, she shifted and Blayne released her shoulders. He stuffed his hands in his jeans pockets.

"I really should go," she said softly.

Concern entered his eyes. "I'll worry about you if you leave."

The softness and sincerity in his voice dissolved her heart yet another degree. She sighed. "That's emotional blackmail."

He cocked one eyebrow. "Yes, it is. But it's true."

Afraid of the heaviness in the air she asked, "I don't know, Major, what will all your girlfriends think if they find out I'm here?"

"I don't have a girlfriend."

Nothing like fishing and getting a clear answer. Satisfaction made her say, "I find that hard to believe. I mean, that you don't have a girlfriend."

"Believe it. Most women won't tolerate seeing a guy only a few times a year."

"That's why I don't think I could fall for a soldier. Too complicated."

Disappointment entered his eyes, and she instantly regretted her cool, detached statement. "I thought all relationships are complicated. Why should dating a soldier be any different?"

A little ashamed, she said, "You're right. Relationships take work no matter the occupation."

"I have some buddies that are married, but most aren't. If a man is in the Special Forces, the work it takes to keep the relationship going can be tremendous."

"But it can be done."

"Of course. If the couple works at it and there's commitment and willingness to stick out the tough times."

"I'm not so sure most women are willing to let their husbands get shot at and maybe never return from a mission. And some of the wives aren't that independent."

He paced over to the breakfast bar and sat on one of the stools. "Graham seems to make it work and he has a wife and two kids."

"He's not Special Forces."

Blayne grinned wryly. "Yeah, that does seem to royally fuck things up." Her eyebrows rose at his language, and he immediately looked contrite. "Sorry. Living with dirty, stinking, tired men for months does that to me. I sometimes forget to clean up my language."

"Don't worry about it. My mouth gets me into trouble sometimes, too."

"I can imagine," he said huskily.

His gaze latched onto her mouth, and by the rapt expression on his face she wondered if he visualized her lips molding to his and then tasting his body. No, this man had no compunction about showing her with his expression what he wanted from her. He appreciated a woman, made her feel special. How would those incredible, muscular arms feel around her? Would he slide his hands down over her back, or would he be bold enough to cup her ass cheeks? Would he tenderly caress her lips, or would his tongue take instant possession?

As she watched him, she did a little exploring, too. Her gaze drank in his broad shoulders and his jeans curved over his thighs. She imagined one rock-hard thigh wedged between her legs.

Jemma's face went hot and words popped from her mouth without thought. "Stop it."

He snapped to attention, his gaze clearing. "What?"

"Picturing my...you...us..."

He laughed, then crossed his arms and peered at her like an instructor inspecting a student. "Spit it out, Sweets."

Temping, very appealing to spill the answer and see what reaction she'd get. "Never mind. Let's return to the subject of getting a life."

"I think the subject we were on was fascinating enough."

Despite the incredible urging inside her to succumb to his flirtations, to let everything hang out, embarrassment made her squirm. She looked at the floor. "Can it, Forbes."

"Okay, if it makes you more comfortable, we can talk about our secrets again."

"Kleptomania *was* my one secret. Not much happens in my life. Nothing exciting anyway."

"That's a shame. You don't want a little adventure?"

"Depends on the adventure."

That's it, Jemma. Roll with it.

"What *wouldn't* you do?" he asked.

A little frightened of the energy pinging back and forth, she returned to her chair and tried to look casual and unaffected. She slid down a bit so her head rested on the back and clasped her fingers over her stomach. "Bungee jumping is out, I think."

"Yeah? Sounds like a piece of cake."

She made a little snort of disbelief. "Of course it seems no big deal to you. You rappel out of helicopters and down the sides of mountains all the time. You run through jungles with a heavy backpack and don't think twice about it."

He laughed, and the deep, rolling sound warmed her like a hot toddy spiked with too much whiskey. Her heartbeat quickened, breathing escalating the tiniest bit.

A playful glimmer entered his eyes. "So you think life is dull?"

She sighed and sat upright again, far too nervous to do otherwise. "Maybe not dull, but something is definitely missing." Caught up and wanting him to understand, she leaned forward. "Maybe I need to look for a new hobby."

"No more art museum?"

"Oh, I'd stay with the museum, but I'd volunteer somewhere else, too."

"I've already tried filling my schedule with too many activities. It keeps your mind off things you don't want to think about for a while. It keeps you from thinking about what you really want in life."

Is that why she stayed so busy?

Aware of his scrutiny pinpointing her like a sniper rifle, the truth came out in all its baldness. "Blayne, just because that's your situation, it doesn't mean I need a lot of activities to keep me happy. I can be quiet sometimes."

His attention didn't waver. "You're right. I didn't mean to imply that. I guess I was talking about myself."

"There are things you need to forget?"

When he nodded she saw sadness in his eyes. "Yeah."

She took a chance. "Want to talk about it?"

Uncertainty entered his eyes; she saw an insecurity she never expected to see in a man like this. Then again, maybe she didn't give Blayne all the credit she should for hidden depths.

She admired his obvious intelligence, his clear physical attraction. Yet intellect didn't explain all riddles in the human mind. She wanted to know more about the real man and not the façade.

His eyes narrowed and she wondered if she'd pushed him too far. "There have been some situations. Some missions where I've seen people killed and it takes a lot of internal processing." He tapped his fist on his chest. "I usually talk it out with buddies who are willing to listen. Graham is really good at that."

Pleasure filled her. She liked what she heard. "I'm surprised."

"That he's a good listener?"

She sighed. "No, that you're willing to talk about things that bother you. So many men aren't. It can cause problems down the line."

"Yeah, well, I've figured out keeping everything I think inside me is a sure way to self-destruct. I've seen it with other soldiers and it isn't going to happen to me. We haven't had any men in my unit come unglued, but I've heard about others losing it and becoming violent toward their wives or girlfriends or pulling some other incredibly stupid stunt." When she frowned, he asked, "Is that one of the things that worries you about getting involved with a soldier?"

"No. Not at all."

"What is it, then?"

Oh, damn. She'd never expected their conversation to come to this. She couldn't lie to him, though. Not when she enjoyed this new friendship they'd discovered.

"It's not the soldier part, per se. I've dated a couple of guys in the Army before, but they weren't serious relationships. It's all the things we've talked about. Not just the long separations or the moving or any of that."

Blayne's expression tightened. "Is it just Special Forces soldiers you don't want anything to do with?"

She could tell him she'd desired him for two years but

refused to do anything about the attraction. Instead the words wouldn't leave her mouth.

He filled in for her. "Graham doesn't want you to get involved with soldiers like me."

She put her hands to her suddenly warm cheeks. "Oh God. He actually said that?"

"Yep. I took it as a very nicely worded warning."

She managed to meet his dark, warm eyes. "I'll wring his scrawny neck."

He laughed. "I'd like to see that. Graham loves you, but he's got to understand if you want wild monkey sex with a soldier, that's up to you. It isn't his business."

She wanted to hide, but at the same time putting this out in the open made her feel better. At least it would no longer be a secret. "He doesn't trust easily."

"Your father is part of the problem, right?"

Surprise hit her. She didn't think he knew about Dad's Army career in Vietnam. But Dad hadn't been any type of soldier. He'd participated in missions he couldn't explain to her or her mother.

"Graham told you?" she asked.

"What he could. What he knows about your dad's experiences."

"Then you can understand Graham's reluctance. He remembers some of Dad's problems." She shook her head. "I think he's afraid I'll get involved with…"

She couldn't say it.

Blayne nodded. "Someone who would hurt you." He sighed and gestured emphatically. "I can understand him wanting to protect you. But I don't see you as the type of woman who lets her father and brothers dictate your life."

Truth became uncomfortable in a whole new way. Scary, in fact. "I've wondered on more than one occasion if I've unconsciously structured my social life around my family's desires. I'm hoping it's been my decision."

"I want to hear how you plan to get that life you so desperately need. I see your brain boiling. What's your first impulse? Don't hold back."

She wanted to tell him, but at the same time this game terrified her.

"Trust me," he said softly.

Oh, man, those words sounded so good. With that overwhelming sense of excitement mixing with fear, she jumped into the deep end of the pool. "I don't know. Maybe this next summer I'll shop for one of those barely there bikinis."

His eyes widened. "Now that's a beautiful image."

Despite the pleasure coasting through her libido at his compliment, she had a difficult time believing he really thought she warranted beautiful.

"Right." She rolled her gaze to the ceiling, then back to his cheeky grin. "But thanks anyway."

"I'm serious. You in one of those tiny bikinis? That would be awesome."

"Are you trying to embarrass me?"

Humor mixed with a smoldering heat in his gaze. "I'm telling you what I really think. You're very pretty, Jemma."

Intrigued and flattered, she let pleasure pool deep inside and radiate outward. She wanted to reach for him and show with her body how much she loved his compliment.

"Thank you," she said. "Then I'd book a trip to a Mexican resort and soak up some heat."

"You wouldn't go alone, I hope?"

"I might."

He frowned. "I don't think I like that idea."

Surprise made her frown. "Here we were talking about me being my own person and making my own decisions. I'm a grown woman. I can take care of myself."

"Of course you can." His gaze took on a serious note; reluctance battled with determination in his eyes. "I don't think it's safe for an American woman to go there alone. Let's put it this way, I'd be damned worried about you."

While she didn't want to cause him anxiety, the fact that he cared that much thrilled her in a secret way.

"I'd worry about the kind of men you'd meet and what they'd expect of you," he said as the gravity turned to humor.

"You mean some handsome man would sweep me off my feet?"

"Yeah."

The challenge in his eyes made her ask, "Why should that alarm you?"

"Like I said, it can be dangerous there."

She smiled. "It can be dangerous anywhere, Blayne."

"I realize that, believe me."

"So I shouldn't go to Mexico."

"Not without me. I could keep you safe."

As she searched his eyes for answers, she planted her hands on her hips. "My own personal bodyguard?"

"That's right."

His careful scrutiny made her feel incredibly vulnerable and yet protected. Amazement warred with common sense. She ached to reach for him, to press against his hard strength and feel the protection he offered. A man, other than her brothers and father, had never expressed this type of concern for her. It was heady and a little unbelievable.

Don't wonder, get the straight up answer.

"So if I decide to go to Mexico, I should call you up first to make sure you're available?"

"You got it, Sweets." His grin almost looked sheepish. A mischievous light entered his eyes.

"What would everyone think?"

"Why should you care? Like you said, you're a grown woman."

She smiled. "You never give up, do you?"

He didn't speak for a long time. For a flicker Jemma thought she saw pain flash through his eyes. His voice was raw with unvarnished emotion. He left the stool and sat on the couch. "Actually, I have given up before."

Silenced, she pondered if she should probe deeper into his meaning. She found her voice. "When?"

He closed his eyes and she imagined the hurt he must feel. "This last mission when I let them send me back."

She frowned. "How exactly were you supposed to prevent them from sending you back?"

Blayne opened his eyes. "I shouldn't have got hurt and caught the damned flu."

She laughed and his eyes darkened. *Oh, good, Jemma. Insult him.* Eager to show her regret, she left her chair and sank down on the couch next to him. Before she could give too much thought, she smoothed her hand over his back.

Hard muscles moved under her fingers and he shivered. "I'm sorry, Blayne. How did you hurt your knee?"

He kept his gaze nailed to the coffee table. With his big, capable hands clasped together he looked like a thinking man, someone who didn't do things on impulse or hazardous propositions. But she knew he did like risk, or he wouldn't be in Special Forces.

"I can't talk about the last mission." His voice was tight and hard. "At least not the details."

"You were going to see Graham and talk about it to him, right?"

"He's got the security clearance."

"Ah." The single word said it all.

"You understand, right? It's not that I don't want to tell you."

"Of course I understand."

Some of the tension left his solid frame. "Huh. Maybe I wouldn't tell you even if I could. You know what they say about war being hell?"

"Yes."

"This time it was more than hell. I hurt my knee trying to get to another soldier who was down. Two bullets hit my vest and tossed me flat on my back."

"What?" She reached out and gripped his shoulder. "Oh, my God."

"I couldn't breathe at first, and it made me think the bullets had penetrated my vest."

She shivered simply thinking about the possibility that he could have died. Her mind whirled around the idea he wouldn't be here right now.

"That's horrible," she said so softly it came out as a whisper of sound.

"My sternum was sore and my ribs, too. It knocked me on my ass, and somehow I managed to twist my knee at the same time. I was lucky as hell. I could have broken ribs, punctured a lung, you name it."

She took a shaky breath and tears came to her eyes unbidden and unexpected. "Oh, Blayne."

Warm and seeking, his gaze held hers and the harshness left his expression. He turned towards her. He captured one of her hands and held it. His tenderness was her undoing.

Oh, damn.

As he tilted her chin up, his brows pinched together. "What's this? Do I see tears?"

She inhaled deeply. "I was thinking about what might have happened to you."

A long silence captured them, and her hand trembled a little in his. He released her chin, but his lingering gentle touch went straight to her soul. "Might haves are nothing to worry about."

She gave him a wobbly smile. "Oh, I get it. It's *not* okay for me to blubber over you being in danger, but it is okay for you to escort me to Mexico as a bodyguard."

"Something like that." He paused, his gaze searching hers. "How *would* you have felt if something happened to me?"

Her throat tightened. "Something *did* happen, Blayne." She swallowed hard. "If you were on a mission and didn't come back..." No, she couldn't finish the thought. He'd understand her feelings went far deeper than she'd recognized until now. "I don't spend much time thinking about soldiers in harm's way. It hurts too much. I'm so thankful Graham is here and not out there getting shot at."

There it was in black and white. If anything happened to Blayne, she'd be devastated. It was painfully, indelibly true. Yes, she'd vowed never to love a soldier, but as he looked into her eyes right now, she understood it didn't matter.

Pain clutched at her soul. It was too late *not* to care.

A slow, achingly tender smile touched his lips. His fingers pushed into her hair and he cupped her neck. "Thanks."

"For what?"

"Being so damned sweet and caring."

She ached for a chance to feel masculine power and strength wrapped around her. And if she was truthful, deep inside her willing body. Her heart picked up the pace, her breath shorter as her pleasure edged into the danger zone.

Jemma couldn't believe how much she'd learned about him in a short time. She'd seen rough, tough, and ready-for-battle as the biggest part of him, but now she realized he owned a profound reverence for life and living to the fullest.

She couldn't think of a thing to say. Danger crackled in the air, but not the kind on a battlefield. No, this felt steamier, hotter, and imbibed with sexual energy.

Was he closer? She felt it. Needed it. The embrace, the kiss, everything.

Blayne released her and the tension snapped. Jemma bolted, standing up and walking around the coffee table. She took up position at the breakfast bar as he had earlier.

Nothing like experiencing a narrow escape. For a few seconds everything inside her stilled. She'd found excitement, desire, and need in his touch. Yes, she could have inched forward and risked kissing him.

He yawned.

Off-balance and disconcerted, she asked, "Why don't you take a nap?"

He stood and sauntered toward her. "You're not going to run out on me while I'm sleeping are you?"

"Would I do that?"

When he stopped near her, he placed one hand on the breakfast bar. Damn his hide. He smelled so good and he probably knew invading her space drove her crazy.

"You might. But I won't sleep if I think you're going to sneak out into this snow." He edged closer, his voice soft but deep and caressing. "Stay here."

"That's emotional blackmail again, Forbes."

"Yep. I'm feeling pretty damned emotional right about now."

Startled, she arched one brow. "Oh?"

"I've never met a woman like you before. You're about the sweetest, warmest..." He swept the back of his index finger over her jaw line. "Damn. And so soft."

His gaze traveled to her lips again, a lingering caress of hot attention begging for release. Energy tingled between them. His finger trailed down her neck, sending shivering excitement darting into her breasts and groin. He paused, fingers measuring the pulse there.

Blayne must have felt her chaotic heartbeat. His brow wrinkled a little. "You look frightened. You know I'd never hurt you, right?"

"I feel safe with you."

"Good. You had me worried there."

He removed his physical touch, but the force of his personality made her feel as if he encircled her body, sheltering, warming, driving her into a sexual craving she hadn't experienced before.

"Every time I look at you," he said, "I can think of only one thing. I didn't want to feel this way, but here it is staring me in the face."

She was afraid to guess, though the devouring expression burning in his eyes told the truth. He looked like a man who wanted a woman. Badly.

But just any woman? That wouldn't do. She might want him, even without love. But he had to want her specifically. "I'm not in the market for a seduction, Blayne. I can't."

He didn't appear angry or surprised, his expression revealing nothing but the enduring sensual yearning she'd seen moments ago in his sin-rich eyes. "You can't or you won't?"

"Both."

Before she could take a breath, he slipped his hand into the hair at the back of neck and moved in slow and steady. "Then maybe you'll give me something to remember you by."

Chapter Three

Jemma could have pulled back, could have said no. But despite her assertions, she couldn't wait to finally taste him.

Blayne's mouth captured hers, a blending stroke of mouth against mouth, breath into breath. Exquisite yearning parted her lips to his subtle coaxing. Her thoughts went inward, the ecstasy of his touch bursting into life. The energy crackled and flowed around them. She could feel it in the hot, demanding power she sensed right under his surface. Potent and male, he held her like a precious item, something he cherished above all things.

From the first day she'd seen him, Jemma had wanted this, though she spent far too much time pretending she didn't. Now she knew he cared, he liked her, he wanted *her*, and she could enjoy each beautiful sensation.

Fire raced along her veins as she responded with full abandon. He might be a fierce, deadly warrior, but the way his mouth treasured hers and the way he stroked her hair, spelled nothing but gentle lover. As he tangled his hands in her hair, he tilted her head back a little, as if wanting more access to her secrets. Caught up in sensations, she drifted into excitement as he caressed her back with slow deliberation. His big hands cradled and cherished while his strength empowered her desire. With subtle movements his hips nudged hers, and as his erection pressed against her belly, she gasped into his mouth.

God, it felt out of this world. She almost reached down to test him, to measure his length and width. Imagining his strength sliding in and out of her wet, swollen depths made Jemma whimper with longing. All around her the world faded to touch and maddening desire.

His body moved against her with the subtle pressure of

seduction, his chest rubbing against her breasts, his hips brushing against hers. She clasped his shoulders as an anchor, her world tumbling into wild abandon. She palmed his hard pecs, delighting in the evidence of his strength. Hard, pillar strength bunched and flexed under her fingers. She couldn't stop touching, exploring, opening her heart and mind to sexual feelings more wonderful than she'd fantasized.

As his touch became bolder, she released the last of her inhibitions. She moaned softly when his hands traveled down to her ass and squeezed. Massaging, he cupped and caressed with steady kneading.

Seconds blended as her body responded to his call. Shivers of delight heated her skin. Her nipples tightened, begging to be touched and sucked. Aroused didn't begin to describe the need building within her core.

And he kissed her with the veneration reserved for a princess. Kiss after small kiss, he explored, a traveler over her senses. He savored and cherished until she couldn't stand the dizzying excitement and her body responded in a way that held no doubts. Between her legs a hot yearning pulsed hard and demanded. Blayne's cock strained big and hard against her stomach. She was falling over the edge of no return.

Blayne thought his head would explode. He had to get inside Jemma before he burst like a fucking schoolboy. He couldn't remember the last time he'd wanted a woman so much, when he'd ached with a frenzy that resembled the need to fuck after a long, hard battle. This yearning was far worse.

Why had he waited so long to kiss her? His body ached with the need to take her places neither of them had ventured, to brand her with every hammer and thrust of his cock deep inside her. And he knew she *would* be wet for him. The rhythm of her breathing, quick and excited, the way her hands stroked over his biceps, his chest, and plunged into his hair said one thing.

She wanted him.

Fuck, yes.

She felt so wicked in his arms, his little bundle of mind-blowing sin. He wanted to show her with his tongue and his lips that he could bring her to ecstasy. His heart pounded a frantic rhythm, his body screaming for completion. She moved in his arms sinuously, a desirable, incredible woman he'd wanted to nail since the first day he'd seen her.

And he did want to nail her. Hard, fast, and furiously. Denying anything less would be pure lie.

But he couldn't take her hard the first time they had sex. He would frighten her with his strong need and overt desperation. No matter how much he wanted her, he'd take this slow and bring her to orgasm after orgasm until she ached to be filled with his cock and begged for it. He wanted to hear her liquid, tantalizing voice screaming his name.

The way he felt now, he could fuck her all night.

Blayne's tired bones should have warned him off, but he knew he'd feel one hundred times better if he could slide deep into Jemma's hot, wet center and find oblivion from intrusive thoughts and dreams.

He must have her.

Deep in Jemma's belly, a new pulse began, demanded they finish what they'd started. His tongue parted and plunged, thrusting deep into her mouth. She moaned as he invaded with the demanding rasp of his tongue against hers. Each blatantly sexual movement drove her higher, her craving for him growing by the second. She responded, tangling her tongue with his until he groaned against her lips. She gasped as he started a dance, a rhythm sweeping her into fairytale lands and silk-spun visions of naked bodies writhing on satin sheets. Her fingers plunged into his hair to feel the silken strands, and he groaned against her lips as she caressed him. No, no doubt about it now. He wanted her with a passion asking for nothing less than total surrender.

In a sensual haze, she barely felt his hands under her sweater and opening her bra. Then he cupped her, testing her small rib cage. She writhed against him a little, but he was unrelenting. His tongue tortured as he pumped and stroked in her mouth, the rhythm so much like sex. She clenched her vaginal muscles as the pleasure gathered strength.

He broke the kiss and worked his way to her ear, his tiny nips along her jaw making her shiver with delight. She caressed his shoulders, wanting more. Seconds expanded into infinite minutes as his tongue stroked over her sensitive earlobe and she gasped in pleasure.

Tears of total happiness burned her eyes as he nibbled on her ear, then stuck his tongue inside.

Oh, God. I can't stand this. It's too good.

Her hips undulated, demanding he give her what she needed. His lips brushed down her throat, bathing her skin with licks and kisses. When he found her lips again she kissed him with voracious hunger. Taking the initiative, she swept her tongue over his lips and he opened to her hungrily. A soft growl left his throat and he twisted his mouth over hers, taking her tongue deep into his mouth.

With gentle, loving caresses he touched the sides of her breasts and she gasped in delight. He broke their kiss, and when she dared look into his eyes, she saw everything she wanted and more.

Blazing with sexual need, his dark gaze devoured her. He slid her sweater upward. Almost as if he feared hurting her, he cupped each breast and molded her in the hot embrace of his palms. She shivered as pleasure shot through her nipples, hardening them into almost painfully aroused beads.

"Please," she whispered.

He backed her toward the couch, then with a swoop of his arms, he picked her up. Startled but pleased, she waited to see what he'd do. She smiled in delight and his sensual grin sparkled in his eyes. He sat down on the couch with her in his arms, then tipped her onto her back. Leaning over her, he pushed up her sweater and his fingers rasped gently over one nipple. She moaned as the feather light caress drove her into mindlessness. She closed her eyes, little moans of startled pleasure leaving her throat.

His mouth came down on hers and Blayne kissed her deeply. He clasped her nipples and plucked them, a steady tempo matching the stroke of his tongue in her mouth. Shivering in startled amazement, she enjoyed his seduction. Soon the pace overtook any thoughts but his fingers tormenting her breasts and his mouth weaving a heady desire she could never escape.

Jemma tore her mouth from his and gasped. "Blayne."

As he plucked and stroked one nipple, he tortured the other with long licks and gentle sucks. She writhed under his ministrations. He cupped both breasts in his big hands and held them prisoner as he tweaked and stroked, suckled and laved with hot attention.

She groaned, the dampness and heat deep inside her growing to desperate craving. She dared look down at his dark head. Shoving her fingers into his hair, she kneaded his scalp as he treated each nipple to relentless attention.

Surely they'd reached the point of no return.

The phone rang.

Instantly he released her, his breath heaving in and out of his lungs as he stared at her. "Damn."

Whether he cursed because they'd been interrupted or cursed because they'd been making out, she didn't know.

Again the phone rang. Twice. Three times. The answering machine started to pick it up. He disentangled himself and lunged for the cordless phone on the breakfast bar. Halfway mortified that she'd been lying on his couch, she stood and walked to the breakfast bar, too.

Blayne barked a reply into the phone, his clipped voice sounded mighty pissed at the interruption.

Weak-kneed, she sank down on a stool and stared at him. Then she clipped her bra back together and pulled down her sweater. Her fingers trembled.

He jammed his fingers through his short hair, scrubbing as if the motion might wake him from a daze.

Oh, my God. I've just made out with Major Forbes. I was ready to strip off my panties, part my legs and let him have me right here. Right now.

A smile parted her lips.

Oh, yeah.

"Graham." Blayne's voice sounded rough-edged and deep, and Jemma liked the idea she'd created that rich note in his tone. "Yeah, how's it goin'? I stopped by your office around lunch. How did you know I was back in town?"

The pause as he listened gave her a chance to think. Did she want overprotective big brother Graham to know she was here?

Get a hold of yourself. You're a grown woman, for pity's sake. If you want to screw the entire United States Army that's your business, not your big brother's.

She winced at the thought. She wasn't a slut puppy, although part of her felt wanton beyond control. The burning attraction she felt for Blayne didn't consist of only lust, but feelings she couldn't comprehend. In any case, the situation propelled her into dangerous waters. If she touched him again she knew she wouldn't turn back.

Seconds later Blayne glanced at her, and the way his gaze surveyed her body said the desire hadn't worn off. "Don't worry about her Graham. She's safe." A shit-eating grin covered his mouth as he laughed. "Because she's right here with me. Look, I'll talk to you later. Maybe in a couple of days we could get together for that beer. Yeah, there's something I need to tell you. Here's your little sister."

She shook her head, panic taking hold. Her hand automatically took the phone and she was forced to talk to her brother. "Hey, Graham."

"Is there something *you* should be telling me?" Graham asked, his voice tight.

Oh, great. Is this where he starts twenty-questioning me?

"Nice to speak with you, too." She looked around the room. No sign of Blayne. "How's the snow at Fort Carson?"

"Piling up. What about at Blayne's apartment?"

She glanced outside. "Snowing harder than it was an hour ago."

A sigh echoed from him. "You shouldn't go out in this. Then again I'm not sure it's safe for you there either."

"What? Why isn't it safe?" The line clicked off. "Hello? Hello?"

The phone was dead, no dial tone. She hung up, then lifted the receiver again. Nothing. Great.

"That would be my question." She jumped at the sound of Blayne's deep voice. "What's not safe?"

Did she really want the truth? "Well, I suppose he could be talking about the weather, but I got the impression that isn't what he meant."

With a wry grin he moved closer to her. "What do you think he meant?"

"Maybe he sees me as the little sister who needs protecting. Big brother instinct, you know."

His grin made her heartbeat accelerate. "Did he hang up on you?"

"No, no, nothing like that. The line is dead."

"Damn. Well, I guess even if he wanted to scold you about being stuck here with me, he can't now. At least not for a little while."

He brushed her cheek with the back of his fingers. She almost whimpered. Then he leaned in and captured her lips quickly. He didn't linger, but did a hit and run. Her heartbeat increased, excitement at having him near driving her toward something she didn't know if she wanted.

He turned away and headed down the hall to his bedroom. "Make yourself at home while I take a short nap. See ya in about twenty minutes."

*****

While Blayne slept, Jemma took time to check out his bachelor quarters. She realized she'd received the wrong impression when she'd first walked inside. She strolled to the fireplace mantel and looked at framed photographs that sat there.

One of the five-by-seven photographs showed a night she remembered well. Blayne wore military dress blues and stood next to her and Graham.

The Christmas military ball from a year ago.

She smiled at the fond memories resurrecting in her mind. The party had almost turned into a bust for her; her date decided he'd rather dance with other women. Infuriated, she'd almost left. Blayne, who had arrived at the ball without a date, had graciously danced with her. She closed her eyes and recalled the two fast dances they'd shared. Free and happy, she'd experienced the exhilaration.

Now she knew the attraction she'd felt for him all this time wasn't one-sided. She touched her lips and sighed. She played it over again; his warm lips teasing, coaxing, seducing reactions from her she'd never imagined resided deep within her. Hunger. Need. Incredible passion.

She perused other photos. A large eight-by-ten featured his mother and father.

A fantasy played in her mind as she imagined standing beside him in a family portrait, a new addition to his photos.

God, I need to take a step back. A few minutes to remember why I'm here.

One kiss didn't make a lifetime. It didn't make one night.

Of course, she'd done far more than kiss him. At the memory of his hands and mouth on her breasts, she quivered in renewed excitement. Nothing had prepared her for the desire, the craving to know him inside and out.

Feeling a little nervous, she looked at the *Life* magazine on his coffee table, then she wandered to his bookshelves. Eclectic was his middle name. He owned copies of Shakespeare, Twain, and other classics. Alongside more conventional fare were mysteries, suspense and adventure novels. Michael Crichton looked like one of his favorites based on the number of titles on his shelf.

Feeling thoroughly snoopy, she examined his DVD collection. Damned if he didn't have quite a few of the same movies she did. After that she noted his music selections ranged from smooth jazz, hard rock and classical.

She turned to the stereo equipment. Maybe if she played soft music she could get her mind off the way it had felt snuggled in his arms, and the way he'd made love to her mouth and breasts.

Like many men, he owned an elaborate setup including a large television, radio, DVD player and CD player. The huge array of buttons on the equipment scared her. It would be her luck to push the wrong button and startle him straight out of his nap with a huge blast of sound.

Nah. I can figure this out.

After a couple of false starts she popped a CD into the player. Seconds later the mellow, soothing tones of jazz eased into the room. Relieved the music played softly, she sank into the easy chair and closed her eyes, a little weary. She sank into a hard sleep almost immediately.

When Jemma awoke she realized the room had grown darker. Blurry-eyed, she glanced at her watch. Three o'clock. She sat bolt upright, her eyes wide as she realized she'd slept over an hour.

She left the chair and tried the phone again. Still dead. Then she headed to the window. What she saw made her groan. Sure enough, the snow blew almost horizontal and the wind howled with furious persistence. Snow piled up against the wheels of cars in the parking lot.

Great. At this rate she would be trapped for the night. While she shouldn't be affected one way or the other, the thought of staying in his apartment overnight made her nervous and filled with anticipation at the same time. Right now she didn't have an alternative.

She heard a soft moan.

Concerned, she headed down the hall. He'd partly closed the bedroom door, and when she eased it open, it didn't make a sound. The shade over the single large window was closed, leaving the room in semi-darkness. She crept forward and looked down upon him. A sweet tenderness in her heart made her move nearer, a craving to help him weather storms, the ups and downs in life.

What images did he see when he closed his eyes? Was his soul marred by the battles he'd fought, every combat zone permanently printed on his heart?

She swallowed hard as she allowed her gaze to caress him. Did any man deserve to be so disgustingly hot?

She'd imagined this moment, this delicious revelation in her dreams, in her night fantasies.

Lying shirtless and spread-eagled on the bed, Blayne represented delicious in a strong, alpha man. Muscular and drawn in authoritative, intimidating lines, his body gave new meaning to the words heart-attack-hunk. In repose, his features softened slightly. But somehow he retained awareness, a spring-load quality that spelled danger. Each taut line and defined curve promised sheer supremacy. In dim light she could still see his rippling, defined muscles. Wide shoulders looked capable of taking on huge responsibility. He possessed powerfully built arms, and she loved how protected she'd felt with those bands of strength around her. Defined pectoral muscles were sprinkled with dark hair that trailed down to his washboard stomach and into his waistband. Her mouth almost watered.

She sucked in a breath. Of course he owned a chest to-die-for. The man worked out and kept in shape. Mesmerized by the site of his chest moving up and down in sleep, she gave into voyeuristic enjoyment.

He groaned and muttered, "Look out, Glabowsky! Don't—"

His hand reached out, then his brow wrinkled as if he felt pain. He clutched at his chest with one hand.

Alarmed, she sat on the bed. She reached for his shoulder, pausing as she hesitated to touch his hard, masculine body. When she did touch his shoulder, his skin felt smooth over a rock-solid frame.

"Blayne? It's all right. Wake up."

He jerked, his eyes popping open, staring like a wild man. He grabbed her arm and yanked. She tumbled forward with a startled squeak. She tried to keep her balance, but fell onto the bed next to him in a heap. Sturdy arms wrapped around her waist.

Plastered almost nose to nose with her, his fierce expression frightened her until his gaze cleared in recognition and his grip loosened. But he didn't let her go. Instead he turned her onto her back and his legs twined with hers. Her head was cradled on his arm while the other hand slipped down her arm and cupped her waist. One of his solid thighs wedged between her legs and pressed upward. She gasped as her clit responded to the wicked pleasure, and she arched against him instinctively.

Oh, man, he felt fantastic. Every inch of his big body pressed into hers. Lying half under him should have panicked her, but instead she reveled in the thrill. Heat radiated from his skin and his intoxicating male musk delighted. His breath touched her lips.

He scowled. "Damn it, Jemma, don't sneak up on me like that. Did I hurt you?"

Shaky, she said, "No, but all I was trying to do was wake you up. You were having a nightmare."

Easing his frown, he asked, "A nightmare?"

"You don't remember?"

He sighed and nodded. A shiver racked his body. "Only too well."

"Want to tell me what it's about?"

Although darkness encroached on the room, she could see the intent in his eyes, the recognition of her body cradled alongside his. "God, Sweets, you feel so good under me." The hand cupping her waist slipped down, down over her hip, then wandered down to caress her thigh. "This is all I want to talk about." He reached up to stroke her face with his palm, the touch so exquisite and gentle she shivered with sweet, hot needs. "Not war and nightmares. And me doing something I should have done out in the living room an hour ago. Hell, I should have done it two years ago."

Anticipation spread like lightning in her veins. "What should you have done two years ago?"

"I should have kissed you. I should have told you how attracted I was to you. We could have been in bed a lot sooner."

Amazed and so turned on she couldn't speak, she knew what happened between them now would be up to her. If she said no, he would stop, but if she allowed him to kiss her once, Jemma knew she couldn't resist.

His thumb ran over her lips, and the brush against her sensitive skin made her writhe with the barest of movements. "Speak to me, Jemma. Tell me what you want. When I kissed you earlier I was worried I frightened you."

Total honesty meant telling him she wanted down and dirty sex. So, for once in her life, she would be candid to the quick, even if he rejected her. Even if he left on his next assignment and didn't return. She would have this moment, this night.

Desperate, she palmed his face and enjoyed the prickly rasp of his stubble against her fingers. "I want you."

Fire leapt into his eyes. "The first time will be fast. I'm aching so bad I don't think I could last long."

"I want you hard and fast and deep."

With a wicked, hungry grin that said he liked what he'd heard, Blayne laughed softly. "Sweets, I never realized what a reckless woman you are."

Only for you.

His mouth came down on hers, hungry as his tongue plunged deep and started a cadence that spelled *Fuck* with a capital letter. She knew by his kiss, by the way his hands touched her, that he was right. Their first time wouldn't be tender, wouldn't be an agonizingly long lovemaking session. No, this would be raw, primitive fucking.

Heat built inside her, starting a chain reaction of physical sensations she couldn't control. Her breasts felt tender, the nipples extra sensitive. Her lower body seemed permanently on fire, heat and dampness igniting between her legs. He shifted and she felt his erection hard and long against her thigh.

Breath suspended, she realized the slow smooth jazz melody had extended into a new age tune with a sultry, exotic tone. Steamy, the song throbbed into the bedroom with a pulsating beat spelling urgency and desire.

Pulling back, he stood by the bed and unbuttoned his jeans. Despite his vow they'd make love fast, he slid the zipper down at an agonizing pace. He hissed in a breath as he hooked his fingers in the waistband and took his black briefs down with the jeans.

Holy, holy God.

She'd ogled his chest, admiring the endless stretch of male muscle, but the dark hair trailing over his stomach bushed around a thick, long cock. Blayne's penis was bigger than any she'd taken inside her before. Not porn star huge, but gorgeous male perfectly proportioned to his big male body. He looked delicious, and part of her wanted to take him in her mouth and suck him until he spewed down her throat.

Before she could reach out and touch him, he said, "Take off your clothes."

She didn't need more urging. She slid off the bed, never taking her gaze from the glorious male in front of her. Desperate to feel his nakedness against her, she yanked her sweater over her head and tossed it aside. Her bra, jeans, socks and panties followed seconds later in a heap on the floor. Every concern she might have had about shyness evaporated under his hot, appreciative survey. Without a word, he backed her toward the bed and they fell upon it in a tangle of arms and legs.

Her breathing accelerated, her body flushed with heat. She might burn up before he took her, if he didn't take her right this minute.

She'd always thought groping was something uncouth high school boys did in the backseats of cars. As they explored each other like ravenous animals, she realized a mature man and woman in desperate need of each could thrash and roll and grope with the best of them. He covered one nipple with his hot tongue, lapping and sucking as he slipped his fingers between her legs.

As he traced her wet labia with one finger, she gasped and bucked against his hand. He groaned against her nipple, the vibrations tingling into the hard nub and making her echo his sound with one of her own. "Damn, baby, you're so hot and wet already."

His boastful male satisfaction didn't diminish her yearning and excitement. Instead it fueled and heightened her arousal. Jemma shuddered against him. "God, I can't stand this."

"What do you want?" His eyes went animal, the most primitive part of him hovering on the brink. "What do you need, Sweets? Tell me."

She'd never told a man what she wanted before, and a man had never asked. She could allow every inhibition dissolve into dust in Blayne's protective arms. This realization came to her, forbidden, and more exhilarating than anything she could have imagined.

"Fuck me," she whispered, her voice hoarse and aching with desire.

"Yes," he growled.

As he lowered his hips between her thighs, his cock nudged

her soft folds. His tongue penetrated her mouth, dipping inside to rub with a continual, deep stroke.

He ripped his mouth from hers, his breath coming harshly. "I almost forgot. Hold on."

Jemma moaned softly as he headed for the bathroom and she heard him ripping open a condom package. Seconds later he returned, his heavy cock sheathed. He tossed several other condoms on the nightstand. Oh, yes. It looked like he had a long evening planned.

Now. He would take her now.

As he settled between her legs again, he made sure to keep most of his weight off her by propping up on his forearms.

This was it.

As he kissed her, he slid between her folds and eased his thick cock into her tightness.

She tore her mouth from his, her female power roaring inside her. "Hard. Do it hard."

With a groan he muttered, "Yes, ma'am."

He drew back for power and plunged so deep she gasped and arched her back in stunned ecstasy.

"Yes," he said again, his voice guttural. "God, you feel so good."

Hard as steel and so thick it stretched her, his cock felt hot against her walls. She'd thought she'd had sex before, but what had she known?

This...this incredible hardness buried deep inside her was *sex*.

She shivered and slid her arms around his neck. "Please. Now."

"Don't let me hurt you," he rasped. Without further preliminaries he withdrew and jammed his cock high and tight into her once again.

She gasped, her eyes wide as she sobbed with incredible excitement. "Yes, yes."

He took her mouth, his tongue fucking her mouth as his cock fucked her cunt. He started a hard, driving movement, jack hammering between her thighs. Each insistent, ramming thrust into her took Jemma to a new height of craving, her hips rotating beneath his as he powered his way into her.

An incredible tingling built deep inside her as his cock rubbed her G-spot fast and relentlessly. Back and forth, back and forth, the steady piston action of his hips driving her to the beyond. Burning with amazing, stunned ecstasy, she moved with him, her body learning a rhythm of push and retreat. She understood more of her heart and soul through the heart-bursting physical connection. Sex became an intoxicating, loving, primal mating on the most basic scale.

As she leaned up and licked one male nipple, he tasted salty and hot. Jemma gripped his shoulders, her fingers digging in a little as she held on for the ride.

Blayne groaned her name against her lips, his breath harsh and rapid. "Come on. Come for me."

As he rammed deep, she gasped in stunned ecstasy. She came, her hips lurching upwards, her back arching as a tiny moan of fulfillment left her throat and bursts of bliss fired in her clit.

"Oh, yeah," he rasped.

Jemma's reaction set him off, a male animal out of control and reaching for the top in no uncertain terms. She felt like he might fuck her forever.

God, she hoped so. The harder he thrust, the more she wanted him. She couldn't get enough.

Although she'd experienced a satisfying orgasm, sensation piled upon sensation and demanded more from her. She opened wider to each punctuating thrust, each ruthless requirement of his body on hers, then pulsated and clenched over the rock-hard man moving inside her.

His voice raw with passion, he whispered erotic words against her ear. "God, you're so hot." When she whimpered, pressing her breasts into his hard chest and lifting her hips, he praised her. "That's it. Oh, shit, you like that don't you, baby?"

She groaned low in her throat, soft little pleas for more.

Instinctively she knew what he wanted, felt it in her bones. She grabbed his ass cheeks, digging into them with her fingers. As it anchored her, she rotated her hips, and at the same time, tightened and released over the hardness plunging inside her.

Punctuated by increasingly fiery lunges, he demanded more. "God, that's it. Fuck me. Come on, fuck me."

His harsh erotic demands turned her on so much her blood seemed to boil, her breathing heavy as he hammered deep. She complied, writhing under him, possessed by sheer mental and physical ecstasy she'd never encountered with such searing intensity.

Sweat tickled her forehead, their bodies musky with exertion, and their breaths hot. Her body couldn't say it, but her mind could.

Yesyesyesyes.

Jemma's orgasm burst inside her without warning.

She screamed against his mouth. As her walls tightened and released against his cock, he burrowed into her again and again. A wave of heat blasted into her womb, then extended outward like an atomic reaction. She shivered and moaned as it spread down her legs into her toes, fanning out and up into her chest and into her arms and head.

He growled low in his throat and kicked up the pace. He buried his face in her shoulder. Thrusting strongly, he took her toward a new revelation, a second ecstasy not far behind.

Orgasm ripped her yet again, pushing a shriek from her throat.

With a snarl he burst. As his hips continued to move, he moaned harshly again and again and again. With a last shudder of fulfillment, he sank upon her and lay still.

And the truth moved over her in a huge wave, reality

stunning, beautiful and frightening.

She loved him.

Chapter Four

Blayne awakened sometime later, a languorous contentment flowing into his mind and body. He lay face down in bed. He couldn't remember falling asleep, and as he cracked one eye he realized the room had gone almost dark.

Shit. Maybe for the first time in his life he'd passed out after having sex.

He smiled. Man, he'd never experienced sex so mind-blowing. Something wild roared inside him, ready to take her now, hard, fast and without foreplay. While he'd never considered himself a sex machine, he had enough desire pouring into him this minute to grow at least a couple more raging hard-ons before the night finished.

He rolled onto his back. His groin ached with the memory of his first plunge into her body. He went into the bathroom and removed the condom, then returned to the bed.

Whether she realized it or not, Jemma qualified as one incredible, sexy woman. He'd sensed her vulnerability, an unwillingness to believe she could share a sexual experience beyond the norm.

He thought, even when he'd started to thrust into her hard and fast and she'd begged for it, that she might be a little inhibited. *Hell, no.* He'd fucked her through her orgasms, pumping into her as she'd moaned and quivered.

Jemma.

He realized she lay curled up with her back to him, and he inched nearer to her. As his index finger brushed over her spine, she shivered. Tangling his fingers in that flame-glorious red hair felt terrific. He loved plunging his fingers into it. The hide and seek of her hair covering her breasts, then revealing them drove him into a serious state of lust.

If he was lucky, she'd want to fuck him senseless again. He reached over for another condom. As he sheathed his aching cock, he knew this time would be slower. She deserved care and consideration, and part of him still worried he'd hurt her, despite her breathless cries of climax.

He brushed his palm along her back to her hips, then snuggled up behind her. She pressed back against him with a soft sigh. He wasn't one hundred percent sure she was awake after all. He smiled. She would be in a minute if he had anything to say about it.

Nudging his cock into the crease of her buttocks, Blayne drew her back until he could slip his right arm under her body and pull her against him.

He wondered if she'd enjoy getting fucked in the ass. The very idea made his cock harden. Not that he would suggest it to her right away. They needed time to explore. Then again, if she gave signs she wanted it tonight, he wouldn't have any trouble accommodating her needs. Whatever she wanted, he'd be damn sure to comply. He wanted her screaming out his name, begging for another orgasm. So whatever it took to get her off, he would give it to her.

As she snuggled against his groin, he sucked in a breath. He palmed her breast, cupping and stroking, reaching up to trap her nipple between his fingers. She moaned again and arched, her breast pushing tighter into his hand. Fingering the already hard nipple, he plucked her, loving the sensation of the bud elongating under his touch. He rubbed his cock against her ass, making sure she could feel how much he needed her. After tracing the soft skin around her belly button with his index finger and feeling her shiver against him, he lifted her leg up over his thigh so he could reach the soft curls covering her cunt. Seconds later his fingers dipped between her thighs to find her wet and hot.

"Oh, yeah," he whispered against her ear.

With a delicate quiver she moaned. "Blayne."

He plied her flesh, his middle finger drawing a circular pattern around the lips of her wet sex. He rubbed all around her swollen clit. When she squirmed against him, her tiny moans telling him how much she loved it, he eased three fingers deep into her.

Curling his fingers upward, he found her G-spot and started to massage. Her cream moistened his fingers. He fondled her hard nipple, brushing across, over and around the delicate area until she twitched against him, her muscles reacting to arousal. The more he massaged her, the more liquid hot cream spilled over his fingers. Blayne felt her walls shivering as her need to climax quickened. He loved driving her into madness, making her want him as much as he wanted her. When she started to beg, he thought he'd lose his mind.

"Please, Blayne."

"What, honey?"

"I'm dying here."

Her plea spurred him onward and he increased the pressure against the sweet spot inside her. Fluttering his tongue against her earlobe, he whispered, "So soft and wet and tight."

Her breathing increased, her desperate moans rising higher as she suddenly gasped and a high-pitched squeal of delight left her throat. Her wetness tightened around his fingers as he stroked inside her. He drew his fingers out as she relaxed in his arms. He opened her legs wider, then pushed his cock deep into her sopping wet cunt. She gasped and moaned, pushing back against him.

Heaven hit him between the eyes as he moved slow and deep and pressed in as far as he could go. He rested there, gritting his teeth as her channel shivered around him. Blayne's eyes closed on a ragged moan as he drew back, then plunged again, slow and steady pumping. For long minutes he continued the pace, drawing out her excitement as he pushed and pulled back, keeping each thrust deep so that he touched high inside her. He reached down and plucked at her clit while his cock tunneled inside her, using his other hand to torment her breast with steady tweaks and flicks.

"Blayne." She whimpered and writhed against him. "Please."

Her pleas spurred him on, but he refused to move faster. Soon she moaned nonstop, her begging and sobbing for breath mixing with his urging. The pace remained steady and it seemed forever that he moved back and forth inside her heat.

With a quaking gasp she came again, her long drawn-out climax slipping from her with a low moan of overwhelming ecstasy. Her cunt gripped him in steady, muscle-melting throbs.

Her satisfaction pushed him over the edge. With a burst he came, pushing up high so she could feel every pulse of his cock. He grunted as climax took him into the deepest pleasure he'd ever known.

*****

Jemma awoke to almost total darkness. She blinked and looked at the bedside digital clock and it read six o'clock in the evening. Amazed and a little dazed at everything that happened between her and Blayne that day, she decided she needed distance to think.

More than anything she needed to decide if she could survive having her heart broken. Now that she'd foolishly fallen in love with him, he wouldn't reciprocate her emotions. No way would this Special Forces soldier allow her a permanent part of his heart. Instead he would smile sadly and tell her gently he'd enjoyed their time together, but she had to know how it was, right?

She did understand that his life spelled travel, adventure, and danger. But if he could love her back, could she endure knowing he might die on the next mission? Tears surged into her eyes, and she took a deep breath to suppress a sob. If she wanted to cry she needed to leave the room.

His heavy arm was plastered over her waist, her body nestled to his in a spoon. She savored, for a full minute, the heat and hardness of his big, muscled frame. Shifting her legs against his, she enjoyed his hair-roughened thighs brushing against her. The room held the musky scent of sex, and she inhaled it as evidence of their lovemaking. This intimate moment might be all she possessed soon. When he left and went into battle, she could enjoy this memory.

For while she'd indulged in mind-altering sex, she believed the way he'd caressed her and the tender way he'd spoken was more than a man fucking mindlessly. No, she didn't think Blayne could have sex with a woman and not have it mean something to both of them. She sensed he must have at least some affection for the woman he went to bed with.

Well, if she wanted to leave the bed she'd have to take the risk of waking him. With a little tug she pulled out from under his arm. To her surprise he didn't make a sound. She groped around trying to find her clothes, and after gathering at least her sweater, panties, and pants, she slipped out of the room.

With a soft smile of semi-contentment, her mind blurry with sleep and sex, she negotiated the dark hall. The open curtains in the living room allowed the area to be lit with a soft glow from a streetlamp outside.

She dressed quickly. Her nipples, sensitive from Blayne's relentless suckling and caresses, tingled against her sweater. Now that she'd experienced his wonderful lovemaking, she didn't know if any man from this point forward would ever live up to the tough and tender soldier.

She drifted to the window and looked outside. Under the glow from the streetlamp she could see the wind blew the snow horizontally. She placed her hands on the cold windowsill and allowed her thoughts to drift.

Yes. Intrusive thoughts, this time negative and annoying, shoved aside pleasant reverie.

Blayne was a soldier, all right. A man her father and

brothers wouldn't approve of for her lover and certainly not for a husband. She sighed. *What difference did it make?* As an adult she made decisions about her relationships, not her family. *That's the way it should be.*

Long-held inhibitions took time to erode and so did fear. She needed to find a way around her doubts if she had any hope of a relationship—a friendship at the least—with the man in the next room.

Warm hands slid around her waist and she gasped in surprise as a big body pressed against her from behind. Warm lips touched the side of her neck.

"Blayne," she gasped and laughed. "God, you scared me."

"Sorry."

"How did you sneak up on me like that? I've got great hearing."

"Training, Sweets. Just training. Remember what I do for a living."

Thanks for reminding me. This man could surprise the enemy and inflict damage or death. She shivered at the thought.

"What's wrong?" he asked.

She lied. "It looks cold out."

"Mmm. But we're warm in here." His voice held the rumbling, warm tone of a man satisfied by sex and food, and not necessarily in that order. His hands slid from her waist to under her sweater. "I woke up and you were gone. Are you okay?"

His big hands cupping her rib cage felt so strong and exciting. She leaned back against him. Warm and caressing, his fingers trailed up until he cupped just under her breasts.

"Jemma?"

"Oh, yes. Yes. I'm fine."

His lips touched her ear, his tongue licking at her lobe. "Damn, but you're fine all right. You're beautiful. You also have the cutest ass I've ever seen and being inside you comes damn close to heaven."

She laughed softly in pleasure. "Flattery will get you everywhere."

"Yeah?" Husky, his tone told her he wanted her again. "How far?"

Without hesitation his touch changed, becoming less tentative. She moaned and pushed back against him. Blayne reached down with one hand and undid her jeans. He slid them off her hips and they fell to the floor. Her panties followed. She took a moment to kick them aside, excitement making her bold. As he cupped her breasts, she quivered in raw enjoyment.

With long, steady strokes he plumped one breast, then palmed his way over her stomach to her mons. He feathered her curls, teasing with the tips of his fingers. She squirmed at his feather touch, the tickle making her gasp.

Back and forth he tortured, his palms at first cupping her breasts, then his fingers working her nipples.

He brushed her hair aside and his lips touched her ear. His warm breath tickled her earlobe. "Do you want me?"

"Yes. Of course."

"How much?"

"Now. I want you now."

He licked her ear. "Mmmm."

Encouraging her to open her legs, he slipped his fingers between her wet folds and probed. As two fingers found their way into her center, pushing deep, she groaned in unadulterated joy. Love swamped her whether she wanted it or not, lust following with a surge so hot and unrefined she couldn't think about consequences or tomorrow.

He withdrew his fingers and she moaned a protest. "Don't stop."

With gentle hands he turned her around. She could see his sultry grin in the semi-darkness. "Spread your legs."

She did as requested and he got down on his knees.

Oh, man. Oh, he was going to –

His mouth found her clit.

"Oh, Blayne. Oh my God, Blayne."

Lightning quick sensation darted into her as he initiated a seduction beyond anything she'd encountered before. Oral sex had always been somewhat blasé for her, but as soon as Blayne touched her that all changed.

His touch darted across her labia, then sank deep between the folds to fuck her with thrust after thrust of hot tongue. She thrashed a little against his hold on her hips, but he held her in place. His tongue smoothed across one side of her labia, then caressed the other side with equal slowness. Relentless, he licked and savored. She felt new moisture seeping from her cunt, and he encouraged it by placing his thumb over her clit and starting a slow circling motion. Over and over his thumb flicked and rubbed her clit as his tongue lapped and dined on her juices. Her vaginal walls clenched tighter and she moaned in lust and a desperate need. He slipped two fingers deep into her and pressed upward.

She whimpered and writhed against his hold, but he wouldn't let her come down from the bliss. She could feel it climbing, climbing.

Although she wanted to climax, she felt too excited to make it there.

If she thought his tongue and fingers felt wonderful, she wasn't ready for the staggering sensation of what he did next.

He stirred his fingers inside her, starting a gentle tempo that caressed her G-spot. Moments later he spread her overflowing moisture down to her anus. She gasped. He paused a moment as if to see what she would think. When she said nothing, he did it again, a continual massage until it felt natural for his fingers to move with long strokes in her cunt and his other hand touching her anus.

When she writhed against him, almost ready to beg again, he did something she didn't expect. One finger slipped a little way into her anus. When she gasped he stopped all movement.

"All right?" he asked. "Tell me to stop if it hurts."

"Mmm, please don't stop." Her voice sounded almost choked, and she couldn't believe the pleasure. "More."

He licked her clit and stuffed his fingers higher into her cunt. He pushed gently farther into her anus.

He started a motion. As he licked and sucked her clit he rubbed her G-spot and dipped in and out of her anus with gentle strokes. It took maybe half a minute and the ecstasy drove her excitement up like a rocket and she came. She sobbed, her body twitching in a mind-exploding pleasure that washed through her. Spasms of delight made her slick, engorged walls ripple and contract over his fingers.

When she stopped gasping and shivering, he released her and turned her around so she faced the window. As she stared in mindless bliss out the window of the apartment, watching the crystalline snow carpet the city, she realized they weren't finished.

He retreated to the bathroom and she waited in a heat of anticipation. Moments later he returned. He spread her legs wide, and then she heard him putting on a condom. Seconds later he speared his cock deep into her tight cunt and she moaned. Her head fell forward and she closed her eyes. She gripped the windowsill and sighed as he drew almost all the way out of her, the friction of manhood against female tissues a stunning and delicious sensation she would remember all her life.

"You like this," he said with a ragged, almost begging tone. "God, please tell me you like this. You like getting fucked in front of a window."

"Yes."

He plunged deep inside her again. "Where anyone might see you, Sweets?"

With a groan she pushed back against him, impaling herself on his stone-hard cock.

Then the meaning behind his words breached in full.

Oh. My. God. They stood in front of a window where anyone, if they walked by, could see them fucking. Or at least an observer could see Blayne and Jemma's shadows moving in the night, the sensual meaning behind their writhing bodies obvious.

As he shoved hard and deep inside her, he reached up and drew her sweater over her head. While no one could see them from the waist down, they sure as hell could see her naked breasts. She imagined being down in the lot in the freezing snow, looking up and seeing a naked female body wiggling and moving as a gorgeous male fucked the naked woman into oblivion.

Again Blayne thrust into Jemma. She sobbed as a tiny orgasm blossomed inside her. Unable to stand it, she slipped one hand down and rubbed her middle finger over her clit.

"Are you touching yourself, Sweets?"

"Yes."

"Oh, yeah."

"Blayne, we're doing this in front of a window," she said, scandalized and excited all at once.

"Damn it if we aren't," he whispered roughly as he unmercifully wedged his spike-hard cock into her. "Do you like it?"

His hands caught her hips and he pumped in an unyielding tempo that made her cry out with the most knee-weakening, heady orgasm she'd experienced yet. And when that orgasm started to fade, he kept the pace going as it drove her toward new insanity. Just when she thought it couldn't get better, he slowed his thrusts and inserted the tip of his thumb into her anus. As he fucked her mindless he massaged her with tiny thrusts of his thumb.

As she manipulated her clit, riding cock and thumb, she drove toward another climax, her body flowing with the beat, moving with his driving thrusts. She knew he loved to hear her response, and Jemma allowed emotion to mix with physical need into an explosive combination. She threw back her head and moaned as the intensity increased.

Every emotion, every sensation coalesced. She heard his rapid breathing, the never-ending drilling sensation of hard cock into receptive cunt, the way her vaginal walls seemed to widen and widen, opening her womb to his invasion. She didn't think she could become more excited, any more aroused.

But when he tucked her hips closer and reamed her with short, stabbing thrusts, she writhed in his hold.

Wildly turned on, she opened her eyes and gazed at the blizzard without really seeing it. Winter raged outside, and blazing fulfillment hovered just out of reach.

With a roar he pounded into her, sending Jemma into meltdown, one orgasm splintering into another until tears of bliss ran down her cheeks.

Suddenly he stiffened, and at the height of her last orgasm he growled and shuddered against her. She felt his cock grow bigger and harder for one moment, then the rippling burst as his body quivered in blast after blast of cum.

Jemma sagged in his arms, her heart pounding so hard she could barely suck in a breath. Her sighs echoed with his heavy breathing. He soothed her with kisses along her shoulder.

"God, Jemma." He laughed softly. "I've never met any woman as hot as you, you know that?"

Pleased, she smiled and pressed back into him. His arms tightened around her waist as he nibbled on her ear. "Thank you." Feeling bold she complimented him. "I've never met a man who could make me feel like this before. I've never been multi-orgasmic. This is amazing. I'm…you're very important to me. I don't want this night to end."

He went silent, his movements stopping as his arms stiffened around her. *Oh, hell.* Now she'd done it. At the slightest verbal affection, at a mention of it he pulled inward. She could feel his withdrawal emotionally almost as if he'd shut himself off.

He released her and headed for the bathroom without a word.

Immediately an ache centered in her heart. Damn and triple damn. She quickly returned to the bedroom. She burrowed under the covers, any idea about getting dressed and pretending she hadn't experienced kinky sex in front of a window, disappeared from her mind. But she couldn't deny that she worried about what had happened moments ago. Fear ran in circles inside her. Would he tell her that he couldn't care for her the way she needed him? That he wouldn't get emotionally involved? She heard the water go off, then he returned moments later.

She started to get out of bed, but he slipped under the covers and trapped her against him. "Where do you think you're going?"

With a smile she knew he couldn't see in the darkness, she said, "My turn."

"Hurry back."

This tiny encouragement made sure she hurried into the bathroom and rushed out. When she climbed back into bed, he tucked her into his arms and sighed. She snuggled against his heat and muscles and reveled in the closeness. As his hand swept over her hair and he kissed her forehead, her heart melted a bit. Maybe his silence hadn't meant anything earlier. Maybe she hadn't screwed up her chances with him after all.

She remembered what she'd been thinking before he drove her into sexual madness. Could she afford to feel the way she did about him? Falling in love didn't guarantee anything...happiness, security. Nothing.

Then again, how could she help it? Love swamped her whether she wanted it or not, and with each sexual act she fell more and more in love with him, as if his physical care and pleasure bound them together. While sexual dalliance didn't always equate to love, Major Blayne Forbes tied her emotions in knots and could break her heart into bits.

When he didn't say a word, she spoke instead. "That thing in front of the window was…kinky."

He chuckled. "Yeah. You're a wildcat, Sweets."

"I've never… I mean…that was fantastic. Can we try it again soon?"

Silence covered the room, and she thought he might not answer. Then he spoke. "We can do it anywhere, anytime, any way you like."

Reassured in some small way, she allowed quiet to grow around them, afraid to breach an emotion-filled subject. Instead she enjoyed how he cradled her in his arms, and not long after fell asleep.

Chapter Five

Light speared under the curtains and managed to hit Blayne in the eye. He groaned and levered up on one elbow to look at the clock. Seven o'clock the next morning. He never slept this late, but mind-altering sex apparently acted as a tranquilizer.

He glanced over at Jemma. She lay curled in a fetal position buried in the covers with the sheet pulled up to her nose. She looked too damn cute for words. Although he'd held her most of the night, at some point they'd separated and found lonely positions on the bed. He lay back and sighed. Covering his eyes with his hands, he almost groaned. He *could* wake her up with more sex.

What he should do was an entirely different thing.

In the light of day everything seemed clearer. While he felt much better than he did yesterday, he realized things had become complicated. He didn't know where his career would go from here or whether he could even stay in the Army.

Now he'd just screwed his best friend's sister.

Holy shit.

Graham would be pissed.

He realized he needed to do some deep thinking before this thing with Jemma went any further. Being as quiet as he could, he jumped into the shower. After shaving and dressing, he wandered into the living room and looked out the window. The snow had stopped and bright sun parted lingering clouds. About six inches of snow had accumulated but it looked like it would all be cleared away soon. Now that the snow was no longer an excuse for her to be here, would she run away? Would she tell him yesterday and last night had all been a mistake?

If she didn't, he might.

The phone rang, startling him. He grabbed the cordless before it could ring twice.

"Blayne," Graham's voice said, "I'm glad the damned phones are working again. I'm worried about Jemma. I tried calling her apartment but she's not there." Graham's serious tone went a little harsher. "Did she stay with you last night?"

Blayne cleared his throat. Time to face the music. "Of course she did. You didn't think I was going to let her go out in that snowstorm, did you?"

"No, I suppose not."

"She's fine. You don't need to worry about her."

Graham's sigh sounded somewhere between perturbation and relief. "Sure, man. I know you wouldn't let anything happen to her."

An awkward pause filled the air between them. Finally Blayne said, "Fort Carson even open today?"

"Late reporting. I don't have to be at work until nine o'clock. I could pick Jemma up from your place and take her home."

"Jemma's got her own car here. I need to go to the fort and get mine." He explained how he'd left it there when Jemma drove him home. "She was worried I'd pass out and crash the car."

"How do you feel now?"

"Much better. I guess I needed more sleep."

"I can pick you up and then we can talk."

The tight quality in Graham's voice worried him, and he wondered if he would get the inquisition. "Yeah, sounds good."

"Can I speak to Jemma?"

"She's sleeping."

"No, I'm awake now," Jemma's voice came from behind Blayne, and he swung around.

She'd thrown her clothes on, but her hair appeared tousled. Her blue eyes held apprehension, as if she feared reprisal from her brother. *Damn it, this was way too complicated.*

"Hold on. She's right here."

Jemma took the phone, and Blayne decided to make breakfast. He was hungry as hell. Maybe all that sex had given him a new appetite.

Her voice came soft and clear as she settled on the couch. "I'm fine." A pause formed as she listened to her brother, then more from her. "So you're picking him up to take him to his car. Good." Another pause. "You're coming right now?" Her sigh sounded heavy, and he wondered what else her brother had said. Her silence went on for a long time. "This isn't the time or the place to talk about this, Graham. I'll see you in an hour and even then I don't plan on giving a lengthy explanation to you. Maybe we'll talk about it later."

She hung up without saying goodbye.

Blayne turned his gaze on her as he flipped on the coffeemaker. She remained on the couch, staring into space. *Shit.* The last part of the conversation hadn't sounded good. Concerned, he left the kitchen and stood near the coffee table. He didn't sit next to her, afraid in some idiotic way he shouldn't touch her. Maybe he'd touched her way more than he should after all.

"What's wrong?" he asked. "Is Graham getting on your case about being here? I explained to him I didn't want you to go out in the weather. I thought he understood that."

As she looked up at him, she clasped the phone. "Oh, I think he understands it. But I also think he knows we weren't exactly platonic last night."

Her understatement might have made him laugh at any other time. Right now he felt nothing but cynicism. "And?"

She shook her head. "I don't know. I'll be interested to hear what he says to you. He'll probably call me up later today and give me an earful."

"What do you think about that?"

Doubt turned her pretty face pensive. "I'm not sure I know what to think about any of this." She put the phone down on the coffee table and swept a hand through her hair. "We had a great time last night. It was crazy and wonderful and…I don't know."

Without trying to pry more feelings out of her, he let the words spill. "You're concerned about what he'll think about us being together. It's your life, you know."

She nodded and stood up. She walked slowly to the living room window where they'd fucked like wild animals last night. "I know."

"It's up to you, but as far as I'm concerned you shouldn't let him dictate who you sleep with."

She nodded again, staring out at the parking lot. "But it's not just whether Graham will approve."

He put his hands on his hips, feeling like he might be in for the battle of his life. "Then what is it?"

She turned her back on the snowy world outside and leaned against the sill. "It's what we talked about yesterday before we got involved. You leave for months at a time and you may or may not come back. I don't know if I can take that." A shimmer of tears filled her eyes. "I don't know if I can see you every few months, sleep with you, then let you go."

While he'd heard from other men in Special Forces that some of their girlfriends got clingy, he'd never encountered the problem before. Maybe he'd kept his emotions and his affection shut off so well the women he'd dated here and there hadn't felt more for him. Maybe he didn't deserve a woman like Jemma being concerned about him.

It hit him in the stomach like a bullet.

Tears meant she cared about him enough to get emotional and the idea stunned him. Deep in his gut he realized sleeping with her had made it worse for both of them. Taking her to bed hadn't removed his lust, hadn't taken the edge off of needing her. He craved her right now, as she stood in the window with sun turning her already beautiful hair into a shimmering curtain of flaming red. My God, she looked A-number-one fucking gorgeous.

If he continued the relationship with her, if he wanted to jeopardize his relationship with Graham, he could continue to sleep with her. If she would allow it.

Before he could respond she said, "I…I think I need to give this time. Think about what I'm doing."

He should be relieved, maybe, that she wanted to cool things down and think over what they'd done. Damn, if this wasn't ironic. Usually he left first, telling a woman goodbye after they'd had some fun together. The woman always understood that a few nights together and a little dating didn't mean anything permanent.

Why the hell did he ache inside where he couldn't recall feeling so empty or alone before?

"I think you're right," he said. "Why don't we play it cool for awhile? I'm not sure where my career is going anyway."

That's it, Blayne old boy, play it cool.

She took a deep breath and he saw she'd forced the tears back. Now she appeared calm and composed. "So what happened in the Middle East may affect your career?"

"Yeah. I don't know. Things are up in the air, so it's probably not a good time to start anything when I may not be able to finish it."

Again she gave him one of those precise little nods. "I'd better go take a shower before Graham gets here."

With military precision she left the living room. Blayne returned to the kitchen and poured a cup of coffee. The first sip burned the hell out of his mouth and he cursed. He put the cup down on the counter and stared into its murky depths.

Damn it all to hell.

*****

Blayne stared at the snowy streets as Graham drove his Subaru Outback slowly toward Fort Carson. Tension drew tight in the car, and when Blayne glanced over at his friend, he could tell from the man's expression something might blow at any second.

At the best of times Graham was happy-go-lucky, a tall, strawberry-blond soldier with a tall, muscular build. Pound for pound he figured Graham weighed about the same as him, and yet he knew when it came to fighting he could kick his friend's ass.

Graham might be a soldier, but he wasn't trained quite like Blayne. He wondered if Graham would be tempted to fight him anyway. Trouble was, he understood Graham's fierce protective feelings; Blayne felt the same way about his sisters Polly and Anne.

Graham hadn't twenty-questioned either of them when he'd arrived at the apartment, but he'd given them both a look that assured there would be inquiries later.

It came sooner than Blayne expected.

"What happened last night?" Graham's voice was tinged with sarcasm.

Blayne cleared his throat. "I'm not going to bullshit you, Graham, because we're both adults and Jemma is an adult."

"You asshole," Graham growled before Blayne could say another word.

Blayne gritted his teeth. "Look, your sister's love life is her business."

"Love? You mean this has something to do with love? I can't believe you did this. What did you tell her, eh? Did you give her some hearts and flowers crap you have no intentions of following up on?"

"No, *damn it,* I did not." He glared. "You know me better than that. I don't play games with women. When a woman dates me, she knows right up front what my intentions are."

Liar. You didn't state any intentions to Jemma other than getting into her panties.

Graham grunted. "All right, I'll give you that. But this is my sister we're talking about here, Forbes."

"What she does and who she does it with is her business. She's twenty-nine fucking years old, not sixteen."

Graham went silent for a couple of minutes, his profile granite hard with irritation. "I won't have her hurt."

"Who says she's going to get hurt? You really think I'm that much of a bastard?"

"No."

One word didn't satisfy Blayne, but he figured it might be all he'd receive for now.

Graham swallowed hard. "She needs a man who isn't going to leave and get his ass shot off."

So, just like Jemma had discussed with him last night, her entire family remembered too well what their father had experienced in Vietnam.

"This is really about your father," Blayne said.

"Yeah, that's a good example of what can happen to a soldier in combat."

"Right, but your father came back alive."

"Alive, but not whole. Look, he's doing well these days but every once in awhile he's got these problems, you know?"

Blayne gazed out at the highway as it rolled beneath the car. "Night sweats, nightmares, anger impulse control problems. Yep, I've heard it all."

Silence entered the car as they turned into Fort Carson and passed the gate checkpoint where they showed their IDs to the soldiers guarding the gate.

Once they went through, Graham spoke again. "I want what's best for my sister."

"Of course you do."

"If she falls in love, it should be for a damned accountant or a lawyer who comes home every night. Not a soldier who sees horrible things and is sent back from a mission because his ass has been kicked by a bullet."

An ache centered in the center of Blayne's chest, as if Graham had shot him, too. "They sent me stateside to convalesce. But maybe they won't let me back into the team. I don't know."

For the first time Graham's voice softened, a different worry in his tone. "What? Tell me what happened."

So in excruciating detail he explained how the mission had gone south, some bad intelligence sending the team into an area overflowing with the enemy. Sergeant Dennis Glabowsky had died because of it, and now the man haunted his dreams.

"That wasn't your fault," Graham said as he turned down the street leading to his office. "You didn't have any way of knowing what was going to happen. It was an ambush. You were damned lucky to come out alive. From the way I hear it, you saved some lives."

Blayne gave a half-sarcastic laugh. "Well, I don't think they'll be giving me a medal for it anytime soon."

"Don't be too sure."

Blayne threw him a smile. "For a man who just gave me a butt-chewing over his sister, you're being mighty fucking supportive."

Graham pulled his car into the lot near his office and found Blayne's Focus. The car had a layer of ice on the windshield. Most of the snow had blown off it already.

When Graham pulled into a spot next to the Focus, he shut off the engine. "I guess I am." He stared at Blayne, his gaze contemplative and maybe a little confused. "Look, Blayne, if you need help for the trauma, get help. Don't let it stew inside you like it did my father, okay?"

Blayne nodded. "I'll work through it, even if it means seeing a shrink, all right?"

Though he didn't look one hundred percent convinced,

Graham appeared more relaxed and not as antagonistic. "Still want to have that beer this weekend and talk some more about what happened in the Middle East?"

Surprised at his friend's change of heart, Blayne nodded. "Sure. Now, are you done giving me hell about Jemma, or do I need to sit here and take it up the ass some more?"

Graham laughed, this time the sound genuine and appreciative. "Yeah, I'm done. Look, I'm sorry. It's just that I love her."

"Of course you do. But you can't protect her from life."

Nodding, Graham said, "Guess I should have figured that out by now. Shit, I also should have guessed this would happen between you two."

Stunned, it took Blayne a moment to answer. "Why?"

"My wife made some comments in the past when she's seen you and Jemma together."

Wary, Blayne asked, "Cynthia made comments? That sounds dangerous."

Graham shrugged. "She's very perceptive. Gets me into trouble all the time." A small pause and then Graham said something Blayne never expected. "What if Jemma's in love with you? Have you ever thought of that?"

Blayne didn't say anything for several seconds, surprised down to the root. The concept of any woman being in love with him, least of all sweet Jemma, never entered his mind. Then he remembered Jemma's tears. "I doubt it. In fact, she said she wanted to think about everything that happened." Blayne got out of the car and then leaned down to speak again. "She said she wanted time to think about us. My guess is she feels the way you do. She wants a sure thing, and that isn't me. So you don't have to worry about me breaking her heart."

Another tight aching touched Blayne's soul as he tried to imagine leaving on a mission knowing Jemma would return to her life without him. Maybe dating other men. Perhaps marrying another man.

The pain in his heart surpassed any bullet wound.

One more time he gave Graham a crooked smile. "Shit, if anyone's heart is going to be broken, it might just be mine."

Graham's eyes were aggrieved and surprised, their gray color almost silver in the early morning light. Before his friend could speak, Blayne shut the Subaru door and unlocked his car. As his frozen breath penetrated the cold air, he started the car and allowed the windshield to defrost.

Starting right now, he would hole up in his apartment for a day or two and sleep, think, and dream. Maybe by the time the weekend arrived, he'd know how to treat his misery.

*****

"Crud," Jemma muttered Friday night as she took the first bite of a TV dinner and stared at the evening news.

The so-called Cordon Bleu tasted more like crap than gourmet. Determined, she tried a forkful of green beans and grimaced. Not much better. She took the TV dinner to the kitchen and chucked it into the garbage. Appetite lost, she started a pot of decaffeinated coffee and wandered back into the living room.

As she flopped on the couch she released a drawn-out sigh. Things had seemed flat all week, and she knew why. Although she'd tried reasoning her way out of this stale, almost colorless existence she'd lived this last week of vacation, she couldn't seem to shake the sense she'd lost something precious. She felt as if she'd betrayed herself, given in to belief systems having nothing to do with who she really was.

All because she'd feared what her brothers and parents would say about Blayne when they found out she'd slept with him. Although he hadn't said anything else, she knew Graham had figured it out. For all she knew, he might have given Blayne a stern warning to stay away from her. Or maybe Blayne didn't need admonition; perhaps he decided he didn't want entanglements.

So all week she avoided the subject whenever Graham hinted at it, and she didn't ask if he'd heard from Blayne.

Maybe it was better this way. It didn't matter that her dreams revolved around wild lovemaking sessions with Major Blayne Forbes, and that she still loved him with all her being.

But, oh, her body ached with wanting him. More than once she lay awake at night and fantasized, remembering how his lips felt on her body, how his cock felt moving inside her. Unable to stand the pressure, she'd stroked her clit until she'd experienced a screaming orgasm. It couldn't replace Blayne's lovemaking.

Tears came before she could stop them. Oh, God, she'd messed up everything being wishy-washy and generally stupid. She couldn't blame Graham or her family, only herself. She should have told Blayne how she felt, then if he rejected her...well, then she would know. Nothing could be as devastating as falling madly in love with a man who would never know how she felt because she feared taking a chance.

As Jemma allowed the tears to flow, she put her head back on the couch and closed her eyes. Yes, she'd get over him given enough time. *Maybe.*

Then an idea came to mind, one that could cause as much pain as it might ease. She couldn't allow him to return to his unit and back to combat without telling him what resided in her heart. If something happened to him—

No. She wouldn't think of that. She stood before she could change her mind and ran into her bedroom. After flipping on the light, she went to the small desk in the corner of her room and grabbed her address book. Then she remembered she didn't have Blayne's number. Picking up the phone on the nightstand, she dialed her brother's house.

His wife Cynthia picked up the phone. Rather than asking for Blayne's number right away, she made small talk with Cynthia for a few minutes.

Graham's voice came on the phone moments later. "Hey, sis. What's up?"

Again she chatted with him about mundane things before she asked for Blayne's number. To her relief he gave it to her without question.

Then he asked, "You haven't seen Blayne this week, then?"

"No."

"I have. He's got good news, but I'll let him share it with you."

She sank onto the bed. "How do you know he'll want to share with me?"

"I have a feeling he will."

The smile in her brother's voice made her more than curious. "Graham—"

"Nope, I'm not ruining it. Besides, Cynthia would kill me if I did."

She laughed. "Oh, well in that case, to save you from dire consequences, I'll stop asking."

"And for my part, I'm sorry."

"About what?"

"I was overprotective. I shouldn't have interfered in your relationship with Blayne. I didn't use my skull. I can't control anything you do. Your life is your life and no one else's."

Surprised but relieved they'd jumped the hurdle, she released a deep breath. "Thanks. But it was as much my fault as yours. I allowed you to tell me what I was going to do with my social life. I know Dad won't be too thrilled about Blayne, but he'll have to get used to it." She made a small sound of despair. "That is, if Blayne wants to be with me."

"I have a feeling you're going to hit the jackpot, li'l sis. Wait. Cynthia is giving me dirty looks. I think that means I've said enough."

After they hung up, she dialed Blayne's apartment, afraid and yet excited. The phone rang three times before the answering machine picked up. A mechanical voice, not Blayne's, came from the machine. Disappointed, she left a quick message saying she'd try him back later.

She'd barely put the receiver in the cradle when the doorbell rang. She about came out of her skin, a startled sound leaving her throat.

"Take a deep breath," she muttered as she headed for the door, wondering who it could be.

When she looked through the peephole, her breath hitched in her throat. Blayne stood outside with his eyebrows pinched together as if he was anxious. Happiness to see him glided over her in a tremendous wave. She opened the door, and he gave her a sheepish grin that made him look more like a boy than a warrior.

She gasped when she saw what he held in his hand.

"Hi. These are for you." He handed her a dozen red roses.

Immediately she clutched them to her, drinking in their heavenly scent. "They're beautiful." Jemma's heart sang a new, beautiful song. "Thank you."

As she ushered him inside, she felt a powerful need gathering inside her. She had a lot to tell him, but even more, she *wanted* him. She closed the door and locked it.

Now was the time to let it rip.

"We've got to talk, Sweets."

"I know."

Before she could lose her nerve, she placed the roses on the table inside the entry. Before he could remove his down coat, she slipped her hand to the back of his neck and pulled him forward.

"What—?" he started as she tugged his head down.

She smothered his words with her mouth, kissing him softly and slowly. He stilled, then responded, his mouth twisting over hers. With a groan his arms went around her and he immediately took the kiss to the next level, his tongue plunging deep into her mouth. She returned his ardor, kissing him with a madness she didn't want to contain. His lips demanded, tasting her with a furious desire.

No, he didn't hate her. In fact, he wanted her with a passion she could feel with each breath and sigh. Overjoyed, she slid down the zipper on his coat and he shrugged out of it, still kissing her. The coat fell on the floor. Slipping his arms around Jemma again, Blayne molded her to his body. He deepened the kiss, his tongue making love to her with pure sex and sin.

When he released her mouth, he whispered against her lips. "How did I stay away from you this long?"

"I'm so sorry. I should have told you how I felt when we were snowed in. I should have—"

His mouth swallowed her words, his kisses frantic. He inched her down the hallway, stopping every once in awhile to nibble and explore. His hands found her breasts through her sweater, and when he flicked his thumbs over her nipples, she whimpered into his mouth.

He tore his mouth free and propped his forehead against hers, his breath coming fast and hard. "We can stop and talk if you want."

"Are you crazy?" she asked with a smile. "I want you. Talk later."

Blayne's eyes held powerful desire, his gaze intense, hot, and refusing to wait for anything. He pulled her sweater over her head and tossed it aside. Reaching behind her, he undid her bra, then flipped it away with a quick movement.

He kissed her ravenously as he found her nipples, pulling, tugging on the hard points until she groaned with each movement of his callused fingers on her flesh.

Desire exploded, and as they stumbled their way down the hall, they made it as far as the bedroom door. Gently he pushed her up against the wall, pinning her with his big body. He pushed his cock against her mound, rotating against her clit. Urgency made her greedy, and she worked quickly at his belt, snap and zipper until she freed his cock.

As she smoothed her fingers over the marble-hard column,

he hissed in a breath. She stroked him and he trapped her fingers. "God, baby. Later. If you do that now I'll explode. I can't wait that long."

Every molecule inside her, all the love she possessed for this handsome, wonderful man called her to wild, sexual completion. Nothing would make sense, no more words would be needed until they'd sampled their brand of special madness.

Out of her mind for him, she gazed into his dark eyes and knew she'd love him forever. "I've dreamed about this all week." Despite her arousal, tears popped into her eyes. "I can't stand it any longer. I thought maybe you'd never be in my arms again."

He frowned, his eyebrows drawing together, then his eyes softened as he pressed kisses to her forehead, her cheeks, her nose. "No, Sweets. Don't cry. I'm here and we're together. No more waiting." As she gulped in a breath and a sob threatened, he peppered her lips with tender, soft kisses so unlike the hungry searches they'd explored moments before. "I won't let you go without a fight, Jemma. Please tell me you want to be with me not just for tonight."

Joy danced in her heart, filling her soul with a special, warm glow reserved for a woman deeply in love. "I want you for always."

A big smile parted his lips. "Damn, if that doesn't sound good."

He kissed her as he undid her jeans and slid them down her legs, then removed her panties. She kicked them away. He pressed his thighs between her legs, pressing hard against her clit. He leaned forward and clamped his lips on one nipple, plumping the breast in his hand. As he sucked, she rubbed against him, a soft, frantic moan parting her lips. *Oh God.* She just might come from this.

His breath came in hard pants as he urged her into the bedroom. When they bumped into the bed, he released her. Naked, she got on all fours on the bed and gestured at him with a come-hither look. A crooked grin that spelled wicked things to come parted his lips as he retrieved a condom from his jeans pocket and held it up. He tossed it on the bedside table. With purpose he yanked his boots and socks off, stripped his jeans and briefs away, then pulled his sweater over his head.

At the site of his beautiful, muscular chest and erect cock, her mouth watered. God, she loved his body. She couldn't have conjured up a better fantasy if she tried. She almost left the bed to touch him. Before she could move he sheathed himself with the condom.

"Now," he whispered.

"Yes." Feeling uncharacteristically aggressive, a feral heat blossoming, she grabbed his arm and tugged. "Come here."

He tumbled onto the bed with a laugh and they rolled in a tangle of arms and legs. She came out on top, her body plastered against his from breast to loins. Closing her eyes, she savored sensations. Hard muscles flexed, cradling her as if she were the most precious thing in the world to him. She sighed and brushed her cheek against his chest, loving the touch of his hair-rough pecs against her skin. As her legs intertwined with his, the contrast of hard against soft, cock against wet labia, sent her hormones into riot. Her entire body yearned for joining, for a repeat of their loving. While making love before had been wonderful, she felt everything more intensely this time.

She cherished the brush of naked skin against naked skin, the heat of his hands, the growing ache between her legs. Her long hair cascaded down her naked body, and he reached up to brush aside the hair concealing her breasts.

As she straddled him, he clasped her waist and lifted her over his cock. Without more preliminaries she impaled herself deep, a gasp of ecstasy her only sound. His hardness, thick, long, and hot, arrowed high and tight. Clenching her muscles around him, she rose up and plunged down, keeping the rhythm languid and sensuous. Jemma swiveled her hips, tightening over him with the motion. Throwing back her head, she rose and fell upon his hard heat.

Blayne's breathing increased, his masculine sounds of pleasure growing by the second. She spread her legs wider and placed her palms on the bed for more leverage. She rode him like a wild thing, pounding her cunt over his cock at a furious pace. No waiting for bliss, no waiting for pleasure. Gratification came almost instantly, the blast-off rippling inside her. Rocking and rolling, she did him like an Amazon, a woman who knew what she wanted and from this point forward planned to take it. As need increased, he thrust his hips upward, compounding the ecstasy as his cock rubbed against pleasure points high inside her.

It roared into her, a lightning quick orgasm splintering her into a thousand euphoric pieces. She gasped, her entire body quivering.

Blayne continued to pump, his cock stroking and thrusting with a driving rhythm. Suddenly he stopped, his breath heavy and hot. His fingers stayed clamped onto her hips.

"What else do you need, Sweets?" he asked huskily, his gaze lit with a voracious fire. "How do you want it?"

Spreading her hands over his pecs, she brushed her fingers over his nipples. "I just want you to come."

Blayne pulled her down on the bed and rolled, coming up between her legs with a hard thrust. She moaned, feeling her walls part for him with greedy acceptance and desire for more. Urging him on, she tilted her hips, accommodating each slow, achingly tender thrust. A cadence emerged, a wholly erotic mating that lifted her up where she'd never been. Love and tenderness emerged in her world, and her eyes opened wide as pleasure mounted.

He thought the cock-exploding satisfaction of watching her ride him couldn't get any better. *Man, did it ever.* Although he might blow any minute, he gritted his teeth and held back, concentrating on what he wanted the most. He would get her off again if it killed him; he wanted her screaming, bucking, moaning for it. Who gave a shit if they woke the entire neighborhood?

He would do anything for her. Slay dragons, kick ass, give his life for her.

Blayne adored her, wanted her—

She lifted her hips on a downward thrust and he moaned low in his throat. Now was the time. He drew his hips back and pushed hard.

Fuck, yes.

As she trembled violently, a cry ripping from her throat, he couldn't deny it, couldn't hold body or heart back from the truth. He came with a roar as the last pulsation shook him.

As she imprinted her body and soul upon him, Blayne knew he must tell her what he felt. He drew Jemma into his arms, kissing her nose, her forehead, brushing her long glorious hair away from her face.

With a shuddering breath he confessed, "I love you."

She pulled back a little, her eyes wide and tearful, a smile glowing. She kissed him with gentleness and he loved her more for it. "I love you Major Forbes."

He kissed her softly. "Sweets, are you all right?"

Jemma decided to tease him. "Am I all right? Are you kidding? That was the most wonderful…the most exciting—I can't describe it."

She buried her face against his neck. As tears ran down her face, she thought she'd never recover from the sheer joy screaming inside her.

Blayne *loved* her.

Joy didn't get any better than this. Life didn't get any more wonderful.

After her breathing slowed, she snuggled deeper into his arms and said, "I've learned my lesson, Blayne."

"What's that?" His voice was muffled against her hair.

"I love you and damn the torpedoes."

He chuckled. "Torpedoes as in Graham and the rest of your

family?"

"Yes. No one controls my destiny but me."

Sighing, he kissed her forehead. "I can't tell you how good that is to hear. If you hadn't attacked me in the hall I had this entire speech rehearsed telling you I wanted to be with you. I was going to say I didn't care if Graham approved or not. Then I planned on kissing the hell out of you until you agreed with me."

"I attacked you?" she asked, unable to contain a smile.

He rolled her over on her back and looked down at her, wicked humor in his melting dark eyes. "Yeah." He winked. "Okay, it was a mutual attack."

Returning his unrepentant grin, she traced her index finger down his chest to one hard nipple. She explained how miserable she'd been, how she'd called his apartment and left a message. "Graham said you had something good to tell me?"

"I talked with him on the way to the Fort the morning after you and I spent the night together. I admitted that if anyone's heart was going to be broken, it was going to be mine. I realized I loved you then. All week I've been working things out. Part of me needed the courage to take the chance."

"That's what I've been doing all week. Kicking myself for thinking I couldn't be straight with you." She cupped his head in her hands and dared to look deep into his eyes. "Is there more good news?"

"Yes and no. It depends on how you look at it."

"Go on."

For the first time in her life, she heard hesitation and uncertainty in Blayne's voice. "I'm returning to my unit in the Middle East in three weeks."

The pain, filled with the realization she feared for his safety, hit her in the stomach. "You were worried you wouldn't be back with your men, right?"

"Right."

"Then it's a good thing." She swallowed hard. "And it's a bad thing."

He nodded and they went silent. Finally he asked, "Your love will keep me safe, Sweets. I promise."

Tears returned to her eyes. "I'll accept whatever you have to do. Your Army career is a part of you. I wouldn't have it any other way."

With a groan he said, "I love you. I love you so much."

She smiled around the tears. "Now that's what I like to hear."

"Our deployment might be for a long time. You know how it is."

She nodded. "Yes."

"I want us committed to each other."

He sounded so stern, so military-man that she grinned widely. "How do you propose we do that?"

"I took another chance. There's something in my jeans you've got to see."

She cocked one eyebrow. "I've seen what's in your jeans."

He tickled her side and she giggled. "That's not what I meant."

He stood up and found his jeans.

When Blayne pulled out a little red box, her heart about stopped. He couldn't—he hadn't—oh God. Maybe he *had*.

Heart pounding with anticipation and special delight, she sat up. He got on one knee, naked as the day he was born, and turning the little box toward her, he opened it.

Inside an emerald-cut diamond solitaire sparkled in white gold against the red velvet box lining.

"Oh my," she whispered, her voice choking up. "Oh my."

He took the ring out and slipped it on her ring finger. His eyes twinkled, a mixture of amusement and hope. "Please say that's a yes. Be my wife."

"Graham knew about this, didn't he?"

He nodded, bringing her hand up to his lips for a soft kiss. "Yeah. I decided I'd put him and your father at ease. I called them both and asked for your hand in marriage."

She gasped. "You did?"

"Yep. I could tell it impressed the hell out of them."

She laughed. "So you gave them some satisfaction in thinking maybe they did have something to do with whether or not we were together?"

He shrugged. "For you, I'd do anything. I want you in my life, in my arms forever."

With a tiny gasp of delight, she launched into his arms and they tumbled back onto the floor.

Between each kiss she told him what he wanted to know. "Yes, I'll marry you. Yes. Yes. Yes."

"Thank you, God."

When they came up for air, he said, "I've ached for you all week."

"I fantasized about you."

An intrigued look turned his gaze hot with intentions. "Oh?" He clasped her hand gently and brought it down her belly until their fingers joined in the nest of curls, brushing with tantalizing strokes over her clit. "And did you touch yourself?"

Excited, she closed her eyes. "Yes."

"Show me how you did it, Sweets."

"With pleasure, Major."

Epilogue

Fort Carson, Colorado
Eight months later

Jemma waited with Blayne's family for the buses to show up. Crowds of people gathered in the parking lot, families and friends of the soldiers coming back from the long deployment.

She chewed on one lip with impatience. She knew Blayne's mother, father, and cousin Polly must feel the same thing. His family had flown in to Colorado Springs yesterday just for the reunion.

While she'd been nervous about meeting his family for the first time, Jemma quickly discovered they were friendly people. Blayne's father, Abraham, with his craggy good looks, dazzling blue eyes and slight Texas drawl, looked like an older version of Blayne. Blayne's mother Angela was a slightly plump woman with hazel eyes, light brown hair and a glorious smile that held generous warmth. His adopted sister and first cousin Polly was also tall with light brown hair and as affable as she could be. Their acceptance of her warmed her soul. His sister Anne, a Army nurse, couldn't be here for the reunion since military duty kept her away, but Jemma knew Anne was here in heart.

And while she'd loved getting to know Blayne's family, Jemma could barely stand the hours, the minutes that had passed from the time he'd left eight months ago to this moment. She'd yearned for him with the power of a woman deeply in love.

Nerves prickled in her stomach. No matter how many times she'd envisioned this day, fantasized about being in her fiancé's arms again, Jemma knew once Blayne touched her, she would be in heaven. Now that he was safe and coming home to her, pure delight made her yearning grow stronger each minute.

Her gaze landed on the sparkling engagement ring on her hand, and she smiled. Soon she'd be Blayne's wife.

She felt a warm hand press her shoulder, then Angela's soft Southern voice. "He'll be here soon."

Jemma turned toward his family and smiled. "I can't wait."

Abraham chuckled. "I'm sure he can't wait to see you, too."

Finally two green buses pulled into the huge parking area. Joy did a dance in her heart. The crowd in the parking lot started to cheer and tears of happiness stung Jemma's eyes and ran down her cheeks.

Two other buses parked near the passenger vehicles and within seconds dumped olive drab green duffle bags one on top of the other with careless abandon.

When the passenger doors opened and men in desert camouflage uniforms filed onto the blacktop, her heart started to pound. Her gaze flew from one man to the other.

How would she tell which one was Blayne from this distance? She grinned. They all looked alike.

Then she saw that distinctive, brash walk and knew.

There he was.

After shuffling around to find his duffle bag, he moved toward her and his family.

Other soldiers met their squealing, excited families and friends and the happy atmosphere added to Jemma's elation.

As he came closer and closer her heart felt like it would burst with excitement. He waved and she waved back and smiled. He quickened his pace and when his gorgeous face came into perfect view, more tears welled in her eyes. She didn't try and stop them as they poured down her face.

"Hey, Major," she said as he strode toward her. "It's been a long time."

"Too damned long, Sweets." She saw his lips tremble, as if emotion had taken him by force, too. "Too damned long."

He dropped his duffle bag. She ran into his arms.

As they kissed frantically his hands caressed her back, plunged through her hair. When they parted for breath, he stared into her eyes and she into his.

"I missed you so much," he whispered.

"I've waited for this day forever."

His family, staying back so he could enjoy his reunion with Jemma, finally surged forward to greet him. A round of hugs and kisses ensued. Polly and Angela wiped tears from their eyes, and Jemma thought she saw the sheen of moisture in Abraham's gaze as well.

Abraham clapped a hand on his son's shoulder. "It's damned good to see you, son."

"Good to be back, Dad." He sighed. "And because it's Saturday, our commanding officer has given us two days off before we have to go in for a debriefing."

Jemma, Angela and Polly let out little whoops of happiness and hugged him all over again.

As Blayne turned back to Jemma, he smiled down at her. "Come on." Let's go home. We've got a wedding to plan."

About the author:

Suspenseful, erotic, edgy, thrilling, romantic, adventurous. All these words are used to describe award-winning, best-selling novelist Denise A. Agnew's novels. Romantic Times Magazine called her romantic suspense novels DANGEROUS INTENTIONS and TREACHEROUS WISHES "top-notch romantic suspense." With paranormal, time travel, romantic comedy, contemporary, historical, erotica, and romantic suspense novels under her belt, she proves her gift for writing about a diverse range of subjects. (Writing tales that scare the reader is her ultimate thrill.)

Denise's inspiration for her novels comes from innumerable sources, but the fact she has lived in Colorado, Hawaii, and the United Kingdom has given her a lifetime of ideas. Her experiences with archaeology have crept into her work, as well as numerous travels throughout England, Ireland, Scotland, and Wales. Denise currently lives in Arizona with her real life hero, her husband.

Website: http://www.tilt.com/authors/deniseagnew.htm

Email: danovelist@earthlink.net

Denise Agnew welcomes mail from readers. You can write to her c/o Ellora's Cave Publishing at 1337 Commerce Drive, #13, Stow, Ohio 44224.

Also by Denise A. Agnew:

The Dare

Deep is the Night: Dark Fire

Deep is the Night: Haunted Souls

Deep is the Night: Night Watch

Over the Line

Primordial

Winter Warriors anthology

Charming Annie

Arianna Hart

Acknowledgements

First, I would like to thank all the men and women that serve in the armed forces in whatever capacity. Know that those of us here at home appreciate you.

I would also like to thank my sister Patti of the First Army Augmentation Detachment based out of Fort Gillem, GA., who has been in the Army for almost twenty years. I relied upon her knowledge for everything from ranks to hand grenades. Any errors are completely my own.

Please note, I took some creative license with the floor plan of Walter Reed Army Medical Center to fit the story, any and all descriptions of the hospital come from my imagination, as do the characters.

Dedication

This book is dedicated with enormous thanks to my sister Patti for all her help.

Also, to my "partners in crime" who created such a wonderful family to draw inspiration from. Thanks Denise and Kate (and Bree and Martha) for making me part of the family.

Thanks also to all my online buddies who support and encourage me while I'm writing. You always know when I need a pat on the back or a kick in the pants and I'm grateful for both.

As always, thanks to my husband for putting up with me, and my family for always being there. I don't know what I'd do without you, and I hope I never find out.

Chapter One

Walter Reed Army Medical Center

Taking the stairs in the parking garage at midnight probably wasn't the smartest thing to do, but Major Anne Forbes had an aversion to elevators that went back to the days when her brother would lock her in the closet as a joke. Blayne had thought it was funny to hold the door closed while she screamed and kicked. She didn't find it all that amusing. To this day, being stuck inside a small, enclosed space bothered her to no end.

Annie had just about made it to the floor where her car was parked when the ground quivered and shook beneath her feet, knocking her down the last two steps.

"What the hell was that?" Annie rubbed the spot where her head thunked against the door and cautiously opened it.

To a scene out of a nightmare.

A car had exploded and smoke was blanketing the garage. Several men in black clothes with ski masks over their faces were poised at the elevators with assault rifles. Annie saw one civilian nurse bleeding from a head wound, and several other people crying and whimpering as they were hauled off the elevator. Fire alarms blared, and the noise echoed against the cement walls adding to the chaos.

Her brain had gone on hold, flashbacks to her tour as a field nurse in Iraq raced through her head. Visions of bearded men with fanatical eyes and gleaming knives assaulted her as the smell of smoke and gasoline washed over her. Annie was caught in a vicious film loop of pain and destruction that played over and over again.

She couldn't move. Her fingers froze on the door handle, immobile and helpless. A small voice in the back of her brain screamed at her to shut the door and run for help, but her body wouldn't move. Fire, smoke, the screams of the injured and the shouts of the attackers mixed together until she couldn't tell what was real and what were memories.

A hooded head started to turn, and Annie watched it in slow motion. Suddenly, a hand covered her mouth, and an arm pulled her away from the door. Panic clawed in her belly as she slammed into a hard, male chest.

No! She wouldn't go down without a struggle. Turning her head she tried to bite the hand that held her. Annie fought back using her training, but her captor was too strong.

"Lady, I'm on your side! Calm down, we gotta get out of here." Annie stopped struggling.

As soon as she calmed down, the hand dropped from her mouth and she turned around. And saw the best-looking man she'd ever laid eyes on.

"Come on, we need to go before they decide to start checking the stairwells." Her sexy savior gave her a quick once-over, pausing briefly at her breasts.

"Who're they? And who are you?"

"Later! We don't have time for twenty questions now." He grabbed her arm and dragged her up the stairs behind him.

Annie's brain started working again, and she raced to keep up with the man yanking her arm out of its socket. He was barefoot, wearing pajama pants and a johnny, and she could see the tape from his dressing over his ribs.

Some Army nurse she turned out to be, getting saved by a patient. "Could you at least tell me your name?" Annie asked between gulps of air. How many flights had they already gone up?

"Mace. Mason O'Keefe, Captain, Aviation."

"Major Annie Forbes, Medical." Like her hospital whites didn't clue him in on that. "Where are we going?"

"To the roof. If we can reach the roof before they secure it, we can get out of here and get help. Do you always talk this much?"

Annie shut up and saved her air for the effort of climbing. She'd lost count of how many stairs she'd gone up, but if this hotshot could keep going, barefoot and injured, then she could too.

They were rounding yet another landing when the door above them opened. A scrawny figure in black aimed a rifle in their direction and fired.

"Get down!" Annie yanked Mace's arm back off the steps and dragged him towards the nearest door. Bullets zinged around their heads like pinballs, the noise exaggerated by the cement walls.

Annie hauled open the door and dragged Mace out of the stairwell. She ran blindly through the tunnel that led to the hospital and burst through the first door she came to. Looking around she realized they were in the administration wing. Where could they hide here? She tried to think of a place safe from the lunatic on the stairs.

"Come on, we can hide in one of the offices." She pulled his arm and jiggled the handle on the first door. Locked. The next one down the line was locked too. Panic sliced through her as a drop of cold sweat slithered down her back. That guy had to be on his way down the stairs and they were out in the open.

Running down the hall, Annie's heart pounded furiously in her chest. They were sitting ducks if they couldn't find a place to hide soon.

Finally! An open office. A mop lay in a puddle in front of the partially open door. One of the maintenance workers must have been cleaning the office when he heard the explosion.

"What are we going to do in here? Wait for them to find us and kill us?" Mace held his side a bit, but was barely winded.

"I don't know, but it seemed like a better idea than charging a lunatic with a gun." Annie gasped for air. The adrenaline running through her system made her jumpy and had all her nerves standing on end.

"Whose office is this anyway? Talk about high-class."

Annie looked around for the first time and realized she'd busted into Colonel Michaels' office. "The Chief of Staff, Colonel Michaels. He's a good guy; I don't think he'll mind."

"Does he carry a gun?" Mace asked, crossing to the desk and opening drawers.

"He's a doctor. I don't think he's carried a gun in years."

"He's still a colonel. I'll bet he has something here." Mace continued to rifle around in the drawer.

Annie peeked out the door. "Shouldn't they be following us? I mean it's not like we went that far."

"If they're still securing the upper floors then they won't bother with us until they have more time. Once the hospital is locked down, they'll hunt us down like rabbits."

"Gee, that's comforting."

"Aha!" Mace held up a knife that was easily six inches long. "I knew I'd find something. Come on; let's look for a way out of here."

He hadn't taken two steps around the desk when the stairwell door slammed open.

"So much for your theory, now what?" Annie asked over the thunder of rifle fire.

Mace shot a glance at the window. It was sealed tight with Plexiglas. "Damn. I can't break this with only a knife. We're going to have to try the ventilation shafts and hope they hold our weight. If I give you a boost, do you think you could get in there and help me up?"

"Considering my life depends on it, yeah I can do it." Annie waited for him to pry the grate off the wall and shove it into the ventilation shaft. All the while her ears strained for any sound of the terrorists coming closer. Adrenaline made her knees weak and her heart pound with every passing second.

"It's off." He laced his fingers together and squatted down. "Step in here and I'll give you a boost."

"Just like climbing into a hayloft." Annie stepped into his cupped hands and used his shoulder for balance.

"On three. One, two, three!"

Annie practically flew up to the vent with the force of Mace's boost. Boost? It was more like a launch. Although fit, she wasn't tiny by any means, and he flung her up in the air like she was a toddler. Scrambling to find a purchase on the slick walls of the shaft, she felt a hand on her butt, pushing her inside.

Tucking her legs under her, Annie squirmed and wiggled around until she could poke her head and shoulders out of the shaft. "I'm ready when you are."

Mace put the knife between his teeth and reached up for her outstretched hands. His grip was steely and confident, and she braced her feet against the sides of the shaft so he wouldn't pull her out. Pulling with every ounce of muscle in her body, Annie fought to drag him up.

He must have found something to push himself off with, because one second she was yanking on his hands for all she was worth, and the next he was tumbling in on top of her, crushing her beneath his weight.

"I'm too big to turn around; you're going to have to put the grille back over the vent so they won't know what happened to us."

Annie bit her tongue to keep from reminding him that she had the higher rank. She might be a major, but battle operations weren't exactly her area of expertise. For the time being she'd follow his lead.

Sliding the grille cover out from under Mace's legs, Annie wedged it back into place the best she could. Mace was sliding down her, and she could feel every inch of his muscled body against her back and legs. A sudden jolt of desire rocked her system, driving away the screaming pain in her arms from hauling that same muscled body into the shaft.

This was not the time for her libido to remind her that it was alive and kicking! She pushed away the unwanted heat and tried to ignore the moisture between her legs as she turned herself around to follow Mace.

"Do you have any idea where these things lead?" He looked over his shoulder at her.

"Not a clue. I know we're in the west wing, and that's about it."

"Then we'll follow the shaft where it leads us. With any luck at all we'll be able to find a junction that will lead us up to the next level."

"You really think that's going to happen?" Granted, Annie didn't know too much about crawling along in ventilation shafts, but she didn't think they went up to the next floor.

"Hey, these old buildings are quirky; you never know what you might find."

Mace used his arms and feet to push himself along the shaft. Annie was small enough so she could crawl on her hands and knees, but after scraping her back on the top of the shaft one too many times, she gave up and slid along on her belly. This was going to get old fast.

*****

The stitches in his side were pulling with every inch he moved. Mace tried not to let Annie know about the pain he was in, but he was pretty sure his wound had started bleeding again. If this kept up he'd pass out from blood loss long before he could get out of the building.

There had to be some sort of junction somewhere. The vents couldn't keep going in circles, could they? He felt like he'd been crawling around these dusty shafts for miles. Another grille was just up ahead; maybe she'd recognize the location.

"Hey, Major, we're coming up on a ventilation grille, can you look out and see if you know where we are?"

"Sure."

Her voice sounded a little winded, but she was still moving. Mace slid to the side, careful to keep the knife in front of him and pointing away. He already had one knife slash on him, and he sure as hell didn't want another one.

Rolling over to make some room for Annie, Mace couldn't help but wince at the pain in his side. Hopefully it was too dark for her to see his face, because he didn't want her thinking about him, he wanted her alert and watching for the enemy.

She wormed her way up to him, rubbing against his torso as she tried to see out the grille. Her ass was pressed against his cock in the tight space, and he had to clench his teeth to keep from groaning at the sweet torture.

This was a life or death situation, he shouldn't be thinking with his cock! He had to focus on the mission, staying alive and getting out, not on the sexy number rubbing up against him.

"Do you know where we are?" His voice was a little strained.

"Yup. We're in the office next to Colonel Michaels'. We made a complete circle."

"Shit."

"Well, what's Plan B?"

Plan B? He'd been operating on the seat of his pants for Plan A. He hadn't thought any farther than getting out of the building. Annie squirmed around until she was facing him, and he sucked in his breath.

She really was gorgeous. Big blue eyes stared out at him from an angel's face. Her long blonde hair had long since fallen out of the military bun it had been in and was hanging around her face in wisps. She was covered in dust and still looked sexy as hell. Why couldn't she have been *his* nurse?

"So, what do we do now?" She looked at him like he held all the answers.

Before he could admit to not having a clue, the door to the office below them burst in with a shattering of glass. Two men ran in, spraying bullets across the room. Mace pulled Annie to his chest, muffling any noises she might make. Her body trembled against him, so he squeezed her closer.

"I tell you, I heard voices coming from in here." A tall goon said to the other shorter one.

"I think the tension is finally getting to you. There's no one in here."

"The two I saw in the stairwell didn't just disappear; they have to be on this floor somewhere."

"Well, they're not in here. After your little commando impression, they probably hit the stairs again. Come on, this floor is secure, let's set the charges and move on. We've got a lot of territory to cover before morning."

Mace looked out over Annie's head and watched the shorter one walk out the door. The tall one stood there, looking around, then a smile crept over his face. Pointing the gun up to the ceiling, he let loose with another round of bullets.

Wrapping his arms and legs around Annie's body, Mace tried to protect her from any stray bullets that were flying around. He could hear the plink, plink of them bouncing through the shaft around them.

"What the hell are you doing?"

Mace watched through the grille as the shorter one pushed the gun out of the taller one's hands.

"Are you trying to announce to everyone where we are?"

"I'm just giving them something to think about. If the two of them are crawling around up there, I might have got lucky and hit them."

"And you might have gotten hit by a ricochet bullet too. Dumbass. You are too damn trigger-happy with that thing. Come on, you go first this time, and keep your finger off the trigger."

With his arms still wrapped around the woman shaking in front of him, Mace counted slowly to one hundred. When he was as sure as he could be, he let go of Annie and whispered in her ear.

"I think they're gone, but whisper; sound carries in these things."

She nodded her understanding. "What are we going to do?"

"We're going to wait them out, then seek and destroy."

Chapter Two

"Wait them out? In this little tunnel?" Annie hoped the panic didn't show in her voice. Sliding around in the dark tunnels was starting to get to her. The danger of the situation had kept her mind off the fact that she was in a tiny space, but she wasn't sure how much longer she'd hold it together. Not only that, if she didn't stand up soon, she'd have a permanent kink in her back.

It had to be even worse for Mace, he was so broad and tall that he didn't have half of her wiggle room. The two of them jammed together took up most of the shaft. Her breasts were squished against his chest, and it was like being smashed against a brick wall. An incredibly good-looking, muscular, brick wall.

"We can't stay in here until morning, it's only a matter of time before they get bored and decide to start shooting all the ceilings. We need to find a place to hide. Not an office, maybe an alcove or janitor's closet or something."

Annie's stomach clenched at the thought of being trapped in a closet, but it would be better than this tiny space. She wasn't really claustrophobic; she just didn't like small spaces. And if she kept telling herself that, maybe she'd actually believe it.

"I think there's a closet at the end of the hall, on the other side of the door from the stairs," Annie whispered.

"Okay, I'll go first, you follow. Try to be as quiet as you can, and be careful when we pass the grille openings."

"Yes, sir."

Annie almost groaned as he slid his body past hers, teasing every place he touched. When his waist moved past her, she couldn't help but notice the impressive package he had between his legs. The nearly naked, impressive package.

Her body hummed in awareness, making every atom of her being stand at attention. She was so flustered from the full-body caress, she didn't see the pool of blood on the floor until her hand practically landed in it.

She grabbed his bare foot to stop him and slid up close enough to whisper to him. "Did you get hit? Or has your wound reopened? You're bleeding."

"Don't worry about it, it's only a scratch. Let's get to that closet first, then you can patch me back up."

Letting him slide away from her, Annie tried to see if he was lying to her about the extent of his injuries. He was moving along better than she was, so if that was any indication, he was doing just fine.

Stray bullets clinked against the sides as they passed them. They had been damn lucky so far. Hopefully their luck would hold until they made it to the closet.

What if the closet didn't have a way into the shaft? It wasn't like the janitor's closet would need to be air-conditioned. Doubts chased themselves around and around in her head until she was almost dizzy from worry. Annie bit her lip to keep from voicing any of her fears. She was combat-trained; hell, she'd done her time in the sandbox, she shouldn't be so afraid. But she was. Working as a field nurse hadn't prepared her for this.

It didn't matter. She had to hold it together. As far as she knew, she and Mace were the only two people free in the whole hospital. If she fell apart Mace would have to watch over her and wouldn't be able to go for help. It was imperative that he not know what an emotional basket case she was.

Hell, her father had survived being a POW in Vietnam; she'd damn well survive this.

"Are you sure there's a janitor's closet near the stairs? The end of the shaft is coming up and I don't see any light."

"Maybe it doesn't have a ventilation grille. I mean, it's only a closet."

"If it's a cleaning closet, it should have some way to ventilate it or the fumes from the cleaning products will build up."

"Makes sense. Maybe there's no light on in it and that's why we aren't spotting it."

"Good thinking! Run your hands along the sides and see if you feel it. I might have already missed it."

Annie ran her fingers along the walls, trying to feel for any changes. It was so dark in here she could have already missed it and not have even known.

"We're almost to the end of the line; if you don't feel it, then we'll have to backtrack until we do."

If there really was a grille. They were assuming it was a cleaning closet and needed ventilation. Annie fought down the doubts. Just when she was sure it wasn't there her finger got caught in something. The grille! "I got it! My finger is caught in the bars." Relief swam through her for a blessed second. They were going to get out of the tunnels.

"Stay there, I'll come back to you."

Annie rolled and squished herself up against the wall, trying to give the much larger Mace more room. As he slid down next to her, she felt every inch of his skin against hers. She had never really thought of her back as being an erogenous zone before, but the feel of his body against her back was doing a number on her libido. Sparks of desire shot through her, straight to her crotch.

Large arms encircled her, and his hands ran down her arms until they reached her hands. A shiver of awareness went through her at the contact. Was adrenaline an aphrodisiac?

"I'll get your hand loose, then try to work out the vent. We want to be as quiet as possible; they could still be out there." His whispered words brushed against her ear, and a flood of fluid went straight to her pussy.

"Roger." Her nipples tingled as they pushed against the fabric of her sports bra, and her breath was coming in gasps. She was running for her life and she'd never been so turned on. Annie felt surrounded by Mace's heat and it was doing strange, wonderful things to her insides.

Warm hands twisted her fingers until they came free.

"I've got the knife out, so be careful where you move. I'm going to work on the bottom corners and see if I can free it up enough for us to slide out without taking it off completely."

"I'll push as you pry." *Focus on the mission, not your hormones!*

"On three," Mace counted off and Annie braced her hands against the grate, ready to push on his signal.

"Almost got it," Mace grunted in her ear, sending hot bursts straight to her groin.

A screeching rasp sounded as the grille came loose. Annie's heart was in her throat waiting for discovery. She could feel Mace's heart beating fast against her back, and knew hers was keeping time.

When no one came to investigate the noise, Mace pushed the grille open a little more.

"Do you think you can fit down here?" Mace asked her.

"Sure. I wish I knew what I was landing on, though."

"Yeah, if wishes were horses."

"Beggars would ride. Okay, you are going to have to move a bit or I won't be able to turn around." Annie tried to peer into the darkness of the closet but couldn't see anything.

Mace slipped down, his face brushing up against her rear end and the backs of her thighs. Annie had to clench her teeth to keep from gasping at the contact. She was about to be lowered into God only knew what, and her body thought that this was a good time to get a serious case of lust. Her timing left a bit to be desired.

Tucking her feet up to her chest, Annie stuck her legs through the opening. She squirmed around until her legs dangled into the emptiness below her. Taking a deep breath, she slid further down, kicking out to feel anything with her feet. It was so dark she could be four feet in the air or about to touch the ground and she wouldn't know.

"I've got your hands. I'll lower you a little bit at a time. Let me know if you feel anything."

"Okay." Annie's stomach scraped over the side, her shirt bunching up under her breasts. Thank God it was pitch-black in there! Her feet were still swinging in the emptiness when her shirt halted her progress.

"Stop!"

"Did you find something?" Mace gripped her hands tightly.

"No, but my shirt is caught on the vent and it's wrapping around my neck. If I don't loosen it, I'll choke before I land."

"Can you rip it?"

"With what? You have both my arms. If you unbutton it I can slip out of it and put it back on when you come down."

"Okay, hold onto the edge, I'll try to do this as quickly as possible so you don't fall." Mace let go of one hand, and she had to quickly grab onto the edge of the vent.

"I can't see a freaking thing!" Mace's fingers fumbled around her face, then drifted lower to brush against her breast.

He quickly shifted until he found the buttons that fastened the shirt. The knuckles of his fingers brushed her breasts again, making her nipples tighten painfully. Annie was surprised her blush didn't light up the room.

"Why do they make these things so damn small?" Mace growled, still fumbling with the button.

Annie heard a grunt, then the ping of a button popping off her shirt. Suddenly she was free and started to slide.

"Let go! I don't want to drag you down!" Her grip on the side was slipping. She felt Mace let go, and slid right out of her shirt.

She vaguely heard a tearing sound as she jumped back and fell onto the floor. Her hand landed on something wet that smelled like bleach, and a bottle hit her on the head.

"Are you okay?" Mace whispered from above her.

"Yes. I wasn't that far off the ground. Not the most graceful landing though."

"Any landing you walk away from is a good landing." The smile in Mace's voice was clear.

"Let me find the door and I'll take a peek out."

"No! Wait for me to come down," he hissed.

Annie felt her way around the closet like a blind person, totally disoriented until she felt molding around the door. Running her hands up and down, she found the handle and opened it the merest fraction of an inch.

The hallway was deserted, and the stairway had some sort of device on it with wires and a timer. That couldn't be good.

"It's okay. We're alone down here, and I think we will be."

"Why do you say that?"

"Because there's a bomb on the door next to us."

*****

Get your mind out of your pants, get your mind out of your pants. Annie had just told him there was a bomb next to them, and all he could think about was her walking around down there while he had her shirt in his hands up here.

"Are you sure it's a bomb?" Maybe she was mistaken.

"Not positive, but it has a timer, a fuse, and what looks like C4 all wrapped together and stuck to the fire exit."

"Hold on, I'm coming down. Can you stuff something under the door so we can turn on a light?"

"I could if I could see my hand in front of my face. I think we'll be okay to turn on the light for a few minutes, the hallway is empty, and no one is coming out that door."

It was a risk, but falling and breaking his leg was a bigger one. He didn't have anyone holding on to his hands to keep him from falling all the way.

"Okay, when I get down I'll stuff this johnny under the door."

The light flickered on, and the weak bulb momentarily blinded Mace. Blinking back his tears, he took a look below him to see if there was a shelf or something he could use to step down.

"Hold on, here's a stool, I'll steady it under your feet so you don't have to jump. You've done enough damage to your wound as it is."

Mace tried to concentrate on locating the stool, but all he could focus on was Annie standing there in her bra.

"Go ahead, I'll hold it for you."

"I'm coming." God how he wished that was the truth. He'd be lucky if his dick didn't get him stuck on the edge of the shaft like her shirt did. The feel of her hands on his legs wasn't making him shrink either.

"I've got you. A little farther and you should feel the stool."

"Got it, thanks." Mace balanced precariously on the stool until he was steady. His side was pulling at him again and he could feel the blood dripping down his stomach.

"Let me take a look at your ribs," Annie said when he was finally touching ground again. She didn't seem bothered to be standing there in nothing but a sports bra and white pants. Technically she was covered, but all that bare skin was more than his libido could handle.

"Ah, here's your shirt." The part of his brain that was located between his legs cursed at him for handing the shirt over. The rational part that was worried about getting blown to smithereens wished she'd put it on quickly.

"Okay, I'm decent. Now take off the johnny and let me have a look at you."

The hospital-issue pajamas were filthy, covered in dust and blood. Annie's hands were gentle as they removed the dressing and probed his side.

"You've popped two of the stitches, but that's it. How'd you get hurt?"

"I was breaking up a fight between an officer and two civilians and one of them got a lucky swipe at me with a knife."

"I thought you were in aviation? What's a pilot doing an MP's job?" She dabbed at the blood with a corner of his johnny.

"I am a pilot. I was on leave, just got back from dropping some Rangers." He didn't want to think too much about that mission. He'd been lucky to get them in and come out alive. "I was celebrating with a few other pilots who'd come stateside with me when some drunken assholes started in on us. Next thing I know my buddy is getting pummeled and a knife is flashing."

"Made it out of the sandbox without a scratch and get cut in a bar brawl. How ironic," she smiled wryly.

"Hey, you got to watch your buddy's back."

"Well, right now I'm your buddy, and I say if you aren't careful you'll rip this entire thing open. Hold this to your side and I'll stuff your johnny under the door so no light shows through."

Mace looked around the little closet and tried not to zero in on the way Annie's pants tightened over her ass as she bent down. Looking anywhere but at temptation in whites, he surveyed his surroundings.

"This is the best-appointed janitor's closet I've ever seen," he said after a minute. Amidst all the cleaning supplies, paper towels, buckets and brooms were *Playboy* centerfolds, tool calendars with busty women proudly showing the date and much more, and a whole box of chocolate bars.

"At least we won't starve," Annie said, standing up and helping herself to a candy bar. "Yum, you want one?"

Did she have to look like she was having an orgasm while she was eating? Did all women get off on chocolate? "Sure, have to keep up my energy."

Their hands brushed as she gave him a chocolate bar. Mace felt a jolt of electricity shoot through him. She immediately let go of the candy bar and backed away.

"I wonder if he has a mini-bar hidden in here too." Her voice was shaky and a blush filled her cheeks.

"I wouldn't be surprised to find a bar and a TV in here. Looks like your janitor had a lot of free time on his hands."

"That works out well for us. How long do you think we should wait?" Annie had backed as far as she could go in the tiny space. She was jumpy, and Mace didn't know if it was because of him or the situation.

"I want to have a look at that bomb, then I'll make a decision."

If the bomb was set on a timer, he could probably defuse it. He'd had some training, but not much. If it was any more complicated than a simple fuse and timer job they'd have to come up with a Plan C.

"Hey, look, a police scanner. Maybe we can find one of those news channels." Annie brought the portable scanner over to him and turned it on with the volume down low.

The smell of her perfume filled his nostrils. It was light and flowery and had a hint of baby powder to it. Mace was used to women who wore heavier perfumes that were blatantly provocative. Annie's scent sort of snuck up on him and seeped into his senses.

"— sources from the Pentagon insist this isn't a terrorist attack, and no group has taken responsibility for the hostage situation. Walter Reed remains silent, with no ransom demands of any kind being given. Back to you, Bob."

"If this isn't the act of terrorists, what is it?" Annie clicked off the scanner and moved away. "We better save the batteries in case we really need them later."

"Hell, who knows? I want to go check out that bomb. You wait here." He didn't want her in the line of fire if the thing decided to go boom.

"That's okay! I'll come with you to watch your back. You can't focus on the bomb if you have to keep looking over your shoulder." Her eyes darted around the room, and her body was tense.

"I'd rather not have you in harm's way."

"If that thing goes off, do you really think I'll be any safer in this coffin—I mean closet?"

Her face was pinched and she fidgeted nervously with a loose button on her shirt. What was wrong with her?

"What's going on, Annie?"

"Nothing!" she yipped. "There's nothing going on."

"Then why all of a sudden do you look like a spooked horse? I can't worry about you freaking out right now."

She stepped back and took a deep breath, then another. Finally she looked up at him and opened her mouth. "I don't like small places. And being stuck in here alone while you are on the other side of the door bothers me."

"Excuse me? We spent an hour crawling around a two-foot square tunnel and you were fine." She was claustrophobic?

"That's different, it's not a closet."

"You're not making any sense; it's smaller than a closet."

Heaving a sigh she turned away from him. "Do you have any older brothers?"

"What does that have to do with anything?" Was she nuts? What did his family have to do with this?

"Just answer me?"

"Yeah, I have two older brothers and one younger sister. Why?"

"My brother Blayne is a good man. Special Forces, just got married and everything, but as a kid he was a terror. He used to lock me in a closet and hold the door closed while I kicked and screamed to get out."

"All older brothers torture their younger siblings. It's like a law or something."

"Yeah, but getting locked in small places bothers me. As long as I can keep moving, I'm okay, but the thought of getting trapped in an elevator makes me hyperventilate."

"So that's why you were in the stairwell."

"Yup, right place, right time."

She was calmer now. He just had to keep her talking. Mace fiddled with his dog tags and considered the situation. If he insisted she stay in the closet she could freak out and attract attention. If she went with him, she'd be in danger of getting blown up. Hell, so would he, and she was right, she'd be no safer in the closet if it was a bomb anyway.

"All right, you can come."

"Thank you!" She launched herself into his arms, and suddenly the bomb was the last thing he was thinking about exploding.

Chapter Three

Annie's body sizzled where it touched Mace. She'd been so relieved he wasn't going to leave her in the closet by herself that she just jumped into his arms without thinking. Now it was too late for any intelligent thoughts to find their way into her brain. His body was rock-hard and her breasts tingled from the contact.

His mouth lowered to hers, and her breath caught in anticipation. He grazed her lips with his, once, twice, then finally captured her mouth in a mind-numbing kiss. Annie's eyes closed and she couldn't help but let out a little moan as desire spiraled through her body. Her pussy was growing and swelling with each second, and when his tongue probed her lips for entrance, she gladly let him in.

Dueling tongues tangled together and Annie wrapped her arms around Mace even tighter. She wanted to climb on top of him, to touch him everywhere, to feel everything he could show her. Mace growled against her mouth and pulled her leg up around his waist, pressing her pussy against his raging cock.

The friction sent her already heightened senses soaring, making her nipples harden into over-sensitized points. Mace moved his lips from her mouth to the column of her throat, nibbling his way to her ear. Annie let her head drop back so he could have better access. Shivers chased their way down her spine, exploding in her soaking wet pussy.

Mace pulled her hips against his, rubbing against her already throbbing center. As he leaned back against the shelves behind him something crashed. Liquid splashed against her leg and broke the spell that had her enthralled.

"Holy shit! What happened?" Mace had jumped back and was in a defensive crouch.

"Spontaneous combustion?"

Annie looked down at the bottle of cleaning solution that was splattered against her leg and spreading all over the floor. She quickly bent down to clean it up, hoping the action would cover her blush. Her body was still humming from the contact with his and she couldn't find it in herself to regret her actions. Maybe in a rational world when she wasn't fighting for her life and the lives of every other person in the hospital she wouldn't try to jump some guy she'd only just met. This obviously wasn't normal behavior for her, although she'd never been around a man as good-looking as Mace before either.

"It's just a bottle of glass cleaner," Annie said, breaking the tension.

"Okay. Let's check out this bomb, stay behind me."

"You got it." She had no desire to be any closer to explosive devices than she had to.

Following Mace out of the closet, Annie did her best not to stare at his tightly muscled ass. What was wrong with her? This was life or death and she was fixating on some guy's butt. There was something seriously wrong with this picture.

Mace let out a low whistle as he examined the contraption on the door.

"Looks like you were right, this is set to go off in six hours." Mace looked closely at the bomb, but didn't touch it.

"Can you defuse it?"

"Maybe."

"Maybe? This isn't fixing a bicycle chain here, either you can or you can't. There's not a whole heck of a lot of room for error."

He shot her a look over his shoulder. "If you'd be quiet and give me a little room to move I could get a better look at it and figure out whether or not I can defuse it safely."

Annie stepped back and shut up. She tended to shoot off her mouth when she was nervous, and this whole situation had her jumpier than a mouse on espresso beans. Mace looked at the wires from different angles without touching them. Every once in a while he'd mutter something to himself or let out a curse. Annie was dying to ask him if he had any idea what he was doing, but bit her tongue. The last thing she needed was for him to try to play hero and blow them up.

Stepping away silently, Annie went to investigate the rest of the hall. She kept Mace in sight at all times. It only made sense for her to keep an eye out for the terrorists that were roaming the building. And if having a little space gave her hormones a chance to calm themselves, well that was just a side benefit, right?

Her shoes made no sound as she walked down the corridor looking in all the offices for any sign of the attackers. What could they want anyway? They spoke English, so it wasn't a foreign group trying to make headlines. This was a hospital for heaven's sake!

"Annie!"

She turned around at the sound of Mace's voice. She'd gone farther than she realized and was down the other end of the hall. Jogging back she waved to him.

"I'm here, I was just doing a recon."

"Could you let me know if you are going to take off? One minute you're yammering my ear off, the next I can't even see you. Did you find anything?"

Annie bit her tongue before she said something she'd regret. They were in this together, and bickering wouldn't help. "No, I didn't see any sign of them. I didn't even see where they had trashed any of the offices other than the one next to Michaels'. They must be concentrating on the wards."

"That or they figured this little number would take care of anything they didn't get to. There's enough C4 here to take out the whole floor."

"Who do you think is behind this? They're Americans. Why would anyone want to do this to their own countrymen?"

"Who knows? Maybe they're extremist wackos, maybe they're contracted mercenaries. All I know is, they know their way around a bomb."

"You can't defuse it?" Annie felt her heart drop to her stomach.

"Nope, not for sure."

"And if we open the door?"

"Do you want to take that chance? It could have a motion sensor and go off if we open the door."

"And if we wait?"

"It will go off in six hours."

*****

Mace watched the expressions chase across Annie's face. He really wished he could be a hero and defuse the bomb, but he wasn't certain enough about all the wires to risk it.

"So what do we do now?" Annie asked.

"We can look for another way off this floor, but I have a feeling all the stairways are similarly wired."

"I was afraid you'd say that." Annie slumped against the wall.

Damn, he hated the look of defeat on her face. It pissed him off that he couldn't deal with the situation. If it was only his life at stake he might chance it, but he couldn't put Annie in danger too.

"Why don't we go back to the closet and see if we can pick up any more information on the scanner?" Doing something concrete should help keep her distracted.

"Yeah, I guess we don't have to worry about running down the batteries now."

So much for distracting her. Mace knew how he'd *like* to distract her. He was still achingly aware of her nearness. He hadn't meant to kiss her before, but her body felt so good in his arms, and her lips were so close, he couldn't help but take a little taste. And one taste led to another until he wanted to eat her whole. If he hadn't knocked the bottle of cleaning stuff over he'd have probably taken her against the wall right then and there.

His cock reared up to full attention at the thought. Great, just what he needed in these thin pajama bottoms, a raging hard-on.

Annie had turned and headed for the closet, so he followed her. There wasn't much else they could do. He had to think of a plan, find some way to get them out of this situation. Dying was not an option. There had to be some way out.

Closing the closet door behind him, Mace moved as far away from Annie as he could in the tiny space. He looked anywhere but at her. Who'd have thought pictures of naked, airbrushed women would pale in comparison to a woman in military white scrubs?

Fiddling with the scanner, Mace tried to find the frequency the terrorists were using for their radios. It was a crapshoot as to whether or not he'd be able to pick up their conversations on this tiny scanner, but he didn't have anything better to do right now.

Annie bent over to look at something on one of the lower shelves, and Mace's body sprang into full awareness. Her sports bra pressed up her breasts, and he had a delicious view of her deep cleavage. Choking back a groan, he focused on the scanner again. It was too dangerous to be roaming around in the halls or he'd leave the little room and take a breather.

"So what were you doing in the stairwell anyway?" Annie asked him, her blue eyes looking right into his.

"I had been waiting in the emergency room for one of my buddies to come and get me. The doctors wouldn't release me without someone there to sign for me."

"That's standard procedure; they don't want you getting into an accident or something after you've been given anesthetic."

"I guess so. Anyway, I was waiting for one of the nurses to give me my clothes so I could wait in the lobby when a bunch of guys in ski masks crashed the ER and started firing at anything that moved."

"How'd you get away?"

Mace felt embarrassment curl in his belly. "I was in the john, they missed me so I slipped into the stairway while they were ushering everyone out of the room." He turned his head, unable to look her in the eye.

"Some hero I am. Gunmen are shooting at innocent people and I'm taking a leak."

"Hey, don't be so hard on yourself. It wasn't like you planned on being in the bathroom when they came in, it just happened that way." She laid her hand on his arm, and the gentle contact traveled straight to his gut.

"At least you were smart enough to get away when the opportunity presented itself instead of trying to take on a bunch of armed psychos."

"I still feel like there was something I could have done differently."

"Like get shot? I'm glad you escaped; you probably saved my life. I was in shock when I saw what was going on. I would have stood there like an idiot all night if you hadn't grabbed me when you did."

Mace thought about it for a minute. Maybe she was right, there wasn't a whole lot he could have done against a bunch of lunatics wielding automatic rifles then. And she had been standing there like she was frozen in time. That reminded him.

"What was that all about anyway? Shock?"

"Flashbacks." Her face suddenly closed off and she looked away. "I was in a field unit in Iraq. The last week of my assignment, a group of extremists attacked the place."

"What happened?" The medical units were usually kept away from the action and well protected.

"Not a whole lot actually, it was over pretty fast. There weren't that many of them, and their weapons were ancient. They lobbed a few homemade grenades at us that did some damage to the mess tent and the triage area. A few of them got close enough to attack, but the guards got them before anyone was seriously hurt."

"It's still scary getting shot at." It was his turn to comfort her, and he laid his hand along her cheek.

"Tell me about it. I thought I was over the worst of it, but seeing the car on fire and the men with guns screaming at people brought it all back." She shivered and wrapped her arms around herself.

Mace hated the lost look on her angelic face. He pulled her into the circle of his arms and held her against him. It was meant to be comforting, but he had to angle his lower body away from her to keep from rubbing his erection against her.

Annie shook her head and looked up at him. "You know the worst part? The reason they attacked us wasn't because we were treating American soldiers, it was because we were treating the locals too. Whatever faction had the guns that day didn't want us keeping their enemies alive. I just don't get it. We'd have treated them too if they asked, but instead of taking advantage of the medical care, they'd rather kill everyone."

She buried her head in his chest, and he felt her shoulders shake with silent tears.

"We can't understand everything about them. Their culture is so different than ours. All we can do is offer the help; we can't force them to take it."

Sniffing a little, Annie looked back up at him and gave him a watery smile. "It's the old you can lead a horse to water, but you can't make him drink dilemma?"

Mace laughed. "Yeah, I guess so. People have to make their own decisions, you can only offer to help them, it's up to them to decide if they want it or not."

She sighed and stepped away from him, he suddenly felt empty and cold without her next to him.

"You're right. It just seems like such a waste some times. I was doing better with it after I came home. Working twelve-hour shifts has a way of keeping your mind off things."

"I'm sure." Mace watched her pull herself together, and admired the way she handled herself under pressure. Except for that one lapse, she'd taken the events of the last few hours in stride.

"Have you been able to get anything on the scanner?"

He looked down at the forgotten scanner in his hand. "No, either they aren't talking or I can't pick it up. I'll try again in a little bit."

Annie looked at her watch. "It's close to three in the morning. I should be tired, but I'm wide awake."

"It's the adrenaline; it'll keep you hyped up for a while yet. I'd tell you to try and take a nap, but it's useless. When the adrenaline wears off, you'll crash whether you've had enough sleep or not."

"I don't know where I'd take a nap anyway. There's only this stool here to sit on, and not even that much ground room if I wanted to lay down for a nap."

He laughed. "You've been in the Army how long? And you can't fall asleep anywhere after all this time?"

"I've been in ten years, and no, I can't fall asleep standing up. Can you?"

Mace almost told her he could do a lot of things standing up when there was a muffled thud and the lights went out.

Chapter Four

Pitch-black! She was in total and utter darkness. For a split second, Annie was transported back to her childhood when Blayne locked her in the closet and whispered warnings about the hanger monsters strangling her. A whimper clawed its way to her throat but she fought it down. She was a grown woman for crying out loud! There was no reason to lose her mind over this.

"What happened?" Annie tried to keep the panic from her voice.

"The probably took out the power supply. Fairly standard procedure if you're trying to confine a big group of people. Cut off the electricity and the phones and they can't call for help or communicate with each other. It also increases the hostages' feelings of isolation and fear."

"Oh, makes sense." It was doing a hell of a lot to increase her fear.

"I'm going out for a recon. You stay here. Do you hear me? I don't want you setting foot out of this room in case it's a trap."

Stay here? Alone? "I'll come with you. You need backup!"

"No. If this is a trap I'll need you to bail me out."

"Why don't I go look around and you stay in the closet?" Annie tried to hide the panic in her voice.

"How much do you know about electrical systems or ground operations?"

"Not much."

"That's why I'm going. I'll be gone five minutes tops. If I'm longer, it means I ran into trouble."

Five minutes. She could handle five minutes. By herself. In the closet. Before she could muster another argument Mace was out the door.

Annie tried counting the seconds off in her head. She tried saying the alphabet backwards, doing her times tables, anything that would keep her mind off the blackness engulfing her.

Surrounding her.

Suffocating her.

The walls were closing in! She couldn't breathe! Annie's heart was beating so fast in her chest she thought it would jump right out. Cold sweat dripped down her back, and a whimper tore out of her mouth. She was going to die in this airless coffin!

Lights danced in front of her eyes. She was going to pass out!

"Annie! It's okay! It's just me. You have nothing to be afraid of." Mace's voice may have been gruff, but it was the most beautiful sound in the world to her.

"What did you find?" Annie was breathing as hard as if she'd run a marathon. Relief washed through her in waves making her knees weak.

"I could smell burning wires, but the emergency lights were on. I think they only got the main power supply, but left the generator backup alone."

"That's good, right?"

"Well, it means we're not completely without power. It also means they plan on sticking around here long enough to want some electricity."

"Where does that leave us then?" Annie inhaled deeply. Mace's scent filled her nostrils with each breath.

"We need to stay put a little while. Cutting the power might just be a way to draw us out. We have to stay low so they think we escaped, then we can go after them."

"Stay here? For how long?" Panic reared its ugly head at the thought of spending the night in the tiny room.

"Hey, don't freak out, I'm right here with you." Mace pulled her to him, gathering her against his solid frame.

Some parts of him were more solid than others. The steely hardness of his erection grew against her stomach, swamping the fear with waves of lust. His obvious signs of desire set off corresponding signals in her own body making her pussy lips swell and moisten.

Without thinking of anything other than the need to touch him, Annie pulled his head down and planted her lips on his. Anything to keep the darkness at bay.

He needed no further encouragement, and crushed her to his chest, attacking her lips with the voraciousness of a starving man at a feast. His hands were everywhere, kneading her behind and pulling her closer to his rock-hard cock.

Needing to touch his skin, Annie ran her hands up his bare rib cage. Ever since she'd taken off his johnny to check his wound she'd been drooling over his gorgeous body. With the lights off she couldn't see it, but her fingers were telling her what she was missing.

The hard ridges of his abs felt like mountains under her hands, and she was ready to do a little mountain climbing. His skin was slick with sweat and her fingers slid easily over him. She wanted to see him, all of him, but it was too dark. She'd have to rely on her fingers to show her what she was missing. Cream drenched her panties and she hadn't even gotten his pants off.

"God! I wish I could see your body," she murmured against his neck as she nipped down his throat to kiss his chest. She barely had to bend at all to lick at his tight nipples.

"Not half as much as I want to see yours." Mace pulled the shirt off her arms and yanked the bra over her head.

Her breasts sprang free and she felt the heat of his hands on them, his thumb teased her aching nipples. She dug her fingers into his back, holding on to sanity by the thinnest of threads.

"We shouldn't be doing this, I barely know you." Sanity tried to assert itself.

"It's the situation; extreme stress produces extreme emotions and need." Mace pulled her head back and licked his way down to her breast, drawing her nipple into his mouth.

"Works for me." She'd worry about later when she knew there was going to be a later.

Trailing her fingers down his chest she skirted his wound and went straight for the laces on his pajama pants. She couldn't believe how hard his muscles felt. There wasn't an ounce of spare flesh on his body.

Wrapping her hand around his shaft, Annie felt the velvety smooth texture of his skin covering the steely hardness of his cock. He was definitely rock-solid all over. Her fingers played over his length, making him groan into her ear as he nibbled on her neck.

Annie was so busy exploring every inch of his length, she didn't even realize Mace had unbuttoned her pants until she felt his fingers probing her pussy lips. Even his fingers were thick! Her muscles clenched around him and spasmed at his touch. He was stretching her, filling her, and this was only his finger!

"You're so hot for me, so wet. I want to be in you."

"I'm in-line with that plan," Annie gasped as his knuckle rubbed up against her clitoris, sending shockwaves through her system.

"I don't have any protection. Hell, I don't even have any pockets." Mace's voice was close to a whimper.

"I'm on the pill, and I'm clean as a whistle." Annie struggled to get her pants down her legs and kick off her shoes without letting go of Mace. Dear God, if he stopped now she would die!

"Me too."

Maybe the military's regular blood tests were a good thing after all.

Mace lifted her onto the stool and she balanced on the edge, waiting to feel him inside her.

"Hurry, hurry!" Annie had never wanted anyone so badly before in her life. The wait to feel him inside her was excruciating. Her core was throbbing, and she could feel her juices sliding down her spread thighs. Her legs quivered in anticipation, aching to have him fill her.

"Yes, ma'am!" Mace drove into her, pushing past walls that hadn't felt a man for months.

Annie felt stretched to the limit. She couldn't see Mace, but she could feel every inch of him inside her, filling her to the hilt.

"Good God you're big!" Annie tried to relax her muscles to make room for him.

"Good God you're tight. And hot. And feel so good." Mace peppered his words with kisses to her face and neck.

A volcano of feeling was bubbling under the surface of Annie's body, wanting to erupt. The sensations were flooding her mind, washing away any thoughts but how wonderful Mace's body felt inside hers. When he nipped her shoulder then licked the spot, Annie felt the volcano bubble higher.

"Come for me," he growled in her ear.

"I-I don't know what to do." Her embarrassment was no match against the feelings Mace was creating inside her.

"Just let go, I'll take care of the rest."

Let go? Who was holding on? Annie's body had long since taken control and she was following along for the ride. She was tempted to ask him what he meant when she felt his finger stroke her clit.

Instantly the volcano erupted, shooting wave after wave of pleasure through her body. Hips bucking, Annie held on to Mace's shoulders with all her might. Every infinitesimal quiver of her pussy touched his length and pulled him closer inside her, and even then it wasn't enough. She wanted this feeling to go on and on.

"That's how you do it." Mace pulled a nipple into his mouth, and the pressure set off a new bevy of quivers inside her.

"I guess so." Grabbing his arms for better leverage, Annie thrust her hips up and squeezed her inner muscles at the same time.

The initial explosion was gone, but the aftershocks were still powerful enough to keep her off balance.

"If you keep that up, this won't last very long."

"Oh, I think you've got long enough well covered."

Something he demonstrated by hammering her almost to her womb. Squeezing him even tighter, Annie held on while Mace grabbed her hips and slammed into her again and again. Her world was focused on feeling him between her legs. The hair on his legs rubbed against her inner thighs, sending her nerve endings into overdrive. He was hard, and hot, and felt so good inside her, she never wanted it to end.

His hands tightened on her behind, pulling her harder against him, and he let out a muffled shout before lowering her back against the stool. His cock pulsed inside of her, matching the beat of her racing heart. Before Annie could fully recover from the roller-coaster ride her libido had been on, Mace pulled out of her.

"Shh, I hear something." He covered her mouth with his hand and held her next to him. His body was tense in anticipation.

Mace lifted her off the stool and placed her gently on the floor, pushing on her shoulder in a silent signal to crouch down. Annie curled into a ball, and reached out for some clothing. One minute she was recovering from the first orgasm of her life, the next she was trying to find something to cover herself in case gun-toting lunatics barged through the door. Talk about a buzz kill.

A ray of light from the hallway emergency lights shined weakly through the door as Mace opened it a crack. The light gave Annie a glimpse of Mace as he searched for danger. The part of her mind not absorbed with trying to cover her nakedness marveled at the sheer masculine beauty of the man in front of her.

Broad shoulders she'd only just clung to like her life depended on it were covered in mounds of muscles. She could see his six-pack abs leading to narrow hips and ropey thighs. The shadows hid the package between his legs, and Annie shook herself out of the urge to crane her neck to get a better look.

Arrows of pure lust shot straight to her pussy, singeing her with need. She'd only just had the first real orgasm of her life and already the heat was spreading through her at the sight of him. At this rate she was more in danger of becoming a sex-starved maniac than getting shot by the lunatics patrolling the halls.

"It's nothing. Must have just heard something through the vents." Mace shut the door, cutting off her study of his attributes.

"So what do we do now?" Annie found her bra waded up near her pants, but her shirt was nowhere to be found. She'd have to wait until the power came back on to find it.

"We'll listen to the scanner again. Maybe the news has something to report."

Annie could hear the sounds of him pulling on his pants. If they lived through this, she was going to get a better look at all of him. A nice long look.

Fumbling around on the shelves, Annie found the scanner and turned it on. All she got was static.

"Damn, I must have moved the dial when I grabbed it. Hold on, I'll try to find the right channel." Her hands shook as she turned the knob slowly. Trying to find a frequency in pitch darkness wasn't the easiest thing to do.

"All charges are in place and patients evacuated."

"Stop there!" Mace ordered.

Annie's hand froze on the dial. They must have intercepted the terrorists' radio transmissions.

"Have you separated the civilian employees from the military?"

"Yes, sir."

"Good. Find one soldier to make an example for the press, then we'll deliver our demands."

"Yes, sir. And if they aren't met?"

"Then the hospital is blown sky-high in the morning."

*****

His gut clenched at the coldness in the voice on the radio. Mace had no idea what their demands were, but he knew the government wouldn't meet them. Giving into hostage demands only encouraged wackos to keep trying. They had a few hours until daylight to get out and save all the people in the building.

Hell, he couldn't even save himself and Annie, how was he going to save the hospital?

"Do you want me to try to find the news station or keep it here?"

"Leave it there, we don't want to take the chance of losing it."

"That's what I thought. What are we going to do?" Her voice quivered a bit.

Mace resisted the urge to pull her into his arms and comfort her. That's what he'd meant to do when the power went out; instead, he screwed her brains out in a janitor's closet. Prince Charming had nothing on him.

"I'm going to take another look at that bomb."

"What do you think you're going to find out this time?"

"It seems to me if they are dumb enough to talk on radios that can get picked up by a cheap police scanner, I might have given them more credit than they deserve when it comes to the bomb."

"What exactly does that mean?"

"It means I want another look at the bomb. I think some of those wires are decoys."

"And if you're wrong?" She didn't sound very confident in his reasoning.

"Then I won't touch it, but if I'm right, we might be able to get up those stairs."

"And do what?"

"Divide and conquer."

"Using what?" she snorted. "We have one knife between the two of us."

"First we need to see if we can even get off this floor, then we'll worry about how to take out the unfriendlies."

Mace opened the door to the closet to let some of the light from the hallway in. He didn't want to go searching for the knife blindly. Annie was standing right behind him wearing only the sports bra and her pants. He felt his cock stir yet again. Damn, how could he want her so badly when he had just spent himself inside her?

Her blonde hair was completely loose now and it hung down in a shimmering fall. What the hell was wrong with him? He was supposed to be concentrating on a freaking bomb, not the way the sports bra seemed to push her breasts upward. The adrenaline must be getting to him or something. He'd never had this much trouble focusing on a job before.

"Come on, let's look at that bomb again," he said more gruffly than he intended.

Grabbing the knife off the shelf, he turned and walked out. Annie followed him silently. At least she wasn't tossing out sarcastic comments.

His brain had been churning ever since he heard the scanner pick up the terrorists' transmissions. These guys weren't that sophisticated if they didn't know their conversations could be overheard with regular police scanners. Either they didn't care that anyone could listen in, or they didn't have the ability to scramble the signal.

The more Mace thought about it, the more he realized he might have been suckered. C4 was incredibly stable. Hell, the guys in 'Nam used it in their fires for fuel. There was a good chance he could defuse that bomb; if he could focus his mind on it and not the way Annie's body had milked his.

Don't go there, buddy! Now was not the time to be thinking about sex. If he thought with his dick instead of his brain he could blow them to kingdom come! Another whiff of Annie's perfume invaded his senses. Maybe this was why the Rangers didn't allow women to join? One whiff of perfume and even the best-trained soldier lost his head.

Mace turned to look at Annie. "Stay behind me, and don't go running off without telling me. We don't know that these guys can't get back down here somehow and I don't want you to get grabbed."

"Yes, sir!" She gave him a mock salute, reminding him that essentially she did outrank him.

"I'm not trying to be bossy, I just don't want to have to worry about you, and I will if I think you are putting yourself in danger." Why was he explaining himself?

"I'll stand right by the door and keep my mouth shut. I don't want to do anything to compromise the situation."

Mace turned around and closed his eyes. He needed to get focused and devote all his brainpower to the bomb. Using the same ritual he employed when getting ready for a mission, Mace pulled himself into his zone.

Taking a deep breath in, he held it for a count of three, then let it go slowly. He did that three times before approaching the door. Looking at the bomb again, he noticed that the wires didn't have any recognizable pattern.

Initially, he had taken that to mean that the terrorists had created a sophisticated pattern that he didn't understand. But maybe they were just decoy wires put there to confuse him. If he could find the one that connected the timer to the fuse and disconnect it without detonating the C4, they'd be home free.

If it picked the wrong one, they were dead.

Put that out of your mind. Don't think negative thoughts. The guys he knew on the bomb squad had always told him it took more ego to do bombs than to fly helicopters. If you thought for one minute you'd blow yourself up, your confidence was shot and you wouldn't trust yourself.

Hell, he operated million dollar birds, bringing Ranger teams in and out of places most sane people wouldn't even fly over. He could pull one little wire, no sweat. *Right.*

Looking closer, Mace traced the path from the timer to the fuse. There were several wires wrapped together confusing the trail. Gently feeling each wire, he waited until he found one that was hot. Two of the wires vibrated, and the other three were cold and quiet.

Carefully scraping away the cold wires, Mace examined the timer again. If he could identify the one that led to the timer he'd be golden. He wiped sweaty palms off on his pants and looked again. Three wires to choose from. Only one of them was the right one.

"Can you get me a pair of wire cutters from the closet?" he asked over his shoulder.

"Here you go. I thought you might need a pair." Annie's hands shook as she handed the cutters to him, but her face didn't look the least bit uncertain.

He took the cutters and turned back to the wires in front of him. A drop of sweat slid down his nose. One wrong move— He couldn't think like that! Confident; he had to be confident he was making the right choice.

The three wires that were left were black, green and red. Normally it was "cut the red and you're dead", but these guys made up their own rules. This configuration of wires made no sense whatsoever. Either they were dumb as stumps or so supremely clever they were bluffing him completely.

Mace touched the wires again. All three led from the timer to the C4. The black one was hot, and the green and red ones vibrated. Holding onto the red one Mace waited for a sign. His gut was telling him it was this one, but the limited training he'd had said otherwise. The timer kept ticking away, counting down the seconds until the decision would be out of his hands.

Ticking. That's it! The vibration of the red wire matched the ticking of the timer. Mace carefully took his fingers off the wire. Could the green one be a double timer? He rubbed his fingers against his pant leg and touched the green wire.

This one had a steady vibration, probably hooked to the battery just to throw him off. The red one was it. Taking a steadying breath, Mace lined the cutters up and took a deep breath. Praying to the powers that be, he closed his eyes and cut.

The silence was deafening.

"I did it," Mace croaked out.

"I never had any doubt," Annie said from behind him.

Her face was pale and her lip showed teeth marks, but her smile was beautiful.

"Let's kick some ass."

Chapter Five

Annie used a strip from her ruined shirt to tie her hair back, and another one to strap a screwdriver to her leg. She would have preferred a knife, but the janitor didn't have one lying around. Mace had another strip of the shirt wrapped around his ribs to soak up some of the blood from his oozing stitches. He didn't seem to be in much pain, but he didn't want to leave a blood trail either. So far he hadn't showed any signs of slowing down from his injury. Screwing her brains out hadn't fazed him.

"Let's go over the plan one more time." Mace turned to her, looking intently into her eyes. His emerald green gaze blazed into her.

"It's not complicated. I act as bait and you take the guy out."

"And you don't do anything even vaguely heroic. I don't want you getting in the way of a stray bullet or trying to take the guy out yourself."

"I'm not an idiot. I think I can handle it. You just worry about how we're going to get to the next floor. If all the doors have bombs on them we are shit out of luck."

"I don't think they're motion-activated. Let me worry about the bombs, okay? Are you ready?"

"As ready as I'll ever be." Annie reached forward and kissed him on the cheek. She wanted to plant one on his oh-so-sexy lips but didn't want to get too carried away. She'd never been good with morning-afters.

"What was that for? Not that I'm complaining." Mace brushed his fingers down her cheek.

"For luck. Lead the way."

There was no way she was going to tell him it was because she was afraid they wouldn't make it out of this. She'd keep her self-defeating thoughts inside. Mace had enough on his mind without worrying about her not holding up her end of the deal.

Her gut clenched as Mace opened the door, but nothing happened. Annie tried to let out the breath she'd been holding as quietly as possible. There was a reason she'd gone into nursing instead of the bomb squad. When it came to blood and guts, she was steady as a rock. Explosives were another story.

The irreverent thought that she'd never be able to tell Blayne about this because he'd laugh his ass off popped into her brain. Of course, that would be after he kicked Mace's ass for touching his baby sister. Good thing he was on his honeymoon.

Mace's bare feet made no noise as they climbed the metal steps in the fire exit. The next level up was the surgical unit. Luckily they didn't perform surgery at midnight or who knows how many people would have died.

Annie held back while Mace tested the door. When he deemed it safe, he carefully opened it.

"Follow me. I'm going to do a recon, prepare to duck and run if I give the word."

She nodded her answer and followed his broad back down the hallway. The rooms showed signs of hurried exits and there were medicine carts knocked over in the halls. Were they trying to get to the narcotics? Those were kept locked up in a computerized unit.

"Wait a second," Annie hissed at him. "I want to grab something."

Annie scurried to the narcotics unit and entered her password. Was this on the emergency energy system? She racked her brain trying to remember if the generator powered this or not.

Apparently it was, because the door swung open with a hiss. Annie grabbed a syringe and two vials of Demerol, then hurried back to where Mace was waiting.

"What are those for?" he whispered.

"Insurance."

Mace raised an eyebrow but didn't say anything else. As they approached the nurses' station he raised a hand in warning, then shooed her under a desk. Annie crouched as low as she could and held her breath. Just because she didn't hear anything didn't mean there was nothing there. Mace had already proved his hearing was much better than hers.

Seconds passed and Annie thought her heart would come out of her chest. The blood roared in her ears until she was sure it would alert whoever it was they were hiding from. Her nerves were stretched to the breaking point when a faint echo of boot heels caught her attention.

The footsteps got closer and closer. Annie fought to keep her breathing quiet and even. The screwdriver blade was digging into her leg, but she didn't dare move it. The steps were almost on top of them now.

Then, they stopped. Biting her lip to keep from making any sound, Annie strained her ears to listen for any clue of their discovery. The sound of plastic crinkling was loud in the otherwise silent corridor, and the click of a lighter echoed like a gunshot.

A lighter? Was this guy smoking? In a hospital? Was he really that dumb? This was a surgical floor, for God's sake! There was oxygen in every room. If C4 didn't blow them to hell, this idiot would. Sure enough, the smell of burning tobacco tickled her nose, making it twitch with an impending sneeze.

Not now! She refused to blow this because she was allergic to cigarette smoke! Fighting the urge to sneeze, Annie pressed her face to her thighs and prayed. A drip of cold sweat slid down her back.

Just when she thought she couldn't hold on any longer, the footsteps moved away.

Mace motioned for her to stay still. She was happy to comply. It was going to take a few moments for her legs to reform after being scared boneless. He waved his hand in her direction, telling her to come to him. Annie shook herself out of her fear-induced paralysis and crept over.

"See if you can get him to chase you past that room over there," he whispered directly into her ear.

Annie nodded her understanding and crept out on shaking legs. It was one thing to talk big about being bait; it was another thing altogether to be the one on the hook.

Walking along, Annie tried to make her soft-soled shoes thump as loud as they could in the hall. They were made to be silent so as not to wake sleeping patients, it wasn't easy to get them to make noise. Giving up, she finally just kicked a plastic basin that was lying on the floor. It rattled loudly in the silence of the hallway.

The pounding of feet sounded coming around the corner. *It was about time.*

"Hold it right there!" The gun-toting goon still had the cigarette in his mouth.

Annie turned and ran back the way she came, praying he would chase her instead of shooting. Her shoulder blades twitched with the anticipation of getting hit by a bullet, but she ran anyway. She wasn't sure if it was her heart pounding or footsteps, but she was almost in front of the door where Mace was waiting in ambush.

"I said hold it!" A strong hand grabbed her shoulder and spun her around.

The goon had enough time to give her semi-clad state an evil look before Mace hit him over the head with a portable oxygen tank.

"Get me something to tie him up with. I'll search him," Mace ordered.

Running to the nurses' station Annie snagged a pair of restraints and came running back.

"Put him on the bed and I'll tie him down." Annie drew up a syringe of the Demerol while Mace heaved the unconscious man onto a bed.

Slapping the soft cuffs on the goon's wrists, Annie tied him as tightly as she could, then jabbed the needle into his arm.

"There. That should hold him for the next six hours." Annie brushed a loose strand of hair off her forehead and faced Mace. "What's next, boss?"

"Same thing next floor. I got his radio so we'll be able to monitor their movements."

"Could you find out anything about him?" Annie asked. She'd better grab a few more vials of Demerol. If they had to do this on every floor of the hospital she was going to need a lot more drugs. She grabbed a towel off a nearby cart to hold her supplies.

"From what I could find out before your bondage tendencies came out, I think he's probably in some group of fanatic militia."

"Militia?" She would not even think about the image he called to mind when he mentioned bondage tendencies.

"Yeah. You know, radical fanatics that stockpile weapons and canned goods out in Utah somewhere for the day the government collapses and there's anarchy. Only I think this group decided to give things a little push and try taking over the government early."

"You figured that out in the minute it took me to go get the restraints?" She was amazed at his discoveries.

"Well, he had a tattoo on his ankle that said 'anarchy' and another one with two crossed guns on his arm. Makes me think of a militia group, but I won't know for sure until I see the next guy."

"Right. The next one. Let's go." Annie wasn't sure how many games of cat and mouse her nerves could take.

The sound of a gun ratcheting made her jump. Mace had the goon's automatic rifle and was checking it out. The sight of him in hospital pajama bottoms with a knife strapped to his leg and a weapon slung over his shoulder sent a shiver of fear down her spine. He seemed all business now, no longer the sexy lover in the closet.

"Keep that radio on low; let's see how chatty they get." Mace swung the gun over his shoulder.

"Well, there's one fewer to talk now."

*****

Mace's gut squeezed painfully as Annie walked down the hall to attract yet another unfriendly. How the hell had these guys managed to take hostage an entire hospital when they were dumb as freaking stumps? This was the third time they'd used the same trick, and the idiots fell for it every time.

It didn't say much for their leader. So far the radio had remained silent, no one was checking in to see if all locations were secure. He'd managed to defuse two more bombs and incapacitate three of the enemy. It would be a little easier if he knew how many of them were in the hospital.

The squeak of soles trailed back to Mace and he prayed that this wouldn't be the exceptionally smart unfriendly who shot first and tried to catch her second.

It galled him to use Annie as bait. Prince Charming strikes again. When this was all over, if they got out of it alive, he was going to show her all the manners and charm he had at his disposal.

What was he thinking? They were in the middle of a mission, he shouldn't be thinking about how to get back into her pants!

"Hey!"

Footsteps thumped rapidly down the hall and Mace prepared to jump out and coldcock the next guy. Crouching by the door, his heart leapt into his throat as he watched Annie get tackled by a black-clad man.

Grabbing the knife Mace jumped out and tried to get a shot at the guy, but couldn't find an angle that wouldn't put Annie in jeopardy. Annie was thrashing around, trying to keep him from pinning her to the ground, not making Mace's job any easier.

Finally, Annie must have got a lucky shot in with her heel, because the guy let out a high-pitched squeal and rolled over, clutching his balls. Mace put him out of his misery with a hit to the temple and helped Annie off the floor.

"Are you okay? Did he hurt you?"

"No, just roughed me up a little. I'll live. He did radio in though as he was chasing me. They know at least one of us is loose."

"Shit, I didn't hear anything." Mace checked the guy's ankle for the tattoo that had been on the other guys. Yup, it was here too. Definitely a militia.

"Maybe they're changing frequencies or something. We better hurry, reinforcements could be coming." Annie jabbed the guy's arm with the needle. "How much longer are we going to have to do this?"

"I don't know, but I think this trick is done." Mace wasn't about to tell her his heart couldn't handle seeing her thrashing under a man twice her size again. He'd have to come up with a new plan, one that didn't require Annie to be front and center in the hot zone.

The sound of feet pounding down the staircase jolted him back to his senses. "Get in the bathroom; we'll climb into the ventilation shafts again."

Annie followed his orders without question while Mace finished tying the guy up. Mace shoved him under a pile of spilled laundry to hide him a bit longer and buy them some more time.

Running into the bathroom he saw Annie standing on the sink working the grille off the ventilation shaft. Wrapping one arm around her slender middle, he pulled her off the sink and wedged the knife in the vent to pry it off.

"I'd have gotten it eventually." She shot him a disgruntled look.

"Whatever. Just get in." At least the sink gave him a boost so he didn't have to strain so much to get up this time. His stitches burned like fire, but he couldn't check them out again in front of Annie. While she was catching unfriendlies, he'd been stuffing gauze under the strip of shirt she'd tied around his waist. Blood had soaked through the makeshift bandage and he was afraid he was going to leave a trail.

"Shh, I can hear them in the hallway." Annie had scooted a few feet down the shaft and was listening at the next opening.

Mace belly-crawled his way over to her trying to keep the weapons and radio from clinking against the shaft.

With her finger to her lips, Annie motioned him over to the grille.

"Jud? Jud? Where are you?"

Mace turned his stolen radio off just in time as the guy on the ground keyed his up.

"Command, this is Terminator, I can't find Jud anywhere."

"How many times have I told you not to use names on the air? These bastards have all sorts of devices for intercepting transmissions."

Yeah, Mace called them ears.

"I don't give a shit. We're the ones with the weapons and the ones with the hostages. Let them listen and fear."

Annie rolled her eyes and twirled her finger around next to her head with the universal gesture of crazy.

"You don't know what these brainwashed commies are capable of. Now where is Jud—Justifier?"

"I don't know. He isn't at his post. I didn't catch his message, either. I think there's someone out there." The guy looked around nervously. "I think we should pair up."

"Negative, that's a negative, Terminator. I'm Command, and I say remain at your posts. Our example has been made and the demands delivered. Hold steady to the mission."

"What about Jud?"

"In every war there must be some casualties. He'll be remembered for eternity for his sacrifices."

The Terminator looked like he was going to throw the radio against the wall, but didn't. "Roger. Over and out."

Mace craned his neck to try to follow Terminator's progress. Motioning Annie to stay where she was, Mace slid back down until he could crawl out of the shaft again. If he'd timed it right, the guy should be checking out the room next to the bathroom right about now.

Every thump and clank against the walls of the shaft sounded like thunder to his ears. Good thing he was still barefoot or it would be even louder. Mace had just climbed down from the sink when the bathroom door slammed open.

Terminator pointed his gun, and Mace saw his life flash in front of his eyes. Diving to the side, Mace swiped the guy's legs out from under him and wrestled for the gun. If the automatic rifle went off in the tiny bathroom the ricochet would kill them both.

His side burning; Mace fought for possession of the gun, struggling to keep it from pointing at the ceiling where Annie was hiding.

Or should have been hiding.

"Hold it right there, Terminator, or you'll be the one splattered across the floor." Annie had one of the stolen weapons pressed against the guy's neck and her knee was pushing his shoulder down.

"I thought I told you to stay up there." Mace carefully got up off the floor and grabbed Terminator's weapon.

"Yeah, well, I don't take orders from subordinates. Are you going to bitch about me coming down or are you going to question this guy?"

"I'm not telling you anything. You're just a bunch of communist sellouts! It's because of you we have fags and weirdoes running all over the country." Their prisoner looked almost proud to be defiant.

"Yup, that's me, risking my life so that the communist takeover can be completed. You'll talk, Terminator, or my friend here will dose you up with truth serum."

Annie caught on quickly and pulled a syringe and more Demerol out of the towel she'd put them in.

"Now this won't hurt a bit." She held up the syringe so that light glinted off the point.

Terminator's face paled and he started to sweat. When Annie pushed a little spurt of fluid out of the tip, he gulped audibly. His eyes were rolling in his head as she grabbed his arm and aimed.

"I'll tell you everything! Just get that thing away from me!"

He carried a gun around like it was a water pistol, but was afraid of a needle? There was something wrong with these guys. Mace waved her off and faced his victim. "How many men are in the hospital itself?"

"We've got fifty men spread through out the hospital. Two are guarding each set of prisoners."

"How many doorways are rigged with bombs and where are they?"

The Terminator shut his mouth tightly and Annie pushed the needle into his arm.

"Don't touch me with that thing!" His face was positively green as he looked at the syringe.

"Then tell me what I want to know."

"All the stairways to the main building are booby-trapped." His eyes were darting from side to side as he tried to pull away. Mace got closer to keep him from hitting Annie.

"Then how have you been able to get around?"

"The bombs only work on the timer, not on contact. You can open the doors without getting blown to hell."

"Where are the prisoners being held?" He wanted to get the noncombatants to safety if he could.

"The military personnel are being held in a meeting room. The civilians are in the cafeteria." He was sweating profusely now, and his body was shaking.

Mace nodded to Annie and she gave the Terminator the Demerol.

"I told you everything! Truth serum isn't going to help."

"It isn't truth serum. Night, night, Terminator." Annie pulled the needle out of his arm and checked his pulse as his eyes slowly closed.

"What are we going to do? We can't take out fifty of these guys. And now they'll be looking for us."

Rolling the Terminator in with the other unfriendly, Mace racked his brain for a way out of this situation. They had to do something soon or they'd all be dead.

"Too bad we can't do something with all the bombs you defused," Annie tied the remaining vials of narcotics back up inside the towel.

Do something with the bombs. Hmm.

"That's it! You're brilliant!" Mace gave her a hard kiss on the lips.

"I am? What are you going to do?"

"Set off the bombs."

Chapter Six

"I'm sorry; I must not have heard you right. I thought you said you were going to set off the bombs." Annie looked hard at Mace wondering if the strain had gotten to him.

"I did. We're going to collect the other bombs and plant them somewhere." His emerald eyes were shining brightly at her. "The enemy will think they're being attacked and rush to that area and we can rescue the prisoners and get the hell out of here. Once the hostages are taken out of the picture, we'll let the forces on the outside deal with these guys."

"Isn't that a bit risky?"

"And you running down the hall with two tons of fanatic chasing your ass isn't?"

He had a point; this whole situation was out of control. "Where are you going to put the bombs?"

"I hadn't thought that far ahead yet."

"Maybe you should." Good lord, she was actually encouraging him in this insanity.

"Let's collect the bombs, defuse them and while we're doing that I'll think of a plan."

"And you think these guys are just going to *let* us collect all their explosives?"

"I wasn't planning on asking their permission."

Annie rolled her eyes. This was crazy. They were going to end up blowing up themselves and the whole damn hospital by the time they were done. And she'd thought Iraq was dangerous!

*****

Keeping her weapon at the ready, Annie guarded Mace's back. They'd already had two more skirmishes trying to collect the bombs. She didn't want any more. At least there were two fewer goons to fight.

That was two less to try and kill Mace. Her stomach clenched at the thought of him dying. Her makeshift bandage had held so far, but how much more abuse could his stitches take? Annie resisted the urge to check his bandage again. Time was running out.

Mace's muscles rippled as he hefted the bag of bombs over his shoulder. Annie forced the jolt of lust that shot straight to her core into submission and tried to focus on the problem at hand.

"Why don't we plant them in the garage? It's far enough away from the meeting room and the cafeteria to keep the prisoners safe, but will be loud enough to get their attention."

He appeared to think on her suggestion for a bit. "It could work; we'd have to be careful where we did it and how much we used. The garage might be unstable after already being hit. We should recon the noncombatants first and plan our strategy there before we set off any explosives."

"Let's go to the café first. It will have the most people, and they aren't used to dealing with volatile situations like this."

Annie tried to remember the best way to get to the café without going through the main lobby. They had to backtrack twice when she took them into older parts of the building, but eventually they made it.

"Are you going to unload that somewhere?" Annie indicated the bag of bombs he was holding. She knew in her head that it was stable, but that didn't mean she wanted to be inches from enough explosives to blow up a city block.

"I'll stash it in that closet over there. If anything happens, take it and run for the exit."

"I'm not leaving without you!" Her heart dropped into her stomach at the thought of losing Mace.

Irrational as it was, she'd formed a bond to this man and she couldn't fathom leaving without him.

"Hey, I'm not planning on dying anytime soon, but I can't concentrate if I'm worried about you getting killed. I know it sounds crazy, but I-I have feelings for you I can't explain."

Hope surged within Annie's chest. Maybe he felt the same way that she did?

"Then you'd better live long enough to figure them out. Come on."

Annie watched Mace's back again while he broke into the janitor's closet and stashed the explosives. Her blood pounded in her veins as they crept down the silent halls. The café was in the basement of the building and it was dark and creepy on a good day. With only the emergency lights on and no people bustling around, it was even worse.

Ducking into an alcove, Mace pulled her to his chest and motioned for silence. How could he know if anyone was coming or not? It was so dark she could barely see a foot in front of her. A few endless heartbeats later the sound of clumping feet echoed in the hallway.

"Hey, Brett, you see anything?" A scratchy voice came over the radio down the hall.

Course it's darker than witch's heart.

"Whadda think happened to Jud and the rest of 'em?"

These guys were darn chatty over the radio. The wait must be getting to them.

"Probably got scared and deserted their posts." Brett snorted.

"Probably. You having any trouble with your prisoners?"

"Nah, after the example we made, none of them has the guts to say 'boo'. How 'bout you? You got the commie soldiers in your group."

"Hell no. They're afraid they'll be the next example. I thought this'd be more interesting, ya know. It's just waiting around for something to happen."

"I know. Boring. I was thinkin' of having some fun with one of the nurses."

"Command said don't touch 'em."

"I wouldn't touch her, much. Just make her touch me, if you get my drift."

Annie's gut clenched again. Those were her nurses, her staff. No hick was going to rape one of her friends. She'd tear this freaking hillbilly apart with her bare hands!

Something in her body language must have told Mace what she was thinking, because his arms tightened around her and she couldn't move. She was afraid to struggle and alert Brett to their presence, but her heart pounded in fury.

Mace continued to hold her until the goon walked down the other end of the hall. Even once he determined the coast was clear, he held onto her arm and steered her back to the janitor's closet.

Once inside he let her go.

"Why did you stop me? I could have taken him out before he even knew what hit him!" Annie got right up in his face.

"Yeah, but could you have done it before he radioed his buddy? I'm just as pissed off as you are, but we have to think with our heads, not our emotions."

"He's going to rape one of my nurses! I can't allow that!"

"Stop freaking out and use your training. You can't let the fate of one person jeopardize hundreds of lives."

"What do you know? You're a man. You have no idea what it's like to fear rape."

"It doesn't mean I want it to happen!" Mace stepped back from her and looked her in the eye. "Look, I'll do everything in my power to keep your staff safe, but we've got to do this according to plan or we'll both be dead."

Annie swallowed the fear and anger and tried to focus on what he was saying. If she went charging into the café, guns blazing, she could very well end up killing innocent civilians before she stopped Brett. Even worse, he could radio their location and reinforcements could come down.

But it could be one of her nurses! One of her friends. Annie's mind struggled with the idea of letting one of her friends get hurt. She had to put the good of everyone first, no matter how much it galled her. He was right, damn it. "Let's set the freaking charges."

"That's my girl!" Mace pulled her close and planted a kiss on her.

"But when the time comes, Brett's mine."

"No problem, as long as I get to watch."

*****

Mace set the charges in the parking garage in the farthest spot he could find. The area looked a little weak, but he wanted these guys to take a long time to find out it was only a decoy.

He really wished he had paid more attention to that explosives workshop. At the time it seemed ridiculous. He was a pilot; all he needed to know was what they looked like if they were in his copter. Live and learn. He hoped. He had a lot more living to do.

Looking over his shoulder, Mace felt his breath catch at the sight of Annie holding the weapon on the door to the garage. Her angelic face didn't hold one hint of softness now. He almost pitied Brett. Then he remembered what Brett was thinking and all pitying thoughts vanished.

One of those bastards better not try to rape Annie. Mace would blow the whole hospital up before he let that happen.

Stop! He couldn't think like that. One life wasn't more important than hundreds, isn't that what he just told Annie? He looked at her again and his heart did a slow thump. She was worth more than a million lives, and he'd do anything, *everything* to protect her.

"Come on, Captain, we've got work to do." Annie headed towards the door.

"Yes, ma'am!"

Mace checked the charges one more time and followed Annie out the door. It was a good thing she knew her way around the building, because he would have been lost hours ago.

"I was thinking," Annie started.

"Why do I think I'm not going to like this?"

"Just hear me out. I think we should split up."

"No fucking way! There is no way I'm going to let you loose on Brett." Or leave her open to attack.

"Then tell me how we're going to rescue the military personnel and the civilians at the same time when they're on two different floors? By the time we take care of the civilians they'll have started killing off the others."

Damn. He should have thought of that. He was no good with ground operations.

"There're two men guarding each location, how are you going to take out both of them?" Mace's mind raced as he tried to iron out this new wrinkle.

"The same way you planned to. When the explosives blow I'll shoot the sons-of-bitches with this sucker." She hefted the automatic weapon.

"You could really do that?"

"I've had the same basic training as you have."

"I don't mean physically. Can you emotionally take someone's life in cold blood?"

"It's down to us against them. You're damn straight I could shoot them. I don't want to, but I will if it means saving all of us."

Mace looked at her beautiful face and cringed at the thought of the damage to her soul.

"We have to do this; we're running out of time. Besides, once I take out one of them, I'm sure the civilians will come to my aid." Her face softened and she stroked his cheek. "We don't have any other choice."

She was right, and he knew it. That didn't mean he had to like it. "Fine, but I'll take the civilians; you go after the military personnel. There're fewer of them and less chance that they'll panic when the bombs go off." And hopefully they'll have already subdued the enemy seconds after the explosion.

*****

Annie crouched down behind a huge ficus tree and waited for the explosion to launch her attack. She had been full of bold words for Mace, but the truth was she was shaking in her shoes. It was a whole lot easier thinking of shooting someone who was going to possibly rape one of her friends than it was going into unknown territory.

The roar of the explosion shook the building and shocked her into immobility for precious seconds. Training overcame instinct and Annie ran for the meeting room. One of the goons was running out as she got there and she fired at his legs.

The spray of bullets shooting out of the weapon was faster than she expected and the man went down hard, blood splattering everywhere. She hadn't killed him outright but if he didn't receive medical care he'd be as good as dead. That was something she'd have to worry about later. If the situation was reversed, she didn't think he'd be feeling any remorse.

Kicking in the door, Annie shot at the ceiling and dove to the side, praying the whole time. Return fire came shooting over her head and she scrambled for the cover of a table. Peeking her head over the edge she caught sight of two officers diving on top of the lone gunman while bullets flew.

Using the furniture for cover she crawled her way over to the battle. One of the MPs she recognized from night shift was lying in a corner, his face battered and bloody, and one arm bent at an unnatural angle.

Several other military nurses were clustered in a circle. Annie handed off one of the rifles to the nearest one and worked her way closer to the last goon. Another spray of bullets flew around the room, forcing her to duck for cover.

Shouts erupted and she lost track of the present battle, transported back to the one in Iraq. In her mind, bodies were torn apart by shrapnel, wild-eyed fanatics spouting guttural rhetoric charged at her with guns flashing.

The logical part of her mind screamed at her to snap out of it, but her psyche was frozen in fear. The image of a bearded man pointing a gun at her, then jerking and falling back when he was shot played over and over again. Remembered fear crawled in her belly, and she wanted to whimper with the force of it.

"Major. Major! You can put the weapon down. The prisoner has been secured." Colonel Michaels' voice broke through her daze.

"Yes, sir!"

"Good work, Major. Where are the others?"

Others? "Ah, there are no others, sir."

"You did this yourself?"

"No, sir. Captain Mason O'Keefe is now liberating the civilians. We need to get out before the rest of the enemy realizes they've been duped."

"Duped? You've got a lot to explain." The colonel looked at her with an incredulous expression on his face.

"In all due time, sir. Now we need to leave."

One of the other colonels got up from where he'd been tying up the goon with a telephone cord. "Let's take the fire exits and try to get out by the side of the building. They're bound to have most of the exits covered."

"I'll secure the rear." Annie snapped her spare clip into the weapon.

Michaels looked at her again but didn't say anything. Two of the nurses were helping the wounded MP out, and the one she had given the gun to stopped as she went past.

"What happened to the guy that went out first?" she asked.

"He's lying in a pool of his own blood in the hallway." Annie felt bile climb up her throat.

"Good. He did this to Scott as an 'example' of what would happen if we tried anything. I think he liked doing it too. I hope he dies a slow, painful death."

Annie looked at the wounded MP who was holding his ribs with his uninjured hand and shuddered. Anyone who would enjoy inflicting so much damage they broke bones didn't deserve her remorse.

Colonel Michaels followed the last of the nurses and held the door for Annie. She walked to the threshold and waited for him to get out of the way so she could pull the door closed.

"What are you doing? Get out of here, Major! That's an order."

Colonel Michaels stood in the doorway with hands on hips.

"I'm sorry, sir; you'll have to write me up for insubordination. I have to watch my buddy's back." Annie saluted and ran for the café.

Chapter Seven

Mace's side was bleeding worse now than when he had gotten the original injury. If he had one intact stitch after this he'd be surprised. Blood from the wound he'd earned preventing a rape was dripping down from his shoulder making things look even worse than they actually were.

Trying to ignore the pain from where the bullet grazed his shoulder, Mace concentrated on leading the civilians out of the café. Annie had told him there was an emergency exit somewhere in these tunnels. Another stab of fear hit him in the gut as he thought about her. Was she okay? Hell, was she still alive?

Focus on the job, O'Keefe. He couldn't let emotions take over his brain right now; he had to get these people to safety. The emergency lights were few and far between in this section of the hospital, and Mace flinched at every echo of sound.

They only had a limited time before the enemy realized the explosion was a trick. Once they figured it out, all the remaining unfriendlies would be trying to recapture the hostages. As it was, Mace had taken out four more men than he had planned on.

Thank God he'd told Annie to take the smaller group. They were at ground level and had a better chance to escape without running into trouble.

The thud of a boot heel hitting the floor sounded like a gunshot compared to the quiet shuffling of the civilians he was leading. Searching for options, Mace motioned for them to crouch down behind the huge laundry bins they'd just passed.

Slipping ahead, he strained his ears trying to hear another telltale footstep. If he remembered Annie's directions right, they were pretty darn close to the exit. That noise could have come from someone guarding the door. And since none of his allies wore boots, that meant it was an unfriendly up ahead.

A slight breeze played about his face, teasing him with its coolness against his sweaty skin. If there was a breeze that meant there was probably a door. With his back against the wall, Mace slipped around the corner in time to see the silhouettes of two men standing in an open door. One of them made a pulling motion and tossed something down the hall and ducked for cover.

Shit! He must have pulled the pin on a grenade! Mace had five seconds to throw it back or they were all dead. Running as fast as he could to intercept it, Mace picked up the rolling mini-bomb. Juggling it from hand to hand, praying he had time, he kicked open the emergency exit and threw his best fastball pitch.

The grenade cleared the door, spinning through the air as it went. Mace couldn't follow its progress, his eyes were blinded by the light streaming in. Jumping away from the exit he pulled the door closed and dropped to the floor.

"Get down and cover your heads!" he ordered his followers.

His shoulder screamed in agony as he raised his arms and covered his own neck and head. Seconds dragged out as he waited for the explosion.

And waited.

And waited.

A dud. Ten years scared off his life by a cheap surplus store dud.

Laughing to himself, Mace pushed his weary body off the floor. His knees felt weak from relief, but his job wasn't done yet. He had to get the civilians out of the hospital, and now two enemies knew they were here.

"Anyone know another way out of here? If we go out that door, chances are we'll be met by two guys with machine guns."

Faces glazed by shock looked at him with blank expressions. These people had been through so many traumatic events in the last six hours, they were functioning like sleepwalkers.

"I do."

An older man with "Sanitation Engineer" on his uniform came forward.

"It'll be a tight squeeze with all these people, but there's a side door in the furnace room for repairs and stuff. We'll have to go through one at a time, but I doubt anyone even knows about it."

"Good man. Lead the way."

"Yes, sir!" The grizzled man snapped a salute and turned. "Haven't seen this much excitement since I came home from Korea!" He walked back down the hallway.

Shaking his head, Mace ushered his charges after the janitor. Wonder if it was the same closet that he and Annie had made such memories in? Mace would never be able to look at a cleaning closet the same way again.

The furnace room was indeed a tight squeeze. The exit was a tiny service door, and they had to squeeze by the burner of the furnace to get to it. Luckily with the power out the burner wasn't running or they'd be risking serious burns to get out.

It seemed to take forever for the group to file through. A couple of the heavier women had difficulty getting out, and Mace had a moment of panic picturing them all trapped in the tiny space while the gunmen picked them off one by one. Eventually, the last of them made it through the miniature door.

The janitor stuck his head back in. "Your turn."

"I'm not going." There was no way he was leaving without Annie. He handed the veteran one of the guns he carried. "Take this and get the hell away from the building. The first guy you see in a SWAT team jacket, throw down the gun and raise your hands over your head."

"Are you crazy? They're still a bunch of these guys running around. You'll be killed!"

"It's a risk I've got to take. Thanks for the help, you're a real hero." Mace made sure he had enough ammo then saluted the man and pulled the door closed.

The darkness was overwhelming, and Mace took a minute to get his bearings. Annie should have gotten her crew out by now and be with them.

Should being the operative word.

He was positive that she was still in the building. The two of them were connected in some way, and just as he knew he couldn't leave without knowing her fate, he knew she hadn't left him either.

Jogging down the corridor, bare feet slapping against the tiled floor, Mace thought about where Annie might be. She was familiar with the route he had planned on taking, so she might be headed back to the laundry area.

And if she was, she could be headed right back to two unfriendlies with grenades! Mace began to run.

*****

Annie's thoughts were focused on finding Mace and staying alive. Would she be able to find him? He had insisted that she leave the building with her group, but wouldn't say what he was going to do.

The smart thing would be for him to leave and they'd meet up outside, but he was a hero and she was sure he was up to something. If he thought he was going to single-handedly save the hospital he was in for a big surprise. She was either going to help him or drag his ass out of the building.

Now she just had to find him.

Rounding the corner to the café, Annie saw the body of Brett, pants down around his ankles. She didn't even bother to check his pulse, if he was still alive there was nothing she could do to save him anyway. A shudder ran down her back as she thought about whether or not Mace had stopped him from raping one of her friends in time.

Drops of blood on the floor trailed off towards the laundry. The same direction Mace was supposed to have taken. Was that Mace's blood? Had he reinjured himself, or was that a new injury? Annie felt her heart lodge in her throat as she followed the bright red drops.

The farther away from the café, the harder it was to follow the trail. The halls got darker and darker, and Annie's heart pounded with anxiety. Had he been shot? Was he still alive?

A sudden flood of light blinded her and she instinctively dropped to the ground. Bullets whizzed over her head as she rolled to the side and returned fire. Her eyes watered and she couldn't see what she was aiming at. Trying to look out of the corner of her eyes, she aimed at the silhouettes in the door and kept firing.

As she crawled backwards, Annie tried to think about what she could use for cover. She was painfully aware that she stood out clearly in her whites in the darkness of the hallway. Squeezing the trigger on her rifle, she fired a few more shots to keep them distracted. A muffled scream came from the door. Had she hit one of them? She still couldn't see anything.

Strong hands grabbed her ankles and yanked her back. Panic shot through her and she tried to kick against her captor.

"It's me, Annie! Calm down!"

Mace!

"I think I got one, but I can't tell. The light blinded me."

"You got them both."

That was two more down. "Are they dead?"

"I didn't check, but if they're not, they aren't going anywhere for a while. What the hell are you doing here?"

Annie rolled over and got to her feet. She could barely make out Mace's features, but his dirt-streaked face was the most welcome sight she'd ever clapped eyes on.

"I couldn't leave you. I had to know you were alive."

"When we get out of here, I'm going to show you just how alive I am."

"If we get out of here, I'll hold you to it." Desire surged through her body, augmented by the adrenaline running through her system.

"Honey, you couldn't keep me from you. Now come on, let's get the hell out."

Following his lead Annie jogged after him. As they passed one of the emergency lights she saw blood dripping down his back.

"You're bleeding! What happened?" Annie stopped him to investigate the injury.

"Just a graze, it's more of a burn than anything. Nothing to worry about."

"It still needs to be cleaned."

"Later. Come on, I'll show you a way out."

Mace led her towards the furnace room. What were they doing here?

"Do you know where we're going?" She wasn't really familiar with this area, and if they got lost she wasn't sure she could get them back.

"Yup. I found a back door. Well, half-door." He laughed at his own joke.

Maybe the strain was finally getting to him; she didn't see anything funny about the situation.

The room Mace brought her to was pitch-black and smelled like grease. It was also as small as a closet.

"You're sure we can get out of here?" A slippery shiver of fear slithered down her spine.

"Trust me, have I steered you wrong yet?"

"No. And strangely enough, I trust you with my life." Annie shut her mouth before she blurted out something stupid like "and my heart."

Whatever Mace was going to say in response was cut off by an explosion outside of the room. Dirt and debris rained down on them, and Annie clung to Mace for balance.

Mace pulled her aside just in time as the enormous furnace tumbled against the wall where they had been standing. Annie's knees shook and she bit back a whimper of fear. They were alive, but how long could they stay that way?

"What's going on?" Her voice was breathy with fear. The darkness was closing down on her and she could feel the panic stirring in her belly.

"I think the next grenade they launched wasn't a dud."

"Grenade? You didn't tell me they had grenades!"

"It was a bit of a surprise to me too. Can you let go so I can check out the situation? Will you be okay?"

No! She didn't want him to let her go. Damn it, she was an adult, she could conquer this fear. There was nothing to be afraid of, Mace was right there with her.

"Sure. I'm fine." Cold sweat dripped down her back and she was glad he couldn't see her face and know she was lying.

"I'm right here. You don't have to be scared."

"Who's scared?" *Me, me, me, me*!

"I'm going to see if I can find a flashlight. There should be something here for when they do work on the furnace."

"Check next to the door." Light would make this better. Maybe.

There was a thump and a curse, and then a clatter of something falling. A weak light flickered on and Annie gasped.

The enormous furnace had fallen and lodged itself against the door to the hallway, narrowly missing them. If Mace hadn't moved them when he did they would have been crushed under its weight.

"Oh man," Mace groaned.

"I know, talk about a close call."

"That's not what I'm thinking about. That's the way outside right there."

Annie looked at where Mace pointed. The other end of the furnace was wedged against a tiny half-door. They were trapped.

The fear she'd been holding in check by her fingertips let loose with a vengeance.

*****

In the flickering light of the dying flashlight, Mace watched Annie's face crumple. Tears streamed out of her eyes and her knees buckled. Mace jumped to her and caught her before she dropped to the filthy ground.

"It'll be okay, baby. I promise I'll get you out of here."

"We don't even know what the hallway looks like out there. We might be trapped in here for days!"

She was headed towards all-out panic, and there wasn't anything he could do to stop it. He had to distract her!

Hauling her to her feet, Mace pulled her face to his and kissed her. He could taste the tears on her slack lips moments before she responded to his touch.

And respond she did. One second she was a quivering mass of fears ready to curl into the fetal position, the next second she was a wild woman clinging to him and attacking his mouth with a vengeance.

"Slow down, baby, I'm not going anywhere."

"Don't remind me!"

Oh crap, bad word choice. Mace had to keep her mind off the situation. He was still kissing her, but she was starting to pull away. Thinking quickly he drew her closer.

"Want to play a game?" he whispered as he nipped her earlobe.

"What kind of game?" Her voice had a quaver in it and he didn't know if it was from fear or desire.

"Let's pretend."

"Aren't we a little old to be playing pretend? I mean, isn't the situation a bit desperate for childhood games?"

She scoffed at his idea, but didn't pull back. Mace took that as a good sign.

"This is a great time to use our imaginations. It's just the two of us here; we can be anything we want, do anything we want."

"O-okay. What do you want to pretend?"

"Let's pretend we're in the desert, in a secluded tent." Mace ran his hands lightly over her bare shoulders. He shut the flashlight off and the room plunged into darkness again.

"I was in plenty of tents in the desert, they weren't very fun." Her voice quivered, but she was still standing.

"This isn't field ops; this is a sheik's tent. Gorgeous rugs are on the floor, silk cushions are everywhere." Mace racked his brain to think of what else would be in a tent like that. He had a vague recollection of something like this from a porno movie he'd seen once. "There's soft music playing in the background, and a gentle breeze comes in through the top."

It was working, she was starting to relax. Her hands were stroking his back now instead of clutching him in a panic. He just had to keep it up now.

"What are we doing in this tent?"

Oh boy. What the hell had happened in that movie? "Ah, I'm the sheik, and you're my concubine."

"Oh really?"

"Hey, this is pretend, and I'm making it up. When it's your turn, you can be the sheik."

"I'll hold you to that."

Mace's cock slammed painfully erect at the thought of Annie being in complete control of him. His balls were achingly full and lust was driving him hard. This better be working to distract her, because it was driving him insane!

"As my concubine, you have to do whatever I want, or you'll be punished."

Her breathing got faster, and he could almost smell her sudden desire. Blood pounded in his veins in response.

"What if I don't want to be good? What if I'm a very bad concubine?" Annie's hands stroked his stomach then moved down to cup his sac.

Desire punched him in the gut, driving the air right out of his lungs. He ran his hands up her chest until he reached the elastic of her bra. Very slowly Mace drew the fabric up over her breasts, until her creamy mounds fell free.

"I guess if you're very bad, you'll have to be punished." Before she could react, Mace pinched her nipples quickly, then bent over to draw one into his mouth.

"Oh!"

Mace wished he could see her face. Her rapid breathing told him she was aroused, but he wanted to see what she looked like as he brought her up and over. Licking his way to her other nipple, he eased her pants down her legs until she was completely naked. Slowly he kissed his way to her belly button, then over to her hips, avoiding her pussy completely.

"You're killing me!" she moaned.

"That's the point, you're supposed to be punished." Standing back up, Mace used one hand to part the silken curls between her legs. She was soaking wet, her juices drenched his hand as he parted her pussy lips. Sliding one finger into her tight channel, Mace fought for control as her muscles squeezed him. God, he wanted to feel those muscles around his cock.

Annie moaned and pulled him closer, thrusting her hips against his hand.

"Oh no, you don't. You've been a very bad slave." Smiling to himself, Mace gently swatted her ass.

"Whoa! You just spanked me!" A flood of fluid washed over his hand as he pushed a second finger inside her pussy.

"And you liked it." He slapped her again while driving his fingers deeper into her channel.

"Maybe."

She might not admit it out loud, but her body was telling another story. Annie's hands were squeezing his pecs tightly, and her hips were rocking furiously.

"I think it's a bit more than 'maybe'. I think you're enjoying this little game. Aren't you, slave?" Mace used his thumb to rub against her clit as he spanked her again, a little harder this time.

Teeth bit into his chest as she thrust her hips against him. Mace pushed his fingers deeper inside of her and strummed her clit even faster. At last, a wash of cream flowed over him as her body spasmed.

"Holy shit!" she gasped. "I've never come so hard in my entire life. Who'd of thought I liked kink?"

"Stick with me, I'll show you all sorts of things."

Annie untied his pants and pulled his throbbing cock into her hot, wet pussy. Mace thought he'd die from the pleasure of finally being in her body again.

"I think I'll stick around for a little while at least."

"I can pretty much guarantee it's only going to be a little while."

"So much for the conquering hero." Annie planted her mouth on his and grabbed his ass in both hands. Her hot walls squeezed his cock like a wet fist making his balls ache with the need to release their load. Not yet. He had to hold off just a little longer, it felt too good to end it only seconds after he got inside her.

Reaching between them, Mace slipped a finger against her clit and rubbed. He had to stop moving to hold off his climax, but nothing could keep the desire from throbbing in his veins.

As Annie quivered and clenched around him again, he grabbed her hips and pounded into her hot wet center with everything he had. He could feel the come building at the base of his cock, getting ready to explode into Annie. The stream of semen spraying from his body seemed to go on and on. Mace held on for dear life as he emptied his heart and soul into her.

What had started as a way to distract her had become a catharsis. And an epiphany. He was never going to let this woman out of his life. They'd known each other for less than twenty-four hours, but he felt like he'd known her forever. For the first time in his life, Mace found someone who he couldn't live without.

"One of these days, we're going to have to do this in a bed," Annie said, kissing his neck as she slid away from him.

"Do you think it could be any better lying down?" He clicked on the flashlight and looked at her face to see if the panic had left. She had a satisfied smile on her face, and her angel eyes sparkled at him.

"No, but I'm willing to compare. In fact, I think we should try all sorts of positions and see if they can compare." She gave him a sexy smile.

Mace's cock began to stir again. The moisture from her body hadn't even dried off and he was thinking about plunging back in. "I think it only makes sense to try out all the options before making a decision."

"If we're stuck in here forever, we'll have plenty of time to try." She wrapped her arms around herself and turned away.

He pulled her close to him and tucked her head under his chin. "Don't panic, we'll get out of here."

"How? The furnace is too heavy to move, and no one even knows we're here except the goons who threw the grenade."

"Have a little faith. The janitor who led me down here knows where we are. When the situation is safe, someone will come looking for us. We just have to hold out until then."

"And pray we don't die of thirst or starvation."

"I think you need a little more distracting, Major. You're thinking too many negative thoughts."

Chapter Eight

Annie looked at Mace in the wavering light. Her eyes were drawn to his rapidly growing cock as it stood up hard and tall from the nest of curls between his legs. He was ready so quickly?

"What sort of distraction did you have in mind, Captain?" A curl of anticipation wound its way to her swelling nether lips.

"Turn around." His voice was husky and shot right through her.

"Turn around?" He didn't want her to face him?

"Trust me on this. Turn around and brace your hand on that shelf over there."

"What? Are you going to spank me again?" Not that she'd mind. The combined sensations of having him slap her ass and slam his finger inside her had been mind-blowing.

Annie did as he instructed. The click of the flashlight sounded and the room was again plunged into darkness. Just once she'd like to make love to him when she could see his face. Of course, from this position, she couldn't see his face anyway.

She could feel Mace move behind her, his hand on her naked behind. She felt open and very needy. Being in the dark had lost its power over her. The lust shooting through her system destroyed any smidgeon of fear before it could fully form.

She had other things on her mind.

Mace's fingers ran up and down her back so gently it gave her goose bumps. She could feel her nipples tightening and her pussy lips swelling between her legs. Her breasts seemed to grow fuller too. The position she was in made them hang in front of her and she felt a delicious sense of wantonness spread through her.

"Your skin is so soft." His voice was low and husky in her ear. "I never noticed before how silky it is. I was too busy trying to get between your legs to pay attention to the rest of you. Not this time. I'm going to worship every inch of your body until you beg me to stop." His words danced around in her head, dizzying her with their intensity.

"I don't beg easily." Well, she never had before anyway.

"Good."

His mouth followed his fingers, licking, kissing, and nipping at her back and shoulders. She could feel the slight abrasion of his stubble as he moved over her, and the contrast from his soft lips was erotic. Each touch of his lips sent heat spreading out in ripples through her body. His hands had drifted around and were running over her ribs, sliding up under her breasts then moving away before they reached her aching chest. A hot surge of need followed in the wake of his fingers, silently urging him to touch her everywhere.

A fresh dribble of fluid trickled between her legs, and she was sure there was more to come. Every second that ticked by made her more aware of his movements and her body was burning with eagerness for his touch. Her breath was coming in shallow little gasps. With the lights out, her other senses were hyperaware of what was happening to her, including the nerve endings in her skin. Every caress Mace gave her branded itself on her body.

Annie's heart was beating like a drum and she was waiting in an agony of anticipation for what he'd touch next. Mace's fingers drifted down to her hips and she felt him caress the globes of her rear end. The teasing touch of his fingers made her pussy clench and throb. He spread her legs a bit more, widening her stance and making her long for him to fill the emptiness he'd created.

His lips brushed the underside of her butt, teasing the spot where her thighs met her cheeks. A jolt of pure need shot straight to her center, pulling a cry from her.

"Anything wrong, Major?"

"Ah, no." *I'm just dying in a pool of lust, that's all.*

Her legs were quivering as she waited for his next move. She could feel the cool air of his breath blowing across her wet clit, sending lightening bolts of desire through her. Without thinking, she rolled her hips back to get closer to him.

"Patience, my dear, patience." She could hear the laughter in his voice. He was enjoying this too much.

But not nearly as much as she was.

Mace massaged her calves and he trailed his hands up and down her legs. With each pass he got a little closer to the hot, screaming center of her. Her pussy was so enlarged it was like a separate, throbbing entity between her legs.

A single finger rubbed her outer lips, and she whimpered.

"Ready to beg?"

Yes! Yes! Yes! "No." Her body screamed at her, but her pride wouldn't let her give in.

He stood up behind her, and Annie felt the hair of his chest rub against her back in a long caress. His erection was tantalizingly close to her core, but when she tried to adjust to get him closer he moved back.

"Not yet, baby."

One hand parted her curls and teased her sensitized nubbin, the other kneaded a breast. The dual sensations overwhelmed her lust-dazed mind and all she could think about was having him inside of her. Mace pulled her against him so their bodies touched from shoulder to thigh. Licking at the shell of her ear, he seduced her with love words while pinching her nipple and spearing her center with his fingers.

"Tell me what you want, Annie." His finger stilled on her clit as she was seconds from exploding.

"I want you to fuck me!" Her heart was beating so fast and her blood was pounding in her ears. She'd never make it if he stopped now.

"No."

No? "I want you, damn it, Mace! I want you to finish it and fuck me and stay in my body until I can't think of anything but you!" She almost wept with frustration. His cock was so close to her pussy, and his finger was poised on her most sensitive spot.

"No, I'm going to make love to you until you can't think of anyone else ever again."

With two strokes of his finger Annie came apart in a shattering climax that left her weak and panting. Before she could come down from the stars, Mace bent her over his arm and slammed into her from behind causing another storm of explosions to rock through her body. His hand continued to tease and torment her breasts as he thrust into her, never letting her come down from the stratosphere of desire he'd elevated her to.

"Again. I want to feel you come again."

Again? She'd never come so many times in her life. Mace pulled back until just the tip of his penis was inside her, then drove into her sending her senses soaring. The heel of his hand pressed against a spot below her belly button as he rocked back and forth inside of her. A tingling sensation started almost at the entrance to her womb and spread to her entire body.

Mace thrust into her harder and pressed down a little more until she felt like she was going to explode. When he gave a nipping kiss to her neck and flicked her clit gently with his finger, she came so hard it felt like a flood poured out of her body.

Annie sobbed with release as the strength left her body in waves. Lights danced behind her eyes as Mace continued to pound into her. If he wanted her to come again he was out of luck because she had nothing left to give.

His hand tightened against her breast as he gave a hoarse shout then fell against her back. Their mingled gasps were the only sound in the silent room. Annie had never experienced such mind-bending sex before in her life. This man did things to her body and her mind that both thrilled and amazed her.

"Still scared?"

"Of the room, no. That I may never walk again, yes."

Laughing he lifted his weight off her. Instinctively, Annie squeezed her inner muscles, holding him in her body. "Don't leave."

"I won't." He wrapped his arms around her and pulled her even closer.

Annie's heart did a slow flip as he rubbed his chin over her head. The darkness wasn't so scary with Mace holding her tight.

"What happens if we get out of here?"

"Not if, when." Mace assured her.

"Fine, what happens when we get out of here?"

"We'll have to go through a debriefing, probably have to give depositions about what we saw. We might even have to testify at the trial."

"Not that, I mean with you. Will you have to go back to the sandbox?" She was glad he couldn't see her face. Annie didn't want to be one of those women who pined after a service man when he was long gone, but she had to know.

"Maybe. It depends on what happens with this whole mess."

The thought of Mace going back into battle and maybe dying tore her heart to shreds. How could she live without him?

Hell, she'd only just met him and now she was terrified of losing him. Shock must be wrecking havoc on her brain chemistry, she did not act this way. Ever. She would not be some idiot woman who clung to a guy who was after a cheap fling.

Pulling away from Mace she searched for something to cover herself with. She couldn't see much, but her white pants were easy to find. Hopefully her bra was nearby.

"What's wrong? Where'd you go?" There was worry coloring Mace's voice.

"Nowhere. I'm a little chilly so I thought I'd get dressed."

"Oh. Okay, I'll get the flashlight."

"No!" She didn't want him to see her face until she pulled herself together. "I can get dressed in the dark. We should save the batteries so I can look at your wound. Although what I'm going to wrap it up in is anybody's guess."

"I'd forgotten all about it until now. Guess I was a little preoccupied." Mace's fingers played in her hair and she couldn't move away. His touch was so gentle, so caring, it was killing her.

"Well, I want to make sure it isn't worse than you thought."

"It's not. Here's the flashlight, you can check it out for yourself." He handed it to her and turned around.

Clicking on the flashlight she examined Mace's shoulder. There were nail marks in his back from their first bout, and heat shot between her legs as she remembered how they got there.

"How's it look?"

Damn good. He hadn't gotten dressed yet and his muscular butt was a mighty fine sight to behold. "Ah, you're right, it just grazed you. It already stopped bleeding, just a little antiseptic when we get out of here and you'll be right as rain."

She clicked off the light before he could turn back and face her.

"Shh!" Mace pulled her close and crouched down in the shelter of the fallen furnace.

Annie heard the pop of gunshots being fired in the distance. Another explosion rocked the building, dropping more debris down on them and making the room shudder. There were shouts and more gunshots, and Annie prayed they didn't get shot at by either side.

Two more explosions hit outside their door in rapid succession and she closed her eyes and prayed harder. Mace's body thrummed with tension behind her, but he remained calm. Terror made her legs weak. She bit her lip to hold back the whimper of fear. If he could stay calm, so could she.

Mace reached around her for their weapons and handed one to her. There was silence that seemed to go on for hours, but was probably only minutes. Annie's nerves were pulled tight with the tension. If the fight was over, who had won?

The quiet stretched on until Annie thought she'd scream. At least fifteen minutes later, the scream of ripping metal came from the half door. Annie aimed her weapon at the opening, was it friend or foe coming in? And would they shoot first and ask questions later?

*****

A shaft of light speared Mace in the eye as mechanical claws tore their way through the door and into the furnace. If they were using the Jaws of Life equipment to open the door, it was probably the good guys trying to get in, but he held his weapon ready anyway.

"Major Forbes? Are you in there?"

"Colonel Michaels? Is that you?" Annie answered.

Mace held her arm when she went to go towards the door.

"You don't know if it's safe, and I don't want you getting too close to those jaws."

Annie rolled her eyes, but stayed where she was.

"We've got the building secure, but there was some structural damage to this area. It's going to take a bit to get you out of there."

"No kidding, sir. The hospital's furnace is jammed against both doors."

"What?"

"During one of the explosions the furnace fell over and is now lodged between both doors."

"No wonder it wouldn't open. Now we've got to cut through that goddamn thing too. You may be in for a long wait. I'll see if I can get you some water bottles and MREs."

"Yes, sir."

Military Meals Ready to Eat weren't gourmet cooking, but right about now they sounded pretty damn good. A little bit of water to clear the dirt and the taste of fear out of his mouth wouldn't hurt either.

"Are you wounded at all, Major?"

"No, but Captain O'Keefe is. I could use some clean bandages and some antiseptic. He'll need new stitches when this is over, too."

"Who the hell is Captain O'Keefe?" Colonel Michaels did not sound happy.

"My, ah, partner, sir. He was a patient in the emergency room."

Mace almost snickered. He was sitting there butt-naked with Annie between his legs and she was talking to her commanding officer.

"God in heaven. I want the whole story when this is all over. Right now stay away from this door while we stabilize the structure and get you out."

Mace heard some muffled shouts and the colonel moved away. Annie handed him his pants, or what was left of them anyway.

"These have seen better days," she said, averting her eyes as she moved away from his embrace.

"I'll be glad to get rid of them. You're going to need a new uniform, too, Major. I don't think most nurses run around in sports bras. Too bad."

"I guess it's all over."

Why wouldn't she look at him? "Yeah, if they're using machinery to get us out of here the building must be secure. I told you that janitor would let them know where we are."

"I mean, you and me. You'll be heading back to your unit and I'll be here a few more years."

"I won't be over there forever you know." The thought of losing her sent a cold stab of fear through his body.

"Yeah, but you said it yourself, this is all just a result of the adrenaline exaggerating our hormones, or something."

"Is that all you think it is?" The coldness was spreading. Didn't she feel the same way he did?

"I don't know what I think! All I know is I have never been in a situation like this before, and I don't know how much is adrenaline and how much is real."

"If what we just shared was from adrenaline, I'll bottle and sell it and put Viagra out of business! This is not over, babe."

Mace didn't know what Annie was going to say because another explosion rocked the building. The last thing he remembered was Annie diving for him as his head rang with pain.

Chapter Nine

Mace opened his eyes and winced. He was in an olive drab tent and his head felt like it had been hit with a baseball bat. Where was he? Did he crash? What the hell was going on?

Slowly the memories started to come back to him. He and Annie had been trapped in the furnace room. The wackos had been taken care of and they were waiting to get out. What happened next?

A pain shot through his heart as he remembered Annie telling him that their time together was over. Bullshit! He'd change her mind, by God!

Flipping back the light cover over his legs, he tried to get out of the cot. As soon as he sat up, a wave of dizziness dropped him right back down.

"What do you think you're doing? You lie right back down there this instant, Captain!" Annie came running to his side and straightened the covers over him.

"You're here. I was going to look for you." Mace grabbed her hand and held it tight. She wasn't getting away from him if he could stop it.

"Of course I'm here. Where else would I be?" Her blue eyes shined down on him and she caressed his face with her free hand.

"What happened?" Mace looked around the tent, he was next to a heavily bandaged man who looked like he had gone ten rounds with a heavyweight boxing champ. There was a nurse in a camp chair next to him, holding his hand in her sleep.

"Apparently we missed one of the bombs," Annie explained. "The explosion rocked the already weakened area where we were and that section of the building collapsed. You ended up with a concussion."

"Was anyone else hurt?" Mace searched her for signs of injury. She looked fine. Hell, she looked more than fine.

"No, everyone had gotten out by that point. If you hadn't gotten the civilians out of the café though, it would have been a different story. The entire cafeteria is rubble."

"Did they catch the bastards responsible for it?"

"The ringleaders are in custody, that's all I know. There's going to be some sort of investigation to find out who is behind all of it, but right now things are still pretty chaotic."

"What time is it? I'm so disoriented, I don't know whether I'm coming or going."

"You're not going anywhere, mister. It's a little after noon. You've been out for a while."

Mace let out a low whistle. "I think I was safer in Iraq."

Annie looked sick at his words and tried to pull away, but he held her fast.

"Are you hungry? I could get you a sandwich if you're not too nauseous to eat it."

His stomach growled with hunger at the mention of food. "Guess that answers that question. How about you? Have you eaten?"

"Yeah, I got something while you were unconscious. Hold on, I'll be right back."

She pulled away from him and slipped out the tent flap without a sound. Mace rubbed his temples as he watched her leave. Would she come back? She'd seemed awfully skittish around him. Their conversation was awkward and stiff. Was she just hanging around because she felt guilty?

Could she be the one trying to run away now that things were over? They had done things a little back-ass-wards. He normally at least bought a girl a drink before he slept with her.

Hell, he hadn't even slept with her; he'd screwed her brains out in a supply closet! No wonder she was hell bent on getting away from him. They'd let their raging hormones loose before they had gotten to know each other. What a shock she felt awkward around him now.

He might not know a lot about women in general or Annie in particular, but he did know that she wasn't the type that hopped into bed with every GI she met. There was something very innocent about her, and he just bet she had no idea what to do about him now.

Well, Mace knew what to do, and as soon as he could get out of bed without his brain falling out his ear, he was going to do it. His beautiful Annie deserved a Prince Charming, and he was going to make sure she got one.

*****

Annie knew it was damn cowardly to avoid Mace when he couldn't even get out of bed, but when Colonel Michaels told her to go home, she ran like a rabbit. There was no way she could be around Mace without wanting to either jump him or cry all over the place.

When the support beam came down on him, her heart went stone-cold with fear. She'd been chased, shot at, and almost blown up and that didn't touch the terror she felt seeing Mace buried under a pile of rubble. That sort of gut-wrenching fear didn't come from an excess of hormones and adrenaline.

In some bizarre twist of fate, Annie had fallen head over heels in love with a cocky helicopter pilot in less than twenty-four hours.

Anne Catherine Forbes, who had never so much as kissed on the first date, had not only had the best sex of her life with a guy she'd only just met, she'd tossed all good sense out the window and fallen in love with him. And she'd do it again in a heartbeat.

Unlocking the door to her tiny apartment, Annie dropped her keys on the table by the door and stumbled to the bathroom.

First she was going to take a shower, then she was going to sleep for the next three days. By then Mace would be back with his unit and she wouldn't have to worry about running into him and bawling her eyes out.

She knew all about the military brush-off. Meet a woman in one station and dump her before you go to the next. Well, she'd save Mace the trouble. She wouldn't be clinging and whining when it was time for him to leave. He could go on his way with no empty promises about getting together again when he came back.

Turning the water on as hot as she could stand it, Annie stepped under the spray and let the stinging needles work out the lump in her throat. She'd be strong and send him off with a smile instead of tears. Even if it killed her, he wouldn't know her heart was breaking.

Annie let her tears mingle with the hot water as it ran down her face. How could something this devastating happen so fast? She'd found her heart and lost it all in the same day.

*****

A knock on the door woke Annie from her exhausted slumber. A bleary-eyed look at the clock told her it was ten o'clock in the morning. She'd slept for almost twenty hours! No wonder she felt like her head was stuffed with socks.

By the taste in her mouth, they were dirty socks too. The pounding on her door had stopped. Probably had the wrong address. Annie never got visitors in the daytime, everyone knew she worked evenings and slept in. Could it be the press?

Annie slipped on her robe and crossed to the door. When she peeked through the peephole no one was there. Opening up the door she poked her head into the hallway and looked around. Not a body in sight. On her doormat was a vase of beautiful long-stemmed red roses.

"Oh!" Her heart caught in her throat. Who could those be from? "Don't get your hopes up, Forbes, they're probably for someone else." Even with her cynical side trying to keep her hopes in check, a faint tremor shook her fingers as she reached for the envelope stuck into the beautiful bouquet.

It was addressed to her! So it wasn't a mistake. Her heart beating in anticipation, she pulled the little card out.

Annie –

You are cordially invited to dinner at the Officers' Club, nineteen hundred hours tonight.

Fondly,

Mason.

Fondly? What the hell was fondly? Screwing her damn brains out was a little more than *fond*! Was this his way of brushing her off? He'd treat her to a nice dinner, then tell her it's been fun, but… Probably thought she wouldn't make a scene at the OC. She'd show him a thing or two, boy. She was taking out her shortest skirt and her highest heels for tonight. If he wanted to kick her to the curb, she'd make him eat his heart out.

Picking the roses up and bringing them in her kitchenette, Annie couldn't help but stick her nose in for a deep sniff. Guilt flowers or no, they were still beautiful. Mace might be an ass, but he had style.

*****

Mace was sweating in his dress uniform. What if Annie didn't come? She'd bolted from the camp outside the hospital fast enough. Maybe what he felt was all one-sided after all?

Just when he was ready to march over to her house, a murmur went through the club. A goddess in a screaming red dress and ice-pick heels came into the room. Mace's jaw dropped when he saw that the sexy blonde was Annie. His Annie!

The fire engine red dress was low-cut and only came to the middle of her thighs. As she turned to look for him, he saw that it tied behind her neck and left her back completely bare. All he could think of was one little tug and her breasts would spill free.

Looking around the room, he bet every other horny GI in the place was thinking the same thing. Standing up, Mace waved to her and watched breathlessly as she came over. His tongue was practically hanging out of his mouth by the time she got to the table. Remembering his manners, he was trying to charm her after all, he held out a chair at the table for her.

As she sat, he caught a whiff of her perfume and a glimpse of her cleavage. His body went on immediate alert, all systems go! He had to take a deep breath to control his urge to lay her across the table and see what she had on under the dress.

Down boy! You're supposed to charm her, not attack her!

He cleared his throat before attempting to speak. "Thanks for coming tonight. You look beautiful."

She smiled brightly at him, but it didn't quite reach her eyes. "Thank you for the roses, they're lovely." She looked down at the menu and not at him. "I'm surprised they let you out of the hospital so soon. I figured you'd be under medical care for a few more days."

"I promised to be careful and get lots of rest, so they let me go. I wasn't critical so I don't think they minded. The beds were needed by other folks in worse shape than me." Mace moved away from the tempting view of her cleavage and quickly sat in his own seat, hiding the boner of a lifetime.

Annie took a sip out of her water glass and looked around. "I haven't been to the OC in a long time. It looks nicer than I remember."

"Not nearly as nice as my present company."

Startled eyes turned towards him for the first time. "Uh, thank you. I suppose I'd almost have to look better now. You pretty much saw me at my worst."

"If that was your worst, I'd say you had nothing to worry about. I thought you were lovely then, and I think you're just as beautiful now."

"Oh my." She looked back down at her menu.

"Are you blushing?" Mace was amazed a simple compliment could stain her cheeks so easily.

"Seems kind of silly, huh? I mean, it isn't like we don't *know* each other already."

"We do and we don't. Our relationship started with a bang."

"Literally."

"And we didn't get a chance to go through the normal stages."

Annie looked up at him quickly and opened her mouth, but the waiter chose that moment to relay the night's specials to them. Mace didn't care if he ate MREs as long as he had a chance to work on Annie.

He had no idea what he ordered, but the waiter left them alone and that was all that mattered. Mace reached across the table and held Annie's hand.

"I'm glad you came tonight. After you ran off yesterday I didn't know if I had done something to offend you."

"No, Colonel Michaels ordered me home to get some rest, and I didn't have a chance to get back to you."

"I see." Bullshit.

Her eyes met his again. "Look, if you're doing all this, the roses, the fancy dinner, and everything as a goodbye present, it's really not necessary. I know the drill; I won't put any strings on you."

"Is that what you think this is? A goodbye?"

"Isn't it?" She pulled her hand away and sat back in her chair.

"No, it isn't."

"Then what is it?"

"I like to call it a date." It was his turn to lean back. Let's see how she handled *that*.

"A date?" She looked bewildered.

"Yeah, you know, a guy, a girl, you have a nice dinner than I try to talk you into the back of my car."

"Isn't it a little late for that? You already hit a home run; it seems a little late to be trying to get to first base."

"Now that's where you're wrong. You deserve to be courted, and I'm going to do it."

"Courted? I don't get it. You already got what you wanted; you don't need to go through the dating ritual at this point."

"Wrong again. I'm not even close to getting what I want." Mace leaned forward and captured her gaze.

"And what is that?" A delicate eyebrow lifted.

"You. And not just for a quickie in a janitor's closet. I want the whole package and I'm going to take whatever measures necessary to get it."

"Mace, I'm flattered. Really. I had totally expected you to brush me off tonight. I can't tell you how much it means to me that you want to court me."

"But?"

"But I think once a little time passes and you're on your next assignment, you're going to change your mind."

"Is that a challenge?" He really hoped so. There was nothing he liked more than a challenge.

"No, just the facts."

"As you see them."

"As they are."

"Tell me one thing, just one thing and I'll let this idea go." Mace held his breath. He was gambling here. If she didn't answer the way he thought, he was dead in the water.

"Okay, what?"

"Do you want to end things?"

Mace almost stopped breathing completely as she fidgeted with her napkin and looked anywhere but at him. Finally, when he thought he was going to have a heart attack before the soup course she looked him right in the eye.

"No. God help me, I know it's insane, but no."

"Then sit back and enjoy the ride, baby."

Chapter Ten

Annie's apartment was starting to look like a florist shop. Every day for the past two weeks she'd gotten a delivery of flowers from Mace. Some were wildflowers with little poems attached, some were carnations with just his signature, and there were roses by the score, in every color of the rainbow.

Every night Mace stopped by her apartment to take her out to the movies, for a drive, to dinner, they even went to the circus when it was in town. And every night, he left her at the door with a chaste kiss.

It was driving her insane!

Her body knew what delights he could give her and was not happy about being denied them. One night they had gone on a little country road in Virginia and Mace had pulled the car over so they could look at the stars. He'd wrapped his arm around her shoulders and pulled her close, giving her a little peck on the cheek.

She'd wanted to climb on top of him and tear his clothes off!

Mace in his dress uniform was a sight to behold, but the man in a pair of faded jeans just about stopped her heart on the spot. Annie was so sexually frustrated she thought her pantyhose were going to catch on fire! If they didn't have sex tonight, she was going to have to do something desperate. Like tie him up and have her way with him.

With visions of Mace's studly body spread-eagle and bound to her bed, Annie undid a few more buttons on her shirt and put on the shortest shorts she could find. A knock at the door sounded before she could finish putting on her makeup.

Hustling to the door in case it was another delivery of flowers, Annie was surprised to see Mace in his BDUs—battle dress uniform. Pulling the door open, she got a good look at his face. His eyes were shielded and his expression was serious. A lump lodged in her throat.

"Hey, what's wrong?" She opened the door wider so he could get in.

"I got my orders today. I ship out tomorrow morning for the sandbox."

The lump dropped from her throat to the pit of her stomach. "For how long?"

"I don't know. There's a group of Rangers that needs to be picked up. I've got to do it."

She would not cry, she would not cry. "Of course you do. That's your job."

"I know, but you're my life."

Damn, that wasn't fair. Tears streamed down her face.

"I wanted more time to convince you I was serious about you. About us, but this will have to do."

Mace reached into his pocket and pulled out a ring box. "I had planned on giving you a month or two to get used to having me around, but the military had other ideas. I can't leave without knowing you'll be here when I come back. I love you with all my heart, Annie. Will you marry me?"

Opening up the black velvet box, Mace pulled out a platinum and diamond ring that sparkled in the light of the living room.

She put her hands to her mouth and gasped. Tears were streaming from her eyes as her heart stopped beating.

"Is that a yes or a no?" A tiny drop of sweat ran down his cheek.

"Yes! Of course it's a yes! I didn't need a month. Hell, I didn't need two weeks! I knew I loved you the day we were rescued!"

Jumping into his arms, Annie rained kisses all over his face while tears continued to pour from her own.

"You could have clued me in, you know. I was sweating bullets all the way over here."

"I was afraid to make a scene. I wanted to be strong and let you go with no strings attached."

"I want the strings; hell, this is the biggest string I could find! Start shopping for a dress, baby; when I get home, we're having the splashiest wedding this place has ever seen."

"How about we plan it together when you get back." She refused to say if.

"We can do that, but be prepared for a quick engagement. Once I get back, you'll have a month to get it all organized. I won't be able to wait any longer than that to make you mine." He slipped the ring on her finger and kissed her hand.

"I just want you to come back." Could she stand to lose him?

"Baby, make no mistake, I will be back. Hell, I had more injuries on leave than I ever did in battle. I'll be back."

"How long do you have before you have to report?"

"I have to be on base by ten tonight."

Annie grabbed his hand and pulled him down the hall. "Then we better hurry. We only have two hours to give you enough memories to last until you come back to me.."

Pushing him down on her double bed, Annie yanked off her shirt and pulled off her shorts until she was clad in only her black bra and underwear. She'd been hoping he'd see them, now she was glad she wore them.

"Slow down, baby, I've wanted to make love to you on a bed since the first time in the closet." Mace pulled off his brown tee shirt and untied his boots.

"We'll go for style points on round two, right now I want you hard and fast." She undid the fly of his pants and ripped them down his legs. Grasping his cock, Annie crouched down until she could pull it into her mouth. She'd never gone down on a guy before, but tonight she was willing to discover all sorts of new experiences.

"If you keep that up, I can guarantee it'll be fast."

Mace's fingers twined in her hair holding her to his dick despite her protests. She was dying to feel him inside of her, but wanted to give him as much pleasure as she possibly could. His breath was coming in uneven gasps, and he pulled her away suddenly.

"I want to be inside you when I come. Lay down, I have to get you caught up to my speed." Mace pulled her down next to him and captured her mouth in a blazing hot kiss.

His wandering fingers undid the snap on her bra and pulled it loose, setting her breasts free.

"Oh God, I've been going crazy wanting to touch these beauties."

"I've been going crazy wanting you to touch them!"

"I had to prove to you that I wanted you for more than your body." He sucked a nipple into his mouth and slid her underwear down her legs.

"I believe you, honest! Now fuck me before I die!"

His fingers were so close to her clit she wanted to scream. It would take the barest of touches to send her over the edge, she'd had two weeks of foreplay.

She lifted her hips, trying to get his finger to touch her in the right spot.

"Not yet, baby. I've been dying to taste you."

Taste her? This certainly was her night for new experiences.

Mace nuzzled her breasts and gave her nipple one last lick before sliding his body between her legs. His lips worked their way down her stomach and stopped at her belly button. The feel of his hairy chest against her was making her pulse with need, and the anticipation of what was to come was killing her.

Dipping his tongue into her navel, he swirled it around a few times before drifting lower. When he slid one finger inside her sheath, she almost came on the spot. Mace ratcheted the need burning through her even more by blowing over her clit.

"Mace, I love you. I really do, but if you don't touch my clit right this very second I'm going to kick your ass!"

"Oh, a tough girl. I like it."

The warm touch of his tongue on her nubbin shot her over the edge in record time. His finger drove in and out of her as her body quivered around it. Annie's heart felt like it was going to fly out of her chest before she was done.

She'd barely come back to earth when she felt the tip of his cock probing her entrance.

"I finally have you under me."

"Not for long." Before he was fully sheathed inside her, Annie wrapped her legs around him and flipped him over.

Sitting astride him shoved his cock so deep inside her, it felt like they could never be separated. Rocking slowly she built up the pace, leaning backwards so he rubbed against all the right spots.

Leaning up, Mace kneaded both her breasts in his hands, sending her into a pleasure coma.

"Under, over, as long as I'm in you, I'm happy. Although I must say, the view from this position is fine indeed." Mace's smile went straight to her crotch, stimulating her even more.

"The view from up here isn't so bad either."

Moving forward, Annie held onto the headboard and picked up the pace. Mace fell back and grabbed her hips, driving himself up into her as she bucked against him.

"Come with me, baby." One finger slipped between them to tease her clit yet again.

Annie felt the heat spreading out in waves from her center, growing hotter and hotter. Just when she thought she couldn't take it anymore, Mace slammed her down on his shaft with two quick, hard jerks and she exploded in a shower of stars.

Mace gave a hoarse shout under her then his breath stilled as his cock jumped inside of her. When he opened his eyes and looked into hers, Annie could see all the love he had for her. How could she have ever doubted him?

"I love you so much." She dropped a kiss on his lips before rolling to the side to cuddle up close to him.

"It's about time."

"Hey, anything worth having is worth working hard for, right?" Annie held up her hand and looked at her ring sparkling in the fading light.

"Do you like it? I thought it suited you, classy yet strong."

"I love it. It's perfect, but it could have been plastic and I would have loved it because it came from you."

"You mean I spent all that money and I could have got you plastic? Give it back," he teased.

Annie punched him in the arm. "Idiot. You'd have to pry this thing off my cold, dead body."

"Ouch, hey, watch it, tough girl, you're damaging government property."

"You watch it, Captain. Keep shooting your mouth off and I'll tie you up and punish you." Annie thought of her earlier fantasy and snickered.

"I always knew you had bondage tendencies."

*****

Annie stood silently by and watched Mace get on the cargo plane that would take him to the Middle East. She stood next to all the other wives and girlfriends that watched their loved ones leaving yet again. She prayed silently that he'd come back safely to her.

As he climbed into the plane, Mace turned and spotted her in the crowd. Blowing her a kiss, he lifted his left hand and pointed to his ring finger. Raising her own left hand, she blew a kiss back. She had his ring and his heart, God willing she'd have the rest of him too.

Epilogue

"It's time, Sweetie." Annie's father held out his arm to her and helped her out of the limousine. She was sure she caught the glint of a tear in his eye, but she couldn't hide her smile. It was her wedding day and the world was beautiful.

"You look so handsome, Dad. Thanks for wearing your dress uniform." Annie gave him a kiss on the cheek, then fixed her veil over her head. She and Mace had planned the wedding in six weeks, but it was everything she could have wanted and more.

"Guess I still know how to put one of these monkey suits on. Let's get going; your mother has probably worn out all her tissues with all that crying she was doing."

Annie shook her head and laughed. Her parents had been married for thirty-five years and they were still as in love as ever. She hoped she and Mace could be that lucky.

Her father led her down the aisle where her sister Polly and her new sister-in-law Jemma were already waiting. Blayne was standing up for Mace, an honor Mace had insisted on.

After all, Mace had declared, if it wasn't for Blayne torturing her as a child and locking her in the closet, they never would have met. She wasn't surprised that the two of them got on like a house on fire. It seemed like she was destined to be surrounded by strong military men her whole life.

Her mother was indeed crying into a wad of tissues, her eyes smiling behind the tears. She'd cried just as hard at Blayne's wedding. Annie had said it was in relief that Blayne was finally off her hands.

Mace's eyes were shining at her as her father handed her off with a salute. The butterflies in her stomach started their own flight pattern as Mace held her hand and turned towards the priest. Mace looked so tall and strong standing there, so sure and confident. Then Annie noticed the beads of sweat popping out on his forehead. He was just as nervous as she was. Her stomach immediately calmed and she smiled up at him.

The words the priest spoke as he joined them together were a blur to her. All that mattered was Mace was there by her side. She was sure now that no matter how many times he had to leave her, he'd always return.

Her Prince Charming was here at last.

*****

"Alone, at last!" Mace locked the door to the fancy honeymoon suite of the hotel and undid his bowtie. Annie watched his fingers hungrily. She wanted them undressing *her*. It had been her idea to abstain for a month before the wedding, now she wasn't so sure it was such a good idea. All night long she'd been in an agony of need every time she came within two feet of Mace. When he brushed his rock-hard cock against her pussy during their first dance together, she'd wanted to attack him on the spot.

"It was a perfect day. Just perfect, but I'm glad to have you to myself now." Annie's eyes were held captive as Mace pulled off his formal shirt and undershirt. He had muscles on top of muscles, and she wanted to touch every one of them.

"Same goes, baby. You look stunning in that dress, but now I want to see what's under it."

"Think you can handle it, Captain?" Annie smiled to herself. She had quite a surprise in store for her new husband.

"Give it your best shot, Major." He'd pulled off his pants and was standing there in nothing but black silk boxers.

She sure hoped she could pull off this striptease without cutting to the chase and jumping him where he stood.

Annie moved to the middle of the room and tossed her veil over a nearby chair. She gave Mace a sultry look and turned her back to him. Remembering the last time she'd had her back to him sent a fresh shot of lust through her body. This might be the fastest striptease in history.

With shaking fingers she slowly unzipped her beautiful wedding dress and let it fall to the floor in a puddle of white lace and satin. Wearing only the silky slip and her high heels, she stepped out of the dress and strutted closer to Mace.

"Very nice. I like that little number better than the wedding dress." His cock was pushing the bounds of his shorts, and Annie's mouth watered at the thought of pulling it inside.

"You ain't seen nothing yet." She shot him a wink and slipped one strap off her shoulder.

Moving out of his reach, she slid the other strap off and gave a little wiggle until the slip was also lying on the floor.

The white corset and garters had been a little uncomfortable, but the look on Mace's face made it all worthwhile.

"Holy mother of God!" Mace reached out to touch her, but she scrambled away.

"Not yet, Flyboy."

Kicking off her heels, Annie propped her foot up on the chair and unsnapped the garters holding her stockings up. Slowly she rolled the tubes of silk down one leg then the other. When she was left in only her white thong and the corset, she took a shaky breath and went for the final tease.

"While you were away, I missed you so much. I thought about you every night, about how I wanted to touch you and have you touch me." Looking him dead in the eye she untied the corset and let it fall to the floor. "I would get myself so worked up thinking about all the ways we could make love that I'd just have to take things into my own hands."

Annie ran her hands up her stomach until she grasped her own breasts. Squeezing them and kneading them, she pushed them up higher until she could suck one nipple herself. Another bolt of pure desire slammed into her at her own touch.

Apparently it was working for Mace too because sweat dripped down the side of his face, and his cock poked right through his boxers. Seeing his need gave her courage to go on.

"I got pretty good at pretending I was with you, and you were touching me all over. Especially here."

One hand slipped under her thong and into her pussy. She was so far gone she didn't care that she had wanted to tease him some more first. Annie shoved her fingers inside her pussy and used the other hand to tease her clit. Pumping furiously, she threw her head back and shuddered to completion.

Before she could come back down to earth, Mace swooped her into his arms and attacked her mouth with his. She was surrounded by hot, determined, *aroused* male, and it felt delicious.

"I don't know whether to applaud you or spank you," Mace said when he came up for air.

"I'd pick the spanking if I had my choice." Annie pushed his straining boxers down his legs and grasped his cock in her hands. He was hot and hard and all hers. "But I have something else in mind."

Dropping to her knees, Annie pulled his cock into her mouth and grabbed his muscled ass in her hands. The taste of him rolled across her tongue as she sucked him deeper into her throat. His musky smell filled her nostrils and added to the need building inside her.

Mace's hands tightened in her hair as she moved up and down his length. He was so big and hard she thought she might choke, but it was worth it to know she was driving him crazy. His balls tightened below her mouth, then a spray of come shot down her throat. Annie swallowed rapidly as Mace gave a hoarse cry.

"Woman, you'll be the death of me!" Mace groaned, pulling her up to him.

"At least you'll die happy." Annie gave in to the urge to touch him and ran her hands over his gloriously muscled chest.

Her fingers tangled in his hair and swirled around his belly button before caressing his abs.

"It's going to take me a little while to recover, but I've got an idea of what we could do to pass the time."

Scooping her up in his arms, Mace carried her to the bed and laid her down gently. Running his fingers lightly over her breasts, he smiled down on her. "Do you know how very much I love you?"

His emerald green eyes shined into hers and sent thrills through her. "I have an idea, but you can remind me."

Her blood had caught fire and was burning through her veins as his hands trailed across her breasts and over her stomach. His lips followed and the fire turned into an inferno.

"You are the most amazing woman I've ever met. I love you more than anything in the world. You are my very breath, my reason for living." He peppered his words with kisses as he slid between her legs and moved slowly to her pussy.

"I love being with you, loving you, touching you—" His fingers parted her curls and teased lightly around the opening of her channel before slipping inside. "And tasting you." His mouth descended on her clit as his finger pushed higher inside her pussy.

Hot, pulsing need slammed through her driving her higher and higher. The blood was pounding in her ears and her only anchor was Mace's touch on her body.

"Mace!"

"Come for me, baby."

She screamed as she did. Annie's body convulsed around him as waves and waves of pleasure swamped her.

"Why don't we try it together this time?" Mace licked his way up her body then slid his cock inside her still spasming body.

"I'm in-line with that plan." Annie would follow him wherever he led, from this day forward.

About the author:

Arianna Hart lives on the East Coast with her husband and three daughters. When not teaching, writing, or chasing after her children and the dog, Ari likes to practice her karate, go for long walks, and read by the pool. She thinks heaven is having a good book, warm sun, and a drink in her hand. Until she can sit down long enough to enjoy all three, she'll settle for the occasional hour of peace and quiet.

Arianna Hart welcomes mail from readers. You can write to her c/o Ellora's Cave Publishing at 1337 Commerce Drive, #13, Stow, Ohio 44224.

Also by Arianna Hart:

Lucy's Lover

Rebel Lust

Silver Fire

Enjoy this excerpt from

Always Faithful

Prologue

For Nikki Phillips stepping aboard the non-stop British Air flight to London seemed the toughest decision of her twenty-two years of life. Nikki developed into a self-sufficient, headstrong young woman by her parents rearing. Her last relationship left her drained of self-secure feelings and vulnerable. However, determined to regain her independence, Nikki left the states to start anew in her mother's homeland. Her goal consisted of finding the woman she'd lost and making her a success.

Brandon's attention had captivated her. His masculine beauty touched with slight arrogance kept her interested. His constant selfishness finally sent her packing. Nikki tolerated his belittlement and verbal abuse for their few months together. Why? She couldn't quite put her finger on it. Possibly the thought of having no boyfriend outweighed the thought of being miserable with one.

Brandon attempted to control her every move, dictating what she wore, what she did, and who her friends were. He'd convinced her that she would do as he asked if she loved him. Unfortunately, she'd fallen into his trap. *I will not let that happen again,* she told herself.

After graduating from the University of Texas, Nikki secured a job as a systems engineer for the government. She could leave the baggage behind her in Texas. No more excuses. No man telling her what she should do. This time, she controlled her own mind. She left knowing the strength she once lost could be found by doing so. She took the leap of faith with no safety net.

Chapter One

"Why don't you just loosen up," Brandon said to her as he savagely began unbuttoning her blouse. "You know you want to. All women want it, they just don't admit it."

"I just don't feel like it, that's all," Nikki told him trying to push him away from her. This task was next to impossible in the compact front seat of his Chevy Camaro. "Why do you always want to do it in the car anyway?"

"It's dangerous. There is always that chance of getting caught again."

Nikki looked out the window to the empty field in front of them. The dead end street, now christened "their hideaway," the place Brandon could get his rocks off.

Nikki remembered the mortification she felt the last time they parked there. Both of them lay naked as two jaybirds finishing the dirty deed, when a bright light shone into the passenger side window on them. Brandon thought it hilarious as he pulled his pants up quickly and got out of the car to speak to the officer. Nikki hurriedly refastened her bra and pulled up her pants as the flashlight still beamed in on her nakedness.

Couldn't he turn that damn thing off? Lord knows he should have gotten his thrills by now, she thought to herself.

Nikki grew increasingly pissed off the longer Brandon stood outside the car shooting' the shit with Barney Fife.

"He said that we need to find a safer place next time I want to get in your pants," Brandon said still giggling when he got back into the car.

"I am not going to do it here," Nikki said coming back to the present. "I don't want to have to face my daddy when he has to bail me out for indecent exposure."

"You are such a prude," Brandon said as he removed his member from his pants and began readying himself for invasion.

God, she hated having sex with him. He couldn't care less about her feelings. Surely sex supplied more than just wham bam thank you ma'am. But Brandon sure didn't possess that knowledge. Nikki always felt so used, so manipulated, so unappreciated. Something about him kept pulling her in. There were times he made her feel special. However, looking back she realized it to be only the times that sexual satisfaction consumed him. Surely, being in love provided more contentment than she felt now.

"Fine, if you're not going to pleasure me, than I'll just have to do it myself," Brandon said as he began bringing himself to satisfaction.

A lump grew in Nikki's throat. She swallowed hard attempting to avoid the urge to throw up. Totally disgusted, she looked away as he continued to slide his hand up and down his arousal. She tried to block out the sounds of his moans of release.

"If you're finished, I'd like to go back to the dorm."

"Whatever."

When he pulled into the parking lot at the University he reached across and squeezed her breast and smiled, "So, can I come up?"

Nikki restrained the rage rising up in her chest. "Look, you bastard. I don't want to ever see you again. You are the most disgusting person I have ever met. I can't believe I have wasted so much time being your harlot. You obviously don't need me anymore since you seem so fond of your right hand. Besides, I know that if that doesn't do it, you can call that chick from our English Lit class that I know you've been screwing' on the sly."

Brandon shook his head in disbelief. "How do you—? Well, if you knew how to treat a guy, I wouldn't have to go to anyone else."

"You are a son of a bitch, Brandon. Why don't you just go to hell!"

That night proved to be the last time she saw Brandon on any kind of intimate basis. Shortly after that night, they graduated. She left for England. Brandon would eventually find his way into some other poor, sad, stupid woman's pants; and Nikki swore on all that she held sacred to never suffer men again, at least not in the foreseeable future.

*****

"Where to, Miss," said the expressionless British cabby as he glanced at her through the rear divider of the taxi.

"Hampsthwaite, please."

The cab smelled of smoke and greasy food, and the cabby looked as if he consumed plenty of both on a regular basis. She held on tightly to the door strap as the cabby quickly weaved in and out of traffic during the twenty-minute ride into the village. That last turn, undoubtedly, he took on only two wheels.

The countryside of North Yorkshire fascinated Nikki. The green pastures and purple heather rushed quickly by the window. She loved the looks of the craggy hills and winding roads. She directed the driver. The driver carefully entered the narrow stone and wood gate and approached 28 Hollins Lane, a small cottage typical of the area.

Rosebushes and flowerbeds surrounded the house. Construction of the cottage was of a dark local stone tinged slightly dark green. The dark stones bordered with white wooden trim lent a picture postcard appearance to the cottage. Glass bricks framed the dark green front door. Nikki sighed with approval as she made her way up the steps.

With no small effort, the aging and overweight cabby extracted himself from the cockpit of his cab, shuffled around, pulled out her luggage and carried it to the small front porch.

"Two fifty, Miss," the driver mumbled as he turned back to Nikki.

Nikki pulled out her wallet and handed the cabby the coins.

"Ta love," he mumbled.

Even in August, the bite of the northern wind that trekked down the valley stung her nose. She knew that back in Texas her family endured one hundred degree temperatures about now. Although only sixteen hours ago Nikki had been enjoying the high temperatures, it seemed more like months.

She welcomed the change in climate. However, the drizzle is another issue altogether. A frown spread over her face and the kink that seized her naturally curly hair exposed the remembrance of disgust the weather physically retained on her.

Nikki retrieved the front door key, from the pre-designated rock, and opened the door leading to the narrow spiral staircase. She walked through the entryway and into the den. The fireplace welcomed her and Nikki observed the abundance of kindling and coal left in the wood box by the landlord.

"Bless you, Mr. Dawson," she said to herself.

French doors enclosed the den from the patio, complimenting the beautiful picture window across the room. Nikki stumbled on a fleece blanket, spread over the furnished sofa, and gathered it up swiftly. She then snuggled up to tour the rest of the house.

The kitchen appeared small, but efficient. Nikki snickered when she noticed the piggyback washer and dryer by the small door leading to the backyard. They held a spooky likeness to the appliances Barbie possessed in her Dream House.

As she entered the dining room, Nikki ran her fingers along the antique buffet that complimented a small pine table and chairs. The draft, from the large bay window, made her spine tingle as she looked through to the flower garden and tool shed out back. She spotted the rooftops of the houses behind hers and inhaled deeply the aroma floating from the chimneys. Laying the blanket back on the sofa, she grabbed her luggage and meandered upstairs to unpack.

The exquisite bedroom consisted of a small table and chairs, four-poster bed and a beautiful armoire. The bed displayed crisp white sheets under a fluffy down duvet she imagined crawling under and wrapping herself in oblivion. The windowed wall offered a detailed view of the village. Looking out, Nikki could see the houses stair-stepping down the lane and ending at a small stone bridge. All very quaint, she thought to herself.

Nikki spent two hours unpacking most of her belongings until exhaustion finally took her. She put on her flannel pajamas and crawled underneath the down comforter pulling it just under her nose. A sigh of ecstasy escaped her as she hunkered down lower in the bed. No longer able to contain herself, Nikki squealed with delight flailing her legs under the covers.

"I'm free!" she whispered before the heavy hand of slumber overtook her...

Why an electronic book?

We live in the Information Age—an exciting time in the history of human civilization in which technology rules supreme and continues to progress in leaps and bounds every minute of every hour of every day. For a multitude of reasons, more and more avid literary fans are opting to purchase e-books instead of paperbacks. The question to those not yet initiated to the world of electronic reading is simply: *why?*

1. *Price.* An electronic title at Ellora's Cave Publishing runs anywhere from 40-75% less than the cover price of the exact same title in paperback format. Why? Cold mathematics. It is less expensive to publish an e-book than it is to publish a paperback, so the savings are passed along to the consumer.
2. *Space.* Running out of room to house your paperback books? That is one worry you will never have with electronic novels. For a low one-time cost, you can purchase a handheld computer designed specifically for e-reading purposes. Many e-readers are larger than the average handheld, giving you plenty of screen room. Better yet, hundreds of titles can be stored within your new library—a single microchip. (Please note that Ellora's Cave does not endorse any specific brands. You can check our website at www.ellorascave.com for customer recommendations we make available to new consumers.)

3. *Mobility.* Because your new library now consists of only a microchip, your entire cache of books can be taken with you wherever you go.
4. *Personal preferences are accounted for.* Are the words you are currently reading too small? Too large? Too...**ANNOYING**? Paperback books cannot be modified according to personal preferences, but e-books can.
5. *Innovation.* The way you read a book is not the only advancement the Information Age has gifted the literary community with. There is also the factor of what you can read. Ellora's Cave Publishing will be introducing a new line of interactive titles that are available in e-book format only.
6. *Instant gratification.* Is it the middle of the night and all the bookstores are closed? Are you tired of waiting days—sometimes weeks—for online and offline bookstores to ship the novels you bought? Ellora's Cave Publishing sells instantaneous downloads 24 hours a day, 7 days a week, 365 days a year. Our e-book delivery system is 100% automated, meaning your order is filled as soon as you pay for it.

Those are a few of the top reasons why electronic novels are displacing paperbacks for many an avid reader. As always, Ellora's Cave Publishing welcomes your questions and comments. We invite you to email us at service@ellorascave.com or write to us directly at: 1337 Commerce Drive, Suite 13, Stow OH 44224.

The Ellora's Cave Library

Stay up to date with Ellora's Cave Titles in Print with our Quarterly Catalog.

To recieve a catalog,
send an email with your name
and mailing address to:

catalog@ellorascave.com

or send a letter or postcard
with your mailing address to:

Catalog Request
c/o Ellora's Cave Publishing, Inc.
1337 Commerce Drive #13
Stow, OH 44224

Printed in the United States
33056LVS00001B/262-270